# CRATER LAKE

## BATTLE FOR WIZARD ISLAND

A NOVEL

STEVE WESTOVER

SWEETWATER BOOKS
AN IMPRINT OF CEDAR FORT, INC.
SPRINGVILLE, UT

Other books by Steve Westover

*Defensive Tactics*



ISBN 13: 978-1-59955-960-5

Published by Sweetwater Books, an imprint of Cedar Fort, Inc.
2373 W. 700 S., Springville, UT 84663
Distributed by Cedar Fort, Inc., www.cedarfort.com

LIBRARY OF CONGRESS CATALOGING-IN-PUBLICATION DATA

Westover, Steve, 1974- author.
Crater Lake : battle for Wizard Island / Steve Westover.
pages cm
Summary: Angry at his parents for sending him to stay with crazy Uncle Bart at Crater Lake National Park, Ethan discovers that he will do anything to get them back after they, and all of the other adults in the park, get swallowed into the earth.
ISBN 978-1-59955-960-5
1. Crater Lake (Or.)--Juvenile fiction. 2. Calderas--Oregon--Crater Lake National Park--Juvenile fiction. 3. Adventure stories, American. [1. Adventure and adventurers--Fiction. 2. Supernatural--Fiction. 3. Brothers and sisters--Fiction. 4. Indians of North America--Oregon--Fiction. 5. Crater Lake (Or.)--Fiction.] I. Title.

PZ7.W52712Cr 2012
[Fic]--dc23

2011045302

Cover design by Brian Halley
Cover design © 2012 by Lyle Mortimer
Edited and typeset by Melissa J. Caldwell

Printed in the United States of America

10 9 8 7 6 5 4 3 2 1

Printed on acid-free paper

*To Lindsay, Josh, Elisha, and Samantha—*
*Your love of reading inspires me*

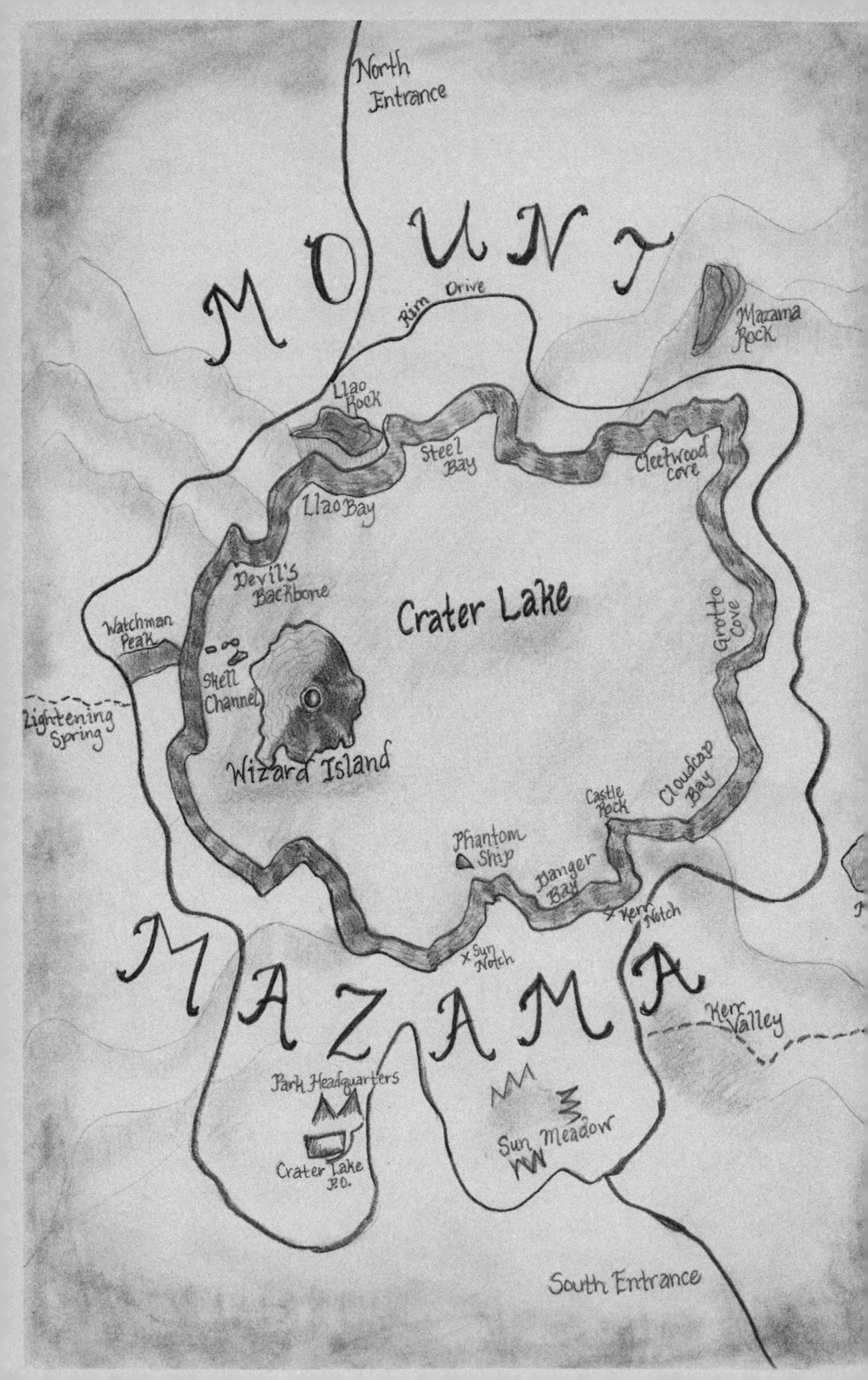
North Entrance
MOUNT
Rim Drive
Mazama Rock
Llao Rock
Steel Bay
Cleetwood Cove
Llao Bay
Devil's Backbone
Crater Lake
Grotto Cove
Watchman Peak
Skell Channel
Lightening Spring
Wizard Island
Cloudcap Bay
Castle Rock
Phantom Ship
Danger Bay
Kerr Notch
Sun Notch
MAZAMA
Kerr Valley
Park Headquarters
Sun Meadow
Crater Lake P.O.
South Entrance

# CONTENTS

Contents

## Contents

# – 1 –

# The Legend

"I can't believe you're doing this to me," Ethan groaned. His mom and dad shared a weary look. Resting his forehead against the cool glass, Ethan stared out the window. "It's abandonment, you know." He looked at his parents and waited for a response, but his mom's lips only tightened. "I'll have issues the rest of my life. Seriously."

Silence.

On the opposite side of the seat, Jordan's curly hair hung across her face as she leaned against the driver's side rear door. She looked like she was sleeping, but Ethan saw her smile.

Ethan covered his lips and whispered in Jordan's direction. "You're a little troll."

Jordan bolted upright. "Mom, Ethan called me a troll again."

"Ethan . . ." his mom scolded.

"What? She's got that crazy hair sticky-outy thing going on," he said with a crooked smirk. "I mean it lovingly."

Jordan scowled. "Chubba-lubbo."

Ethan ran his fingers through his loose curls and smiled at Jordan's lame attempt at mockery. "I'm not chubby. I'm stout."

The vehicle maintained its course, ascending the winding mountain road, every switchback causing the knot in Ethan's stomach to tighten. The barren fields yielded to a pleasant view of ponderosa pines and mountain hemlocks lining the roads and then deepening into groves and forests. With a final turn, the entrance road to the ranger station came into view. Thick posts stood high with a brown wooden sign affixed in between.

*—Welcome to Crater Lake National Park—*

Ethan stared at four large birds atop the sign. Swiveling in his seat to watch the birds through the rear window, he noticed their heads turn, following the car. Ethan flinched. *Whoa . . . weird.*

"Abandoned." Ethan shook his head. "Mom, Dad, I've got to be honest. I expected more from you," he said, hoping the guilt would sink in.

"Son, we talked about this. You complain about never doing anything fun or exciting—well, here you go. A week at Crater Lake will be an adventure," his dad argued.

"If it's so great, why doesn't Jordan have to stay?"

"Because they love me more," Jordan offered. "They'd miss *me.*"

Dad tipped his ball cap and rubbed the bald spot on the back of his head. "Come on, Ethan. It'll be great. Besides, Uncle Bart pulled a lot of strings to make this happen for you. We'll all stay the day, but . . ."

"But Uncle Bart's crazy." Ethan sighed.

Mom fumbled for words of dispute. "He . . . He's not crazy. He's eccentric, and sometimes that can be fun. Yes. Uncle Bart is fun."

Ethan's eyes narrowed as he watched Jordan's grin spread across her face.

Returning his gaze out the window, Ethan stared at the barren ground and the distant wall of mountain. Thick clouds partially obscured snowcapped peaks. "Yeah, this looks thrilling."

Pulling into a parking spot near the front of the ranger

station, Jordan and Ethan gawked as they strained to absorb the view. Surrounded by white pines and fir trees, a lush lawn bordered the impressive outpost. The main entrance at the center of the building reached two stories high in the shape of an A. Halfway up the exterior, a rock facade decorated the building but then gave way to rustic wood planking. To the left of the entrance, two dormers jutted from the steep roofline, and wide-paned windows allowed for a limited view into the building's interior.

Jordan burst from the car, and Ethan followed close behind, eager to rescue his legs from the imprisoning backseat. The cool morning air surprised Ethan as he breathed deeply. He hadn't realized the pungent staleness inside the car until the mountain air provided him with a refreshing contrast.

A small troop of Adventure Scouts sat at a picnic table near the back of the station, rifling through their overnight packs. Nearby, a young couple held hands as they walked toward a trailhead. Middle-aged parents milled the lawn near a flagpole, admiring the scenery, while their teenaged daughter focused on her headphones.

Ethan noticed the teenage girl right away. He peeked once, then twice, but looked away as the girl glanced in his direction.

"Hey, kids! Welcome," a familiar voice called.

Looking up, Ethan saw crazy Uncle Bart descending the stone steps two at a time. He wore forest green shorts, hiking boots with socks up to his knees, and a khaki Park Ranger shirt.

"What do you think of the place? Nice, huh? I'm really glad you could make it," Bart said as he rubbed Ethan's head.

Crouching down with his hands on his knees, Bart looked into Jordan's eyes. "Whoa, you sure are getting big, kiddo. What are you, twelve—thirteen?" Bart asked with a sly grin.

"Eleven," Jordan said with a smug grin but then frowned as Ethan cleared his throat. "I mean, almost eleven," she corrected.

"Ethan, be sure to keep the boys away from this one. She'll have them lining up."

Jordan smiled at the shameless compliment.

Bart greeted the rest of the family, giving hugs and cheek kisses before leading them up the steps to a heavy wood door. "Let's go inside. I've got some cool stuff to show you."

Ethan's eyes widened as he stepped inside the ranger outpost. The interior looked more like a museum of natural history than a ranger station. In one corner, a replica of a Native American wearing simple leather garb and a fur-lined cap stood as a sentry. To the side of the entrance, a full-sized black bear stood on its haunches. Jordan flinched as the creature engulfed her view.

"You're such a baby," Ethan accused with a chuckle. "It's stuffed."

Jordan poked her brother with a sharp elbow.

"Kids," mom scolded. The siblings exchanged gentle shoves but ceased when they recognized their mother's stern "I'm warning you" glare.

Stepping away from Jordan, Ethan strolled around the room, his eyes scanning the interior. Glass viewing cases and a variety of pictures lined the walls, with shadow box displays hanging above. One case contained samples of plant life and information about the environment of Crater Lake, while others had samples of volcanic rock. They had scientific names like basalt, pumice, and scoria, but to Ethan they just looked like lava rock, which was kind of cool. He glanced at a segmented diagram of the volcano, showing the layers of dirt and rock created from the volcanic eruption, but he soon lost interest.

"Hey, Ethan, look at this," Jordan called.

Ethan turned and grinned as he saw Jordan standing in front of the mannequin with her mouth hanging open. He moved closer and examined every detail of the Native's simple wardrobe: the beaded necklace, a waistband, and a heavy leather shawl covering his shoulders like a cape. There was no fancy headdress or a tomahawk, like the cliché version of Indians in the movies.

Ethan stepped to the case near the mannequin's side. "Whoa. This stuff's gotta be hundreds of years old." Arrowheads and spear tips formed from black obsidian and granite lay beside crude statues that looked like they belonged on the end of a witch doctor's staff. "Sweet."

Ethan's eyes halted, locking onto a necklace fashioned from flat round stones, each the size of a silver dollar. The necklace didn't look like anything special, but there was something about it. He couldn't turn away.

Jordan pressed against Ethan, transfixed upon the same necklace.

"You two have a good eye," Bart said from behind, breaking their trance. "I would love to know how the artisan interlocked the three solid stones. It's like a chain of magic."

"I like the colors," Jordan said. "Fiery red and sky blue. And the one in the middle is as clear as glass.

"Are there other stones like that around here?" Ethan asked.

"No. The stones in the necklace are unique as far as I know, but look at this." Bart pulled a similar necklace from around his neck. The flat round stones were not quite as large, and the black leather strap didn't match the original, but still, it was an impressive copy. "After we received that necklace for display, I had a couple of these made. I just got them a couple of weeks ago." Turning his necklace so they could see the back, Bart continued as if allowing them into a strict confidence. "My friend who made this had to cheat. If you look close, the stones on my necklace aren't solid like the original. You know, if it wasn't a conflict of interest I'd make hundreds of these and sell them right here in the gift shop."

"I'd buy one," Jordan offered.

"Well, since I can't sell it, I'll just have to give this one away," Bart said as he fumbled with the clasp at the back of his neck.

Jordan's eyes grew to the size of the stones. "Thank you. I love it."

"You are very welcome. Take good care of it, and it will bring you luck. Hey, it looks like your mom's ready for us to start." With the kids in tow, Bart walked to the center of the room and stood next to the model of Crater Lake.

Jordan "oohed" and "aahed." Ethan acted indifferent, but even he was impressed.

"Now, kids, I want you to listen to Ranger Bart," Mom said.

"Thank you, sis." Turning his attention to the kids, Bart hunched as he moved close. He spoke dramatically in a quiet but earnest voice, as if telling a secret. "Crater Lake is like no place you've ever been, or seen."

Ethan sighed, rolling his eyes. He grabbed his father's elbow and looked up in disbelief. "Seriously?" he moaned.

"Ethan!" Bart's harsh whisper wrenched the boy's attention back. "What I'm telling you could save your life. I suggest you pay attention like your little sister." Indeed, Jordan's attention was rapt, hanging on his every word.

"Like I was saying, the crater is special. I can share many things with you, but some you will have to discover for yourself. We'll start with the basics."

"Should I take notes?" Ethan asked, earning glares of warning from his parents. Bart grinned as he continued.

"Seventy-seven hundred years ago, there was a massive volcanic eruption just a few miles from here. Mount Mazama erupted, casting fiery rocks and ash for miles before collapsing into a massive caldera, or crater. Now, volcanoes erupt all the time, but this one was different."

"What was different about the eruption of Mount . . . Mazamamama?" Jordan asked.

"Mount Mazama," Bart corrected. "The natives tell a legend of two spirit chiefs: Llao of the 'Below World,' who lived deep inside the mountain, and Skell, of the 'Above World.' Chief Llao became angry with the ancient people who lived here. He came out of the mountain and vowed to destroy them with a curse of fire."

"Why? What was his problem?" Jordan asked.

"Good question. I don't know, but the ancient peoples believed Mazama to be a place of power and danger. They stayed away from the mountain. They feared it."

"They sound pretty smart," Jordan said.

"Yeah, well, to protect the people from Llao, Chief Skell came from the sky and stood on the summit of Mount Shasta. From their mountaintops, the two chiefs battled more fiercely than anything ever witnessed on this continent. The battle ended when Chief Skell forced Chief Llao and his followers back into the mountain and collapsed it upon them. All that remains of Mazama is Crater Lake."

"Awesome!" Jordan said.

"So, what about the water? Where did it come from?" Ethan asked, trying to act casual. "What's the rest of the story?"

"Great question. After Llao and his followers were imprisoned underneath the mountain, Chief Skell asked the storm chief, Snaith, to send furious rains to flood the volcanic basin, forming Crater Lake."

Jordan's eyes were wide, her mouth agape. She turned to her mom with smiling wonder, like a child getting her first glimpse of the decorated Christmas tree.

"Good story, Uncle Bart," Ethan said with a chuckle, "but your story has a few holes."

"Oh? Like what?"

"First, I know people make up legends like this to explain natural events. I'm not a kid. It may be more interesting than the truth, but a storm chief filling the crater with water? Come on."

"The truth, huh? And what truth is that?" Bart asked, enjoying the banter.

"The truth that the water probably flowed in from streams and collected over time from the rainfall."

"That's a good theory, Ethan, but there are no streams in or out of Crater Lake. The water is clear, pure, and deep. In fact, it's the deepest lake in the country, the seventh deepest in the world. Personally I think the story of the storm chief makes a little more sense. What do you think, Jordan?"

"I agree. Don't worry, Uncle Bart. He thinks he knows everything," Jordan said.

Bart bent over and placed one hand on Jordan's shoulder. "Good for you." Reassuming his full stature, Bart looked at his older sister and gave a subtle wink.

"There are a couple of other things I want to tell you before you go hiking," Bart said, walking toward the stuffed black bear near the entrance. "I don't mean to alarm you, but there are some real dangers here at Crater Lake. First, the black bear. The black bear is a shy animal and will avoid human contact, unless it thinks you have food. So don't feed the bears. If a bear takes your food, don't attempt to take it back."

"Sounds like good advice—kind of a no-brainer. Who'd be dumb enough to take food from a bear?" Ethan asked.

"You'd be surprised. There are a lot of stupid people. Now, if a bear grunts, snorts, gnashes his teeth, or sways his head, or worse, if he charges, get out of the way."

"More good advice. Thanks."

"If he attacks, fight back."

"Fight back?" Ethan's dad asked. "I thought you were supposed to lie in the fetal position and wait for the bear to get bored."

"No, not a black bear. That's just silly," Bart replied. "Fight!"

"Also, you may see cougars, mountain beavers, and fifteen species of bats, but beware of the Rough-Skinned Newt. It looks like a salamander but has a bright red stomach. If it feels threatened it will rise up and expose its belly. Think of it like a stoplight," Bart suggested.

Ethan laughed as he envisioned a chubby little lizard. "I'll be sure to watch out for the salamander. They probably have big scary teeth," he mocked, holding his fingers to his mouth like fangs.

"No. No teeth, just lots of poison. Natives used to dip their arrows and spears in the poison before going into battle. One rough-skinned newt divided up and eaten can kill seventeen people. Oregon holds the record for the most deaths by newt."

"Oh."

"If you happen to touch one, wash your hands immediately before poison gets into your nose, mouth, or eyes."

Every word that escaped Bart's mouth sounded theatrical yet felt sincere.

"I have one last warning about the most treacherous danger of Crater Lake—the weather. We average almost forty-five feet of snowfall each year—that's four and a half basketball hoops high—so we usually have snow on the ground from October to June. So even though this year is warm and tomorrow is the first day of summer, the snow has only been melted for a short time. Be prepared for anything. The weather can change in an instant. It can trap and kill you."

"Sounds great. Glad I came," Ethan mumbled.

"Don't worry. You'll have a great time," Bart said. "But stay on the trails and respect the dangers of Crater Lake."

– 2 –

# COUGARS

Nathaniel let go of Jenna's hand, and they each sipped from their water bottles. All around them birds chirped and occasional rays burst through the evergreen canopy, warming them with late morning sunshine. Nearing the end of the trail to Watchman's Peak, the young couple relaxed, hoping to savor every morsel nature offered.

Basking in the perfection of his date with Jenna, Nathaniel didn't notice the transformation occurring around him. The rays of sunlight cascading through the trees turned green, and the air became stale, requiring him to take deeper breaths. The cool breeze died, and the birds became mute. Nathaniel wiped the sweat from his forehead, and then he saw it.

Twenty yards away a cougar sat, purring. With one hand Nathaniel tapped Jenna's arm to get her attention. With the other he reached into the side pocket of his cargo shorts and removed a metallic blue pocketknife. His chest heaved, and then he held his breath as he locked the blade in place and extended the knife downward. A nervous chuckle escaped his lips as he exhaled.

"Jenna, do you see the . . . ?" Nathaniel whispered.

Jenna's gasp gave her away. She saw it.

Nathaniel's grip tightened around the cool handle of the knife as he studied the predator. The cougar arose and moved closer with each easy stride. Nathaniel listened to the hungry rumble of the feline's purr.

Extending his arms behind him, Nathaniel felt for Jenna. His arm wrapped around her, locking her into place as his body pressed backward with a cautious step. Jenna held Nathaniel's waist as they stepped backward in unison.

"I'm . . . going . . . to run," she whispered in cadence with her rapid breathing.

"No. Don't. Just stay calm," Nathaniel pleaded.

Hearing a rustle in the underbrush and sensing motion, Nathaniel's eyes darted to the left. Two additional cougars emerged from behind a dead stump. Within moments the cougars were walking wide on either side of but slightly behind their leader.

Nathaniel felt Jenna release her grasp from his waist. He reached back with his left hand, trying to hold her close, but she was out of reach. Her frantic footsteps trampled the pine needles and low shrubbery as she ran from the trail.

Glancing at the approaching cougars, Nathaniel pivoted on his right foot and bolted after her. He dodged trees and ducked below branches that seemed to bend into his path like the attacking arms of a stranger.

Looking over his shoulder, he noticed the center cougar halt while the two cougars on either side sped their chase. For a moment the cougars trotted alongside but then converged behind Nathaniel as he burst from the woods into a grassy field.

Nathaniel lunged forward and dove onto Jenna, tackling her to the ground. He wrapped his arms around her and held tight, covering her body with his, protecting her the best he could. He groaned as he awaited the attack of angry claws and feline fangs on his exposed flesh—but nothing happened.

Lifting his head from Jenna's backpack, Nathaniel's eyes surveyed the area. The cougars were gone. Rolling into the tall grass, he leaned back on his elbows, panting. He peered into the trees but couldn't see past the darkened border. Then his eyes narrowed as he recognized the shape of a single cougar, sitting . . . watching.

Fumbling toward Jenna, Nathaniel stood and grabbed her hand, forcing her from the ground. The air swirled in a soothing breeze, the tall grass swayed, and finches chirped. With his hands on his knees, Nathaniel glanced back to the pine forest, but the cougar had vanished into the shadows.

Jenna placed a trembling hand high on Nathaniel's back. Her fingers slid across his slippery neck. She stood tall, facing her boyfriend. A broad smile enveloped her face, and her eyes radiated excitement. She didn't say a word, but she didn't have to.

Nathaniel knew what she was feeling, because he was feeling it too. The adrenaline. The rush of survival heightened his senses.

"You okay?" Nathaniel asked, tempering his adventure buzz.

Jenna nodded.

"You know, we're not out of the woods yet," Nathaniel said.

Jenna cocked her head and looked at him with a quizzical expression.

"Well, literally we are, but not metaphorically," he corrected. Setting his backpack on the ground, Nathaniel reached around Jenna and held her. Their bodies trembled.

Jenna grabbed Nathaniel's hand and stood on her tiptoes to reach his face. She adjusted his blue bandanna higher on his forehead and then gave him a peck on the cheek.

Nathaniel didn't respond. His eyes scurried back to the dark border. "Those cougars are still out there. I think we should get out of here," Nathaniel suggested.

Jenna's head wagged. "I'm not going back into those woods. Are you crazy?"

After thinking for a moment, he shrugged. "What should we do?"

"Well, the cougars are gone, and we're here, so let's see if we can enjoy the day," Jenna said as she turned toward the east, gazing at the lake below.

Nathaniel swallowed hard and forced an uncomfortable chuckle. "Seriously?"

Jenna nodded.

Nathaniel gulped again. "Um . . . okay. If you say so."

Jenna reached for Nathaniel's hand, pulling his attention from the tree line.

For the first time Nathaniel noticed the awe-inspiring view. They were on the bluff near Watchman's Peak, high above Crater Lake. The thick paddock grass tickled Nathaniel's knees as he walked toward the edge of the cliff. The water inside the crater looked like an enormous sapphire inlaid in a gold ring. The radiance of the water hurt Nathaniel's eyes, but he liked what he saw.

Poking out of the water inside the crater, eight tiny islands led to Wizard Island like stepping-stones. The small islets were covered with grass, but except for a cluster of trees on the largest of the eight, they were barren. Wizard Island rose from the water with pines foresting the sides, surrounding the cap like the hair on the side of a man's balding head.

The view past the lake was clear for miles, and gentle peaks rose in the distance. The setting was perfect and the colors vivid.

Releasing Jenna's hand, Nathaniel sat in the high grass, and then he leaned back with his hands behind his head. He stared into the baby-blue sky at a cloud passing overhead. For the second time in mere minutes, Nathaniel struggled to regain his breath. This time he simply forgot to breathe. He had seen pictures of Crater Lake before, but nothing had prepared him for the awe of his view.

"Incredible."

"Gorgeous," Jenna agreed, basking in the tranquility of Crater Lake.

Hidden in the dark tree line, three cougars purred as they observed the young couple.

- 3 -

# Showing Off

Ethan strolled near the rock wall where the teenage girl was soaking in some sun with her arms propped back. The deepness of her tan contrasted her long blonde hair, buttercup-yellow shirt, and white shorts. It appeared she soaked in the sun often. Ethan grinned. His shy glances became bold gazes.

Strutting toward the rock wall, Ethan concentrated on the girl's tan and welcoming smile, but then the toe of his shoe kicked the back of his oversized sneaker. He lunged forward but never hit the ground. With his stride recovered gracefully, he continued parading along as though nothing had happened.

Jordan kicked at the grass and sighed at Ethan's usual clumsiness. "Mom, Dad—can we go yet?" Jordan hollered from her seat. "I'm bored. I want to see the Phantom Ship."

"In a minute," Mom said, winking at Bart.

"Yeah, in a minute," Ethan mimicked as he strolled by the table. "It's not like there's really a ghost ship out there, you know."

Jordan scowled. "Mom . . ."

"Ethan's right. The Phantom Ship is an island in the lake," Mom said.

"That's not what Uncle Bart said," Jordan huffed.

Bart grinned sheepishly as his shoulders rose.

"Chill out, Jordan. Why don't you just enjoy the great outdoors and the beautiful scenery?" Ethan suggested.

"Yeah, I know what beautiful scenery you're enjoying," she said. "In case you were wondering, her name is Allie."

A wry smile crossed Ethan's lips as he scoffed. "Yeah, got it, Jordan. Thanks."

"Did you talk to her?" Jordan taunted.

"Let's just say, I've got my ways," Ethan said, glancing at Allie.

Jordan jeered, but Ethan ignored her as he made another lap around the lawn. He walked toward Allie, placing one careful step in front of the other. A repeat of his fumbling feet could be disastrous. Ethan's loose curls bounced as he sauntered with his chest puffed out.

"Allie, come on. Let's go!" her father yelled from across the lawn, but Allie didn't budge. "Allie Nichole . . . now!"

Now Ethan knew her middle name too.

"Ooh," Jordan mocked. "Your ways are so impressive."

Ethan approached Allie's seat, determined to speak with her, but before he could open his mouth, she stood and walked away to her calling parents.

Distracted by the gentle flip of Allie's hair, Ethan tripped over his own feet—again. Unlike the first incident, his feet tangled, and he didn't recover. With his arms flailing, Ethan hit the ground, knocking the wind from his lungs. Unable to breathe, Ethan looked up, searching, but Allie was gone. She hadn't seen a thing. Ethan rolled onto his back, panicked by his lack of breath, but then sat up as shallow air teased his lungs. He stood and looked around. Allie was out of sight, and Jordan rolled with laughter on the picnic table.

Ethan soon spotted Allie leaving the ranger station. She was walking toward the trailhead for Sun Notch Viewpoint—the same trail his family planned to hike.

"Mom, Dad, come on! Let's get this show on the road!" Ethan urged.

"Don't you want to hear more about the legend of the Phantom Ship?" Bart asked.

"Not really. Let's go." Ethan strode toward the trailhead with Jordan following close behind.

"What about the 'Old Man'?" Bart pleaded.

"No."

"But it's a fantastic story," Bart protested.

Ethan pretended not to hear.

"I guess we'll have to hear the stories later," Mom said with an apologetic smile.

Pulling on Dad's arm, Mom raced to catch up with her children as they gathered near the trailhead with Allie and her parents.

Although they were natural adversaries, Ethan and Jordan made a powerful duo in the rare moments when their interests aligned. With Jordan's boredom and Ethan's scenic interest in Allie inducing them to action, their parents didn't stand a chance.

- 4 -

# The Living Woods

JENNA HADN'T SEEN THE COUGAR FOR OVER AN HOUR. SITTING in the high grass near the rim of the crater, the couple ate a small lunch. Between sipping water and chomping chips, Jenna searched the tree line with casual glances. But every time her eyes explored, she came up empty. No cougar.

After lunch they held hands as they strolled along the crater's rim, Nathaniel walking closest to the edge. With only a few feet between him and a two-hundred-foot drop, Nathaniel stole a quick peek over the edge and then stopped.

"Check that out," Nathaniel said, pointing toward Wizard Island.

Above the island, level with the height of the crater's rim, four large birds circled, never losing or gaining altitude. They hovered in place, the wind currents from the lake giving them lift.

"What are they?" Jenna asked, fumbling for her camera. She zoomed in on one location, waited for a bird to drift into frame, and then snapped a picture. She looked at the photo display and smiled.

"I can't tell," Nathaniel responded. "Hawks or falcons maybe? They're big." Nathaniel peered back over the edge of the cliff. His eyebrows rose as he saw a lone pine jutting sideways from the cliff twenty feet below. He took a few steps away from the edge, pulling Jenna with him.

Jenna raised her camera again, this time with Nathaniel in the foreground. After reviewing the photo, Jenna stowed the camera in her pack and took a few steps forward, stopping when she felt Nathaniel's resistance in her hand.

In front of them, a cougar sat on its haunches. Turning in place, Jenna looked in the opposite direction. Another cougar sat thirty yards back. With a cougar to the front and another in the rear, and the cliff to the east, Nathaniel and Jenna had just one direction to go: back into the forest.

The baby-blue sky changed to a strange hue of green, and the gentle breeze ceased. The transient clouds stalled like cars parked on a highway. The air became sour and silent.

Jenna faced the piney woods and strained her eyes at the dark border. Seeing nothing, she took a step forward and then another, and another. She peeked at the cougars on either side. The cougars appeared docile, sitting in the uneven grass that swayed despite a complete lack of wind.

Holding Nathaniel's hand, Jenna's grip tightened as she stepped toward the woods.

Midway between the crater's rim and the forest, the two cougars stood as sentinels on the grassy plateau. Jenna stepped into the woods, shooting a glance back at the large mountain cats. She hadn't noticed their unique appearance the first time she saw them because she had been too busy panicking and running.

Instead of deep brown, their eyes were milky blue, and each black paw looked like it had stepped through hot tar. Their sandy-colored coats were shiny, almost glossy. And the cougars were huge, nearly the size of full-grown tigers.

Each step into the woods increased the distance between Nathaniel and Jenna, and their stalkers. The cougars watched with a curious expression.

"We're doing good," Nathaniel said as he clasped Jenna's hand. "Just keep it nice and easy, nice and easy."

Jenna nodded. With her eyes fixed straight ahead, she

lurched forward as her toe caught on a root. She regained her balance, but her shoe caught again on the gnarled undergrowth. The trees leaned together, and the branches collapsed around her; vines hung from the trees, and mangled roots made each step treacherous. Wrinkles gathered at the corners of Jenna's eyes as she squinted into the darkening woods. It felt more like walking through a haunted jungle than a forest of evergreens.

From behind, Jenna heard the soft rumble of the cougars breathing. Looking back, she was startled to see them only a few paces behind. Jenna's heart leapt. She stepped forward and tripped, scraping her hands and knees when she fell into the jagged undergrowth. Ignoring the pain, Jenna jumped up, grabbed Nathaniel's hand, and began racing through the pine jungle. The roots and vines became more unyielding, threatening to pull her down with each step. Brushing at the hanging plant life, Jenna pushed aside tree limbs and ducked beneath dangling vines, but then stopped. The sound of her heavy breathing echoed in her ears. There was nowhere else to go.

"What's going on here?" Jenna screamed, breaking the mountain silence. Her eyes widened with fear.

Vines and roots slithered across her feet. The trees gnarled together, intertwining like a basket, allowing just enough space between the knotted limbs to squeeze through a single arm or a leg. To Jenna's right the forest was like a blackened cave. She couldn't see more than ten feet. Where had the sun gone and when had the forest become this tangled mess?

Focused on the approaching cougars, Jenna backed against a wall of saplings and vines. Feeling an itch on her leg, she looked down and saw slithering grass rising from the ground. A thin root wound around her lower leg. She kicked, tearing the root from its place, leaving it to dangle from her knee.

Looking at Nathaniel, who was standing next to her, Jenna saw a similar vine slither across his upper arm. She grabbed the vine with both hands and ripped it from her boyfriend. Jenna's eyes met Nathaniel's in terror as additional vines and roots came alive, binding them to the forest wall. Awakened plant life wrapped their bodies, inch by inch.

The cougars' purrs turned to severe growls as their piercing eyes illuminated the darkness. Jenna squeezed Nathaniel's hand as the cougars rushed forward at full speed and leapt into the air. She tried not to look but couldn't help it. Her eyes opened and her body tensed with anticipation, but to her surprise, the cougars didn't attack her. Instead they attacked the wall, tearing and clawing, biting and scratching at the binding plants.

"Jenna, fight! Pull—tear. Get free!" Nathaniel yelled.

Jenna's chest heaved with a determined breath as she ripped at vines and roots. With the cougars' aid, she freed her right arm and then clawed at the bands on her left. Then, unwinding a tangle around her waist, she pulled at her legs, kicking and stomping. Leaning forward, she squirmed and then fell to the ground.

Nathaniel slashed and kicked, but he was unable to free himself. Jenna screamed as a heavy vine slithered across Nathaniel's neck.

The cougars continued to fight, biting and scratching at the living forest, which turned the attack on them. In an instant the tangles that bound Nathaniel released, and he fell forward next to Jenna. Slender plants wrapped around one of the cougars and pulled it through an opening in the woven wall.

Grabbing Jenna's hand, Nathaniel raced toward a shaft of light that had broken through the forest canopy. He slashed at the low-lying plant life and lifted his legs high with each step as he stumbled through the forest. The light grew brighter and then turned into a solid beam of sunshine. They continued to race eastward.

Vines dropped from the evergreens and roots shot upward from the ground, recasting the woods in deep shadow. The trees leaned and bent like attacking arms.

Nathaniel swerved toward the wooded border. As the forest prepared to swallow them alive, Nathaniel saw another wide ray of light. With Jenna close behind, Nathaniel put his head down and rushed through the small opening, exploding into the clearing, blocking through the shrubs and widening the breach. Jenna followed him through.

Again, Nathaniel and Jenna knelt on the thick grass of the plateau surrounding the cliffs of Crater Lake. Nathaniel shook his head and asked in a tone less manly than he intended, "What was that?"

Panting, Jenna shook her head and closed her eyes. "I don't know," she responded in stunned monotone. She opened her eyes as her voice wobbled with uncertainty. "No more cougars. No more vines." Jenna shuddered as she tried to shrug off the eeriness of the living forest. "I think we're alone now. We're going to be okay, right?"

Jenna stood, and Nathaniel continued to sit in the grass, his face ashen. The couple stared at each other for a moment and then surveyed their surroundings. Once again, the air became stale and the sky became green as the breeze died. Whatever caused the grass to start swaying wasn't the wind. As Nathaniel stood, the earth jostled beneath his feet, and he toppled back onto the grass.

"Jenna!" Nathaniel yelled, reaching for his girlfriend.

Jenna's fingers reached for him, but the ground rippled outward in every direction. Each blade of grass grabbed, reaching and pulling at the shoes and legs of its prey. Jenna stomped the grass, and Nathaniel climbed to his feet. His eyes widened. Nathaniel looked to the ground and then into Jenna's frantic eyes. The earth opened beneath them like a giant mouth.

Jenna and Nathaniel clasped hands as the ground swallowed them whole.

The stale air gave way to a gentle breeze, and the green sky returned to its natural baby blue. There was no sign Nathaniel and Jenna had ever been there.

– 5 –

# Scouts

Brady grumbled as two of the older Scouts snickered at him. Holding the map at arm's length, Brady squinted as he struggled to read the contours of the trail and the surrounding area. He adjusted the map sideways in his hand, looked for a moment, and then flipped it around one hundred eighty degrees. He stared at it again.

Two weeks ago, when he discovered his Scout troop would be preparing for the campout by learning how to read a topographical map, Brady had made a point not to attend. *Boring.* He told his mom he needed to study for an algebra test. *Right.* That night he had cracked open his algebra book for the first time in weeks, but there was no actual studying going on. He had stared at the page for an appropriate period of time—like he was doing now with the map—and then returned to his video games.

Brady's freckled cheeks turned the color of his bright red hair. The older boys teased him until they recognized the angry look in his eye. Even at fourteen, two years younger than most of the troop, he was still a full head taller, and stronger. Brady's nose crinkled, his eyes became narrow slits, and his lips puckered. His knuckles popped as his fists clenched, but the Scoutmaster blew his whistle, reigning in the escalating exchange.

*Why did I agree to come on this campout?* At school and on

the football team, Brady dominated the other kids, but at Scouts he felt lost. His one good buddy in the troop backed out of the campout at the last minute, but Brady went anyway because his dad bribed him with a case of pudding. *Big mistake.*

As the first Scout assigned to decipher the undecipherable map, Brady failed the Scoutmaster's test. He held out the map, signaling he had given up. The Scoutmaster grabbed the chart by its edges and turned it upright. Brady blushed, embarrassed he couldn't even hold the map properly.

"There. That's better," the Scoutmaster said. "Jacob, would you please show Brady what we're looking at?" The Scoutmaster held the map out for all to see. "Gather around, boys, and take a look."

Jacob looked at his dad and nodded as he moved toward Brady's side. He pointed to the map. "We're here, just over eight thousand feet. You can tell by the way the circles widen and stretch that the trail will decline as we head east."

"Excellent. Now, Brady, we'll be camping at Mt. Scott. It's the highest peak in the park. Can you show me where it is? Remember, the tighter the circles on the map, the steeper the incline."

Brady shrugged but didn't answer.

"Dad, it's here," Jacob said, pointing. "After the trail goes down for a while, we'll start back up, but then we'll hit the steep incline right here. The peak is eighty-nine hundred feet."

"Very good."

Brady's eyes narrowed, and the corner of his lips turned down. He evaluated Jacob in his full Scout uniform and goofy Australian-style hat with the shoelace straps tied beneath his chin. Brady imagined pulling the thick Harry Potter glasses from Jacob's face and crushing them into the dirt with his boot. "Little punk," Brady grumbled beneath his breath.

At five feet one inch tall and a mere ninety pounds, Jacob was small. To look at his scrawny physique, one might expect him to be a sixth grader, not a fourteen-year-old starting his freshman year of high school. But a punk? Despite being a bit of a know-it-all, especially in Scouts, everyone viewed Jacob as a team mascot. Far too small to play sports or win the most beautiful girls in school, Jacob was the ultimate non-threat, Brady decided.

"If everyone is rested, let's get our packs on and head out," the Scoutmaster said.

Two of the boys groaned as they slipped the pack straps over their shoulders and stood. Placing the pack on his shoulders, Jacob held his thumbs beneath the shoulder straps, jumped, and adjusted his pack before connecting the strap around his waist for additional support.

"Follow me," the Scoutmaster said, starting again along the trail. He turned back as the boys fell into line. "Jacob and Brady, you two bring up the rear. Mt. Scott, here we come."

# – 6 –

# The Phantom Ship

Although his dad was the designated caboose on the trail, Ethan fell ten paces behind, mumbling as he kicked at the rocks in his path.

Toward the front of the group, Jordan walked alongside Allie, enthralled with Allie's stories of cheerleading and drivers education near misses. With wild gestures, Allie imitated her clumsy steering ability as she laughed. "Then there was this one time during class that I turned the wrong direction down a one-way street. I seriously freaked out . . . big time."

Allie's dad skewed an eyebrow and scratched his head as he eavesdropped.

"I was banned from driving for a week. Oh, and I flunked the driving test," Allie said with a grin.

"Well, yeah," Jordan agreed.

Jordan looked up and smiled. Allie was like an older sister—friendly, kind, beautiful, helpful, cool, and fun—the complete opposite of Ethan. Removing the hair band from her ponytail, Jordan shook her head, hoping her tight curls would fall to her shoulders, just like Allie, but it really looked more like the "Troll" thing again. Ethan smirked in the background.

At the first rest stop, Jordan tried to roll up the hem of her shorts and pulled her sleeves onto her shoulders to be sportier like Allie, but after a stern look from her mother, she returned the clothing to its natural fit. She was disappointed until Allie patted her on the back and gave her a sly wink.

Walking at the back, Ethan watched his sister's disgusting display of hero worship. Jordan was trying way too hard. Eventually Allie would become annoyed with the little girl and turn her attention to someone more mature . . . someone like him.

Kicking another rock from his path, Ethan sent the projectile forward. It bounced from the ground into his father's ankle. His dad twisted around but didn't scold him.

Ethan lowered his head. "Sorry."

He shook his head from side to side as his chest puffed out with a deep breath. Dad had promised fun and adventure, but this? Very disappointing.

As the families emerged from the trail near the Sun Notch Viewpoint, Jordan and Allie laughed while Ethan remained at the rear of the group in silence with his father. There was an unspoken acceptance, an understanding between them. Girls were the source of all troubles.

Unlike the rugged trail, the paved overlook was bordered by concrete and rock. Only forty-five minutes from the ranger station, the view of the Phantom Ship provided food for the imagination.

Located near the southeast edge of the lake, the small island jutted from the placid water. At first glance, Ethan thought the Phantom Ship looked more like a handful of knives poking from the clear surface than a ship. But as he tuned out the jabbering of his little sister and studied the island, the ship began to take shape.

Near the center of the narrow island, thin rocks rose, and if he used his imagination, he could see the resemblance to a ship's mast and sail. Toward the front of the ship was another soaring rock formation that looked like someone holding up a forefinger and thumb close together. A couple of smaller formations also looked like they could be sails, and between the jagged rocks, pines rose from the inhospitable ground. Ethan's eyes crossed as he stared at the island. His vision blurred, and the dominant island features overwhelmed the details. With his eyes crossed, it definitely looked like a spooky phantom ship. *Excellent!*

Standing near the walled ledge, Allie read aloud from the informational placard. "The Phantom Ship was once the highest peak inside Crater Lake. After centuries of erosion, the sail-like peaks of the 'ship' are all that remain." Allie gazed over the small island. "I like it!"

Jordan cleared her throat. "That's not what Uncle Bart told me. He said the Phantom Ship really was a ship, but then it was *cursed*," Jordan said, placing great emphasis on "cursed."

"Really? And when did he tell you that?" Ethan challenged.

"When you were busy trying to show off for Allie," Jordan responded. "Was that before or after you tripped over your own feet and flopped on the ground? I can't quite remember." Jordan paused. "By the way, I'm loving the grass stain on your shirt."

Pulling his white polo shirt away from his body, Ethan looked. Sure enough, evidence of his clumsiness was imprinted on his chest. He blushed and lowered his head; he didn't have a comeback.

"Cha . . . ching. Point for me," Jordan taunted.

Allie shifted her weight from foot to foot as she glanced around the group.

"I know it sounds weird," Jordan continued, "but Uncle Bart said that the Phantom Ship is the evil leftovers of the bad chief trying to escape from his prison under the mountain."

"Evil leftovers?" Ethan asked. "Kind of like Mom's broccoli casserole."

Jordan didn't even grin. "Uncle Bart said the bad chief . . . what was his name?"

"Llao," Ethan said. His flat tone punctuated his disinterest.

"Yeah, Chief Llao created the Phantom Ship so he could escape from his prison under the lake, but when the other chief . . ."

"Skell."

"Yeah, when Chief Skell saw the ship, he turned it into rock, keeping Llao trapped beneath the crater. Bart said the Phantom Ship is a reminder that as long as Chief Llao is under Crater Lake, his power is weaker than Chief Skell's. But the evil chief is always trying to escape," Jordan said.

"Ooooh, oooh! Wahhhh oohh!" Ethan said with his best ghost imitation. The girls rolled their eyes.

"So what happens if Chief Llao escapes?" Allie asked.

"I don't know, but Uncle Bart said it would be bad. If Llao ever escaped, he would overthrow Chief Skell. Then nothing could stop him."

Recognizing Allie's interest in the story, Ethan chimed in. "According to the legend, Chief Skell became the Guardian of the people after Chief Llao tried to destroy them. Without Skell, the people wouldn't be able to defend themselves against Chief Llao."

"Well, curse or not, I think the ship's pretty awesome. Let's get a closer look," Allie suggested.

Jordan looked at her parents. Dad nodded his approval. "As long as Ethan goes with you," he said.

Ethan played coy at first, pretending to be disinterested, but then agreed when Allie clasped his hand in hers and pleaded, "Please."

Ethan couldn't resist. He smiled as he led the girls to the trail that descended from the outlook. It wouldn't take them all the way to the lakeshore, but it would get them close.

Allie slipped as she hurried down the steep pathway, but Ethan caught her arm and held her up. With an embarrassed grin, Allie released herself from Ethan's grip and then continued, stepping more cautiously on the loose ground.

Ethan followed the girls down the multiple switchbacks. The brilliant blue lake grew larger and the Phantom Ship more ominous. From high above, the rock and the trees on the island appeared average, but as he got closer, the discoloration became obvious. At first Ethan thought the darkness of the trees and rock was due to shadow, but the sun was high in the western sky, shining onto the ship. It couldn't be shadow. The rocks, the dirt, even the trees appeared to be scorched like they had been burned by fire, but the needles on the trees appeared to be intact. The thick vegetation looked hearty except for the rusty-black color that made everything appear dead.

"See, it is cursed," Jordan said.

Ethan shrugged.

As the trail switched to the north, a beam of light flashed across Ethan's eyes. He looked high on the hill but was unable to see the source of the light. Continuing down the trail, Ethan scanned the cliff for crevices or caves. Then he saw it.

Partially hidden in the shadow of recessed rock, midway up the cliff, he saw the figure of a man. The girls didn't notice, so they kept walking, but Ethan stopped and stared. The light flashed again across his eyes. He covered his eyes for a brief moment and then returned his gaze to the cliff, but the man was gone.

"Where'd he go?" Ethan mumbled.

Ethan watched the cliff, but he never saw the figure again. He wondered if he had really seen a man at all. Expelling the image from his thoughts, Ethan returned his concentration to the Phantom Ship and to the cute blonde cheerleader, who happened to be a terrible driver.

* * *

From deep inside the cliff-side cave, a Native American teenager emerged and stood at the edge. The toes of his boots flirting with the edge, he watched the boy and two girls make their final descent to the lower lookout.

A simple black ponytail held the hair out of his face, accenting his handsome Native American features. Transferring his earnest stare to the adults waiting near the lower trail of the Sun Notch Viewpoint, the teenager wrinkled his forehead.

Che-tan stood at attention, his eyes trained on the unsuspecting visitors.

# – 7 –

# Bathroom Break

Though they had not yet begun the rigorous ascent to Mt. Scott, the rest stops became more frequent as the slope steepened. Removing their packs, the Scouts gathered around Jacob as he sat on a tuft of grass beneath a western white pine. In both hands he held a large piece of black basalt.

"Check it out, guys," Jacob said, lifting the rock for everyone to see. The porous volcanic rock was surprisingly light for its size. Jacob passed the rock around so each Scout could take a turn pretending to be stronger than he was. It was only a rock, but it had once been hot lava.

"Cool," one of the Scouts said.

"Put it in your pack," one of the older boys suggested as he handed the rock back to Jacob.

"We're not allowed to take anything out of the park. Not even a rock. We'll leave it here so the next hiker can find it," Jacob said.

"Whatever," Brady said.

Jacob's dad grinned. "Aren't your packs heavy enough without loading them with rocks?" The boys nodded. "You all about ready to get moving?" he asked.

The boys grunted and adjusted, moving toward their packs.

Brady took a step toward his leader and whispered, "I need to go to the bathroom."

"Okay. Go find a tree and let's get going."

"Uh, it may take a little longer than that, if you know what I mean," Brady said with a grimace. He squirmed in place.

"Oh, yeah. Well, Jacob, you and Brady are buddies. Go with him while he takes care of business and hurry back."

"Seriously? I have to take Jacob with me while I . . . you know?" Brady asked.

"Unless you plan on doing it right here where the rest of us can see, he's going with you. If you're out of sight, you need a buddy."

"Fine. Come on, Jacob, before I explode."

Grabbing a fold-up shovel from his pack, Jacob followed behind as Brady hiked up the hill and around a large rock outcropping. He stopped once and chose a spot, but after hearing the chatter of the other Scouts near the trail, he figured he was still too close for any real privacy. Brady continued his search for the location of his personal latrine. He kept walking, with Jacob in tow, searching for a secluded site.

"Hey, pick a spot already? I thought you were about to explode," Jacob said.

"In a minute. I'm going to be a little exposed here. I don't really want anyone walking around the corner while I'm . . . uh, busy." Walking down a small ravine, Brady found an adequate place and gave Jacob his best "go away" look. But instead of going away, Jacob moved closer. Brady gave him an evil eye, but then Jacob held out the shovel.

"What's that for?" Brady asked.

"Do you ever pay attention? Leave no trace—keep it natural. Does this sound familiar?" Brady stared with his usual blank expression. "Brady, dig a hole, go to the bathroom, cover it up. Just don't touch your stuff with my shovel."

"Hey, Jacob, toilet paper?"

Jacob rotated his fanny pack to his stomach and pulled out his biodegradable toilet paper. Counting off five squares, he tore it and handed the paper to Brady.

"Five squares? What am I supposed to do with that? Pick my nose?"

"Well, you'd better make it count," Jacob said, and then walked a short distance, sitting against a tree with his back to Brady. Jacob picked at some knotweed and yellow sulphurflower, waiting while Brady did his deed.

"Come on, Brady. You done yet?"

"Shut up."

Jacob tossed a pinecone at a nearby boulder. "You're taking forever," Jacob mumbled. "Okay, Brady, we need to hustle. We've been gone way too long."

Brady didn't respond.

Meandering through the woods and around the rock fixtures, Brady didn't seem to realize, or care, that everyone on the trail was waiting because of him. Jacob paused and looked back to his straggling buddy. "Come on. Pick up the pace," Jacob urged.

"Shut it," Brady barked. "Just relax . . . and you'd better stop telling me what to do. Don't make me pound you," Brady warned in a semijovial tone.

Jacob shut his mouth and continued walking at a slower pace, allowing Brady to catch up. Moments later, Jacob and Brady stepped from behind a tall rock formation and started down the hill.

"Hey, guys, we're coming!" Jacob hollered, but his voice died in the stale air. He listened for a response but heard only eerie silence. He hollered again as he looked ahead to the spot on the trail where he had left the troop, but he saw nothing. "Guys? Where are you?"

Hopping from the embankment down onto the trail where he had left the others, Brady saw the same large lava rock leaning against a thick root, but the trail was deserted—no boys and no leaders. Even the packs were gone, including his.

Brady turned in place as he searched. "Where is everyone?" he yelled. He ran twenty yards down the trail to search behind a black boulder, but they weren't there. He ran back up the trail, yelling for his group, but there was no response.

"I can't find them!" Brady said, his voice overwhelmed with anxiety. "They're gone."

Jacob sat on the grass and removed his hat, setting it beside him. He picked up the lava rock, tossing it a few inches into the air before catching it. He tossed it again and again as he mumbled to himself.

"Where'd they go? And why would they leave? Is Dad trying to teach me a lesson? Maybe. It doesn't make sense," Jacob muttered to himself.

Brady stood above him, listening to every mumbled word.

"We're all alone," Jacob said, looking up at Brady.

"What are we going to do?" Brady asked, his eyes pleading for answers.

Jacob took a slow, deep breath. "We're going to stay calm." Jacob looked at Brady. "We're only about an hour from camp. If we keep to the trail, we'll be fine. We might even be able to catch up if we hurry."

Brady was surprised by Jacob's composure. He was confident and cool, but best of all, he knew what to do. Jacob's small stature was deceptive, and Brady found himself wishing for a small measure of his partner's courage.

Without the weight of their packs, the duo hiked toward Mt. Scott. They put their heads down and hiked with purpose.

* * *

A short distance into the woods, two large boulders supported a flat slab of stone. Brady and Jacob had passed the rock formation on their search for the perfect latrine, but passing it on their return, they were unaware of a black bear sitting high on top.

The bear watched as the boys searched the trail for their missing friends and as they began their rapid hike toward Mt. Scott. The bear remained still, his pale eyes watching.

## – 8 –

# CONSUMED

FROM HIGH ABOVE THE TRAIL NEAR THE VIEWPOINT, ALLIE'S mom peered over the rock wall. With both hands held to her mouth like a megaphone, she hollered to the wandering kids below. Allie didn't hear her mother's call, and Ethan pretended not to.

The lower lookout was well worth the hike. It felt like an untamed wilderness where natural dangers lurked behind every tree and under every rock. Ethan even hoped he would find a rough-skinned newt. The thought of possessing a natural poison factory excited him. He didn't know what he would do with a rough-skinned newt if he found one, but nothing dastardly, probably. With a myriad of basaltic boulders to climb and rock alcoves to investigate, Jordan, Allie, and Ethan explored the trails. They weaved in and out of piney groves and through narrow passages chiseled in rock.

"ALLIE!" her mom yelled again. The sound of her voice carried as the wind died.

Ethan turned toward it. *Darn it.* Now she knew he could hear her call. Ethan nudged Allie's shoulder and pointed toward her mother, who was standing just off the trail below the viewpoint. Allie waved, and Jordan raised both arms over her head, jumping up and down.

"Come on. Time to go!" her mom hollered.

Motioning for Allie to return from her explorations, her mom suddenly stiffened. Her feet sank into the pumice like it was quicksand. Attempting to step out of her canvas sneaker, she tried to pull her leg from the volcanic sand. It didn't work. She swallowed hard and struggled harder as the sand covered her ankle. Her body wiggled and contorted as she attempted to free herself, but her heavy feet wouldn't budge. The sand pulled at her heels, sucking her deeper with each passing second. She twisted her body and looked up to the viewpoint.

"Ronnie!" Her voice echoed around the mountain as she screamed for help. Her chest heaved with each rapid breath.

Leaping over the short wall of the overlook, Allie's dad landed on the soft slope and slid the rest of the way to the trail on his backside, with his hands positioned behind him like a rudder. Ethan's parents scurried from the ledge, meeting up with Ronnie in time to meet his shocked expression with their own.

The panic was contagious. Ronnie froze, watching as his wife's legs were immersed in the sand to mid-thigh. No one knew what to do. Then, grabbing her hands, he pulled with every ounce of strength. A popping sound from her shoulder and a scream of pain caused him to stop.

Allie's mom looked at her husband. She tried to speak, but gentle sobs rendered her words unrecognizable. Tears streamed down her cheeks. Allie's dad hunched over and wiped the tears from his wife's face, his eyes swollen and red.

From below, the adults' behavior looked very strange. Allie couldn't see what was happening, but it became clear as she watched her mom descend further into the earth.

"MOM!" Allie screamed, but the flurry of activity surrounding her mom continued. Allie's eyes widened as she stood on the lower trail, paralyzed with horror.

"Here! Grab this!" Ethan's dad yelled.

Allie's mom grabbed hold of the stick while the other adults attempted to pull her out. The sand was now waist deep. "I can't hold it," she yelled back, her hands slipping from the stick.

With another stick, Ronnie dug into the soft pumice near his wife's body, but with each stroke, more sand gathered in even faster. Dropping to his knees, he scooped the volcanic sand with his hands, but she sank further, the sand covering her chest and then her neck.

"RONNIE! ALLIE!" Her panicked screams filled the air before being muffled by the sand.

Allie's dad scooped the sand fiercely, turning it red from his bleeding fingers, but his efforts were in vain. His wife's eyes closed and then the sand covered them. Her blonde hair disappeared next, and then she was gone.

Allie stood in astonishment as her mother disappeared into the ground. Shocked silence enveloped the mountain. Then Ethan lifted his eyes skyward as he heard the soft squawking of four large birds circling above the adults, like vultures above roadkill.

Ronnie knelt on the path next to his wife's grave. His bloody hands covered his face as he sobbed.

Once again the ground near the path was firm. Ethan's parents held each other and placed a consolatory hand on their sobbing friend's shoulder. Then, without warning, their feet dropped six inches into the ground. Glued in position, they could do nothing as the suction pulled at their heels. Their panicked eyes met, and they struggled against the inescapable earth.

Wailing and thrashing for escape, Ronnie disappeared first, the dirt covering the crown of his head. Ethan and Jordan's parents followed, gasping for breath before the dirt covered their faces and muffled their screams. Mercifully, they descended faster than Allie's mom. She had been the appetizer, and the other three adults were the main course.

"NO!" Ethan yelled.

Running up the trail, Ethan, Allie, and Jordan navigated the switchbacks to their parents' last position near the overlook.

"MOM! DAD!" Ethan screamed. Hunching over with his

hands on his knees and breathing hard, he looked up to the trail hoping his parents would reappear, but they were gone. Ethan turned to look at the girls running up the hill behind him. "COME ON! HURRY!"

Ethan resumed running, willing his exhausted legs to keep pumping, but before he was able to sprint thirty more yards, he fell face-first into the dirt. Panting, he flopped onto his back and stared into the green sky at the large birds circling above. Fuzzy blackness encroached from the corners of his eyes, and he felt dizzy. The birds disappeared just as quickly as his parents had. Ethan sat up, but his eyes rolled back into his head. Everything went black as he collapsed forward into the dirt.

Sitting on a large stone, Allie bawled at the loss of her parents. Under her eyes, mud was streaked from where she had wiped the tears with dirtied hands. Jordan kneeled on the ground next to Ethan with her head buried against his back. Ethan lay motionless with his face against the dirt. His slight breath blew against the dry soil. Then Jordan felt movement.

Rising up on his forearms, Ethan rolled. His back hit against the large rock and came to rest on Allie's feet. His eyes blinked as he tried to make sense of his surroundings and adjust his eyes to the sunlight. "What happened?"

Scooting over on her knees, Jordan flung her arms over her brother, putting her head on his chest and giving him a tight hug. "I don't know," Jordan answered with a sob.

Ethan's blinking slowed as his mind made sense of his foggy memories. Then he remembered. "Mom! Dad! Where are they?" Ethan asked, sitting up and looking up the hill.

Lowering her head, Allie didn't respond, and Jordan just held on tighter. "We've got to go find them," he said, pushing against Jordan to release her grip, but neither girl seemed ready to follow him up the slope. "What are you two waiting for? Let's go." Ethan stood and started to walk up the trail, each step wobbling.

"We've been up there already. There's nothing left. No

one . . . Ethan, there's nothing left," Allie whispered. "They're all gone."

Ethan stopped and shook his head in disbelief. "That's impossible," he said as he turned back to the girls. "I'm going up there."

Just off the trail, below the viewpoint, Ethan scoured the ground for any kind of clue to his parents' whereabouts. He saw a couple of large sticks the adults had used while trying to free Allie's mom, but there was no other evidence they had ever been there. Nothing remained, not even his dad's ball cap.

Ethan closed his eyes. He wasn't there when his parents needed him. Standing on the spot where he believed his parents last stood, he stomped his foot mostly in anger but hoping the ground would suck him in too. No such luck.

After hiking the remaining distance to the viewpoint, Ethan waited. With his back to the lake and the Phantom Ship, Ethan sat on the low stone wall. He glanced over his shoulder and saw the two girls making their way up the trail. He turned back around, resigned to waiting.

* * *

From a recess high in the cliff, the young Native American watched the kids below, and then, without hesitation, he stepped from the edge and dove off the side. Che-tan's arms tucked tight against his body and his head aimed at the ground as he hurtled downward like a missile. Then, in one fluid motion, his arms rose to his side. His flesh exploded, turning into four large birds of prey, their wings catching the wind and lofting upward, back into the sky above Crater Lake.

– 9 –

# Lost

THIRTY MINUTES. JUST GIVE ME THIRTY MORE MINUTES," Brady pleaded. Sitting on an upended stump near the deserted campsite, he massaged his throbbing legs. They hadn't wobbled so much since two-a-day football practices last summer.

"Do you really want to be on the trail when the sun goes down? We'll freeze. Come on, Brady. We need to get going," Jacob prodded.

"Get going? Where? I followed you up the stinking mountain. Where next, boss?"

Thirty minutes sounded good, real good. Brady dreaded the prospect of hiking back down the mountain to the ranger station, but the sun was already falling toward the horizon.

Jacob groaned as he sat, propping himself up on one arm. "Brady, I'm not your mom waking you up for school," he said, placing one knee on the ground. He paused while he mustered additional strength. "You big baby. We have to go *now.* We don't have a choice."

Brady tilted his head back, squinted his eyes, and inhaled before releasing a sustained scream. "Aughhhhhhhh!" The sound echoed down the mountain.

"You feel better?" Jacob asked.

Brady grinned for the first time in hours. "Actually, yeah."

Jacob stood, shook his legs, and hopped into the air, almost collapsing as his full weight reconnected with the ground. He steadied himself and then began his decent, lumbering down the mountain, moaning with each step.

Brady's long strides and downward momentum carried him down the steep slope of Mt. Scott. Glancing over his shoulder, Brady knew he was getting too far ahead of Jacob, but he felt like a boulder rolling down a hill that couldn't be stopped. At the bottom of the slope, Brady slowed and waited for Jacob to catch up.

The sun fell further in the western sky, and the piney air cooled under the deep evergreen shadows. Brady shivered as a cool breeze stole the heat away from his sweat-drenched shirt.

Jacob panted as he looked to the horizon. He removed his glasses and polished the lenses with the front of his shirt. "Once the sun sets, it's really going to get cold up here." Jacob listened as insects buzzed nearby. He removed his hat to swat at a mosquito near his face. "The rest of the hike should all be downhill past Sun Notch Viewpoint and on to the ranger station," Jacob said.

Brady responded with a grunt.

"We're making better time than I expected," Jacob said.

Brady just sighed. With each heavy step, he thought about the Scout leaders and the older boys sitting at picnic tables, laughing and enjoying cold sodas while eating a late supper. The thought of their comfort turned his face red, and a mellow growl escaped from his lips.

Both boys caught their second, or maybe their third, wind. With renewed vigor they trudged along, only stopping once for a breather.

"How close are we?" Brady asked, wiping the sweat from his forehead.

Jacob thought for a moment. "About an hour."

Eager to make their triumphant return to the station and the waiting scouts, Jacob and Brady pushed on.

# - 10 -

# CHE-TAN

"CAN YOU BE ANY SLOWER?" ETHAN YELLED TO THE approaching girls with an annoyed laugh.

With a hand on the younger girl's back, Allie prodded Jordan up the trail. "Chill," Allie yelled back.

Ethan's head lowered. "Sorry. But the sooner we get back to the ranger station, the sooner we can figure out what's going on around here."

Jordan's nose crinkled, and she squinted bitterly as she approached her brother.

"Hopefully Bart will have some kind of idea about what's going on. Maybe he'll know what happened to Mom and Dad," Ethan said.

The girls finally reached the overlook. They sat on the low wall just as Ethan was standing.

"Let's go," Ethan urged, earning him two weary scowls. "Come on, guys, I know you're tired, but we need to tell Uncle Bart what happened," Ethan said.

Allie exhaled through puckered lips. "Ethan, just give us a couple of minutes."

"But—"

"You can run ahead if you want, but I've got to sit for a minute," Allie said. "We'll catch up."

Ethan considered the offer but then sat back on the wall

next to Jordan. "I think we should stay together. Something weird is going on around here. I'll wait. We'll go together," Ethan said, his head cocked back, tilted to the sky.

Throwing his legs over the side of the wall, Ethan turned back toward the Phantom Ship. Allie and Jordan rested, facing the opposite direction. High above the ship, four birds hovered. Ethan wiped away the tear at the corner of his eye as he considered the loss of his parents, all because they wanted to look at a stupid island, in a stupid lake, in the stupid crater.

Ethan watched the birds floating in circles. He thought he could hear them squawk but then realized the birds were too far away. The noise seemed to be getting louder, closer. It was high pitched and piercing. Maybe it was just a whistle in the wind.

Leaving their hovering pattern above the Phantom Ship, the birds flew toward the viewpoint. Maybe it *was* the birds he was hearing. But no, the sound was coming from behind him. Pulling his legs back over the wall, Ethan set his feet on the cement and looked in the direction of the commotion.

Allie stood, and Ethan followed, peering up the trail to the north. Over a slight rise, the chattering, squawking sound burst over the hill as two teenage boys in Scout shirts sprinted down the trail, screaming in terror.

The four birds from the island drew near and then circled Jordan, Allie, and Ethan, who were too engrossed in the spectacle of the screaming boys to pay the birds much attention. Then the birds fell into single file with the largest bird at the front. The lead bird dove toward the outlook, passing between the two screaming Scouts and the others. Three birds followed behind their leader. Ethan nearly got whiplash as he swiveled to follow the birds swooshing past him near the ground. The birds disappeared into the trees.

Allie locked onto the boys running toward her. "What's up with those guys?" she asked. Then, behind the running boys, at the top of the rise, Allie saw a black bear come to rest. The speeding boys approached the viewpoint with no hint of slowing.

"BEAR!" Brady yelled as he neared.

A little ways behind Brady, Jacob ran as fast as he could, his chest heaving. "BIG bear!" he added.

Standing near the trail, Ethan watched as the boys ran by. Then as the trail bowed to the left, their feet skidded to a stop. Looking at Allie, Ethan followed her eyes up the trail and observed as the bear turned in place and headed the opposite direction, back over the rise and out of sight.

Ethan turned to the Scouts who were standing in the middle of the trail with their hands on their knees, gasping for air. He wondered what had made them stop, but then he saw it.

Moving toward the boys, a shadow emerged from the trees and joined them on the trail. It wasn't a person, and it wasn't a bear, but what it was Ethan couldn't quite tell. It glided toward the Scouts.

Jordan grabbed at her brother's hand to keep him close, but Ethan's feet were already carrying him closer to the specter. Approaching the other boys, Ethan stopped and looked. His head cocked with confusion.

Standing in front of him and the others was not some mystical phantom but another young teenager. There wasn't anything frightening about him at all. He was a normal person in jeans and an open flannel shirt. Ethan blinked and then looked at the other boys. Where was the specter? The shadow he had seen just moments before? The lowering sun was playing tricks on his eyes. The other boys seemed even more surprised, but Ethan recognized their relief.

Stepping in front of the Scouts, Ethan approached the young man and extended his hand. "Hello."

The Native American teen adjusted his black ponytail as he looked at the outstretched hand. He seemed to recognize the gesture as a peaceful offering but didn't take hold. Ethan held the pose for a moment and then lowered his hand when it seemed clear he would not receive a shake.

"I'm Ethan," he said. Motioning toward the other boys,

Ethan urged them to continue the introductions.

"I'm Jacob, and this is Brady," the smallest boy offered, pointing to the other.

The boy seemed to understand but didn't reply, nor did he make any introductions himself. Looking past the boys, he nodded to the girls waiting twenty yards behind. "I am sorry for your loss," he said with a mild accent.

Brady and Jacob looked at each other in confusion, but Ethan understood. Ethan squinted. "What do you know about it?"

"Please, do not fear me. I am here to help. Bring the girls closer. I will not hurt you."

Brady and Ethan looked at the average-sized young man and then at each other. An incredulous cough escaped Brady's mouth. For his age, Brady was huge, over six feet tall, and muscular. Even Ethan was a little taller than the plaid-shirted kid. Turning toward Allie and Jordan, Ethan motioned for them to come closer.

Allie grabbed Jordan's hand and walked to the boys.

"Don't worry. He says he won't hurt us," Brady scoffed as he noticed the girls' hesitation. "I'm Brady," he said as he caught Allie's eye.

"This is Allie," Ethan said, pointing to the older girl, "and this is Jordan."

"Dang, little girl. You look like you lived through a famine," Brady said.

"Hey! That's my sister," Ethan protested.

"And you look like you caused it," Brady continued.

Ethan glared at Brady and clenched his jaw but didn't respond. Then, he returned his gaze to the Native American. "Now, who are you?"

"I am Che-tan. I have been watching you, and I know what has happened."

"What happened? What are you talking about?" Jacob asked.

"You are alone—all of you," Che-tan said. "I watched as your parents were consumed by the ground," he said, looking at Allie.

She lowered her head and closed her eyes, trying to block the tears.

"On the cliff. I saw you on the cliff," Ethan said.

Che-tan nodded. "And my friend watched as your group was swallowed into the Below World," he said, looking at Jacob and Brady with pity.

"I don't know what you're talking about, but you sound crazy," Brady accused.

Jacob scowled at Che-tan. "We got separated from our group, that's all. They're waiting for us at the ranger station. In fact, we need to get going so we can catch up."

Shaking his head, Che-tan mumbled some words no one could understand. He paused. "There is no one left at the ranger station. They have all been devoured. I am sorry."

"Devoured?" Brady asked. "What a nut job. Come on, Jacob, let's go. If you guys want to come with us, you're welcome," he said, looking at Allie. "But you, Mr. Che-tan Nut-job, you're not invited."

"No. Stay. I am here to help. There is hope for your family and friends, but there is not much time," Che-tan said.

After tapping Brady on the shoulder, Jacob motioned for them to go.

"Wait, guys. I think we should listen to Che-tan. Something really weird is going on here," Ethan said as the boys double-timed it down the trail. "Seriously, guys. Just listen for a minute. What can it hurt?"

Ethan, Allie, and Jordan watched as Jacob adjusted his hat. The Scouts hiked out of sight.

"What happened to my mom and dad?" Jordan blurted, her voice cracking. Her brow furrowed, and wrinkles covered her forehead.

Che-tan's eyes burrowed into Jordan as he considered answering the question. "I will tell you what I know." Che-tan paused. "The earth has consumed everyone at Crater Lake who has reached the age of sixteen, including your parents. They have been imprisoned by an evil spirit chief, but we can save them."

"What did you just say?" Allie asked in a low monotone.

"The time is short. If they remain in the Below World at noon tomorrow, they will be lost forever with no chance for redemption."

Ethan stared.

"What should we do?" Jordan asked.

"There is still a chance, but it will be difficult. When the midnight moon strikes the moon dial on the Phantom Ship, the hiding place of the prison key will be made known. You must acquire the key and unlock the prison."

"Midnight? Moon dial? Prison?" Ethan repeated, shaking his head. "What in the world are you talking about?"

Che-tan continued. "You will begin your quest to rescue your parents. It must be done tonight—at exactly midnight. You must decide now what you are willing to do to save them."

# – 11 –

# Free Shopping

BRADY CIRCLED THE RANGER STATION, SEARCHING FOR THE missing group of Scouts, a park ranger, or a janitor—anyone at all. Walking a short distance into the surrounding woods, he checked the trailheads and outhouses while Jacob looked inside. Cars remained in the parking lot, and a motorized cart idled near the side of the building.

Brady massaged his temples and ruffled his fingers through his hair as he thought. His breathing was shallow and rapid. *Where can they be?*

Inside the outpost, the lights were on and the cash register hung open. Jacob pulled a water bottle from the cooler and guzzled it and then opened a second bottle, drinking it at a more modest pace.

"Hello. Anybody in here?" Jacob hollered as he searched. "Anyone?" Jacob listened, but there was no response.

Grabbing a souvenir cloth bag, Jacob began shopping. He hesitated at first, but then, finding a pen and paper near the register, he began making a list of everything he took: six large bottles of water—including the two he just drank—three packs of beef jerky, five candy bars, one family-size bag of Doritos, a bag of sunflower seeds, one newspaper, one flashlight. From the apparel section of the gift shop, he grabbed a forest green hooded sweatshirt and stuffed three others into a second bag.

He also picked four stocking caps from the shelf and a fleece blanket.

He completed his list, which included the two souvenir bags, and left the list on top of the cash in the register. He scrawled the words "I owe U" at the top of the list and signed his name. Closing the register, he headed outside to find Brady.

Sitting atop the picnic table, Brady stared into the trees. "They left me out here to die," he was muttering to himself as Jacob approached. Lowering his eyes from the woods to his small friend, Brady chuckled at the sight of Jacob wearing the hoodie and stocking cap with two large bags dangling from his arms.

"What's all that for?" Brady asked.

Jacob glanced at the lowering sun. "There's only about another half hour of daylight, and it's getting cold. Those other kids are still out at the viewpoint. Did you see what they were wearing?" Jacob asked.

"Not really. Same as us, I guess."

"That's right. Shorts, T-shirts. There's no way they'll survive out there dressed like that. We need to help them."

Throwing his head back with a sigh of displeasure, Brady rolled his eyes as he looked into the sky. "They have their new friend, Che-tan. They'll be fine."

"Brady . . ."

"Jacob—what? They're not my problem. If they get cold, they can come back to the ranger station like normal people. I think we should wait right here. We can sleep inside until morning and then figure out what we need to do. I'm tired."

"I know you're tired. So am I, but I need your help. We'll meet up with the other kids and come back here for the night." Jacob watched Brady, who masterfully avoided eye contact. "Well, I'm going with or without you. I hope you sleep well."

With his bags full and the large blanket hanging from his shoulder, Jacob walked back to the trailhead for the Sun Notch Viewpoint.

Brady watched what would normally be a spectacular sunset. The sky was ablaze with a myriad of reds, oranges, and purples. With a groan, he stood and lumbered inside. Grabbing a hoodie from the rack, he put it on and then placed a stocking cap on his head. He grabbed a flashlight and a blanket and headed for the door when his attention was diverted.

Brady focused on the model of the Native American standing in the corner, and then his eyes wandered to the glowing display case. Underneath the glass, a gentle strobe of red, blue, and white light shone outward, casting its warmth onto the ceiling. Brady moved closer and peered down at the unusual necklace. His mouth sagged open, and his eyes glazed over. Glancing around the room to ensure no one was watching, Brady raised his arm and crashed his elbow into the display case, shattering the glass. Careful not to scrape his arm on the jagged edges, he reached inside. With his fingers, Brady pushed aside a large piece of glass that covered the necklace and then pulled the unique item from the case.

Holding the necklace outward, he examined it. The necklace mesmerized him. Wrapping the leather band around his neck, Brady tied it in a knot and tucked the three interlocked stones under his hoodie.

Hidden beneath his clothing, the strobing glow of the necklace and its hypnotizing spell went dormant. Exiting the ranger station with supplies in hand, Brady hurried to catch up with Jacob.

## – 12 –

# Tall Tales

Ethan eyed Che-tan, skeptical of the tall tale he had just been told. "So if I'm hearing you right, you're saying that our parents were sucked into a prison in the 'Below World,'" he said, making quotations with his fingers, "by an ancient spirit chief?" Ethan's head shook listlessly. "Get real. I was willing to listen to you because I know something strange is going on, but Brady was right: you *are* a nut job."

Che-tan frowned.

Grabbing Jordan's hand, Ethan looked at Allie. "It's going to be dark soon. I've listened to all I can stomach. Let's get back to the ranger station."

"No, Ethan. What about Mom and Dad?" Jordan asked. "We can't leave them."

Che-tan nodded. "You are correct. You cannot leave your parents. If you do, they will be imprisoned forever."

Pulling Jordan's hand, Ethan attempted to lead her away, but she held firm. Jordan looked at Che-tan with pleading eyes.

"Look, Che-tan, if you want us to believe your story, you've got to make sense," Allie said. "Convince us. We'll listen for a few more minutes," she said, looking at the others. "Right?"

Che-tan's stoic face allowed for a mild grin. "What would you like me to explain?"

Ethan's eyes narrowed and his lips tightened. "Okay,

number one, who are you *really*? And don't say 'I am Che-tan,'" Ethan said with his best Frankenstein impression. "I've got to say, that's a very unsatisfying answer."

Che-tan looked confused. "But I *am* Che-tan." He looked at the three kids. It was clear his act wasn't earning him any friends. "Fine, I will be truthful, but the truth is sometimes difficult to accept. Just like you find it difficult to believe your parents were consumed into an earthen prison, even though you witnessed the event."

"Just tell us. Who are you?" Allie repeated.

In an explosion of flesh, Che-tan burst into pieces as four large birds took flight. The flock flew in a tight circle around the kids, rose into the air, and then crashed together at ground level, reassembling into Che-tan. His eyes moved from one kid to the next. Their mouths all hung open with shock. Che-tan smiled.

"I hope now you will trust what I say." Che-tan studied the kids' expressions.

All three nodded in stunned silence.

"I am a Guardian of Crater Lake. I was once counted among Chief Llao's people, but no more. After Chief Skell defeated Chief Llao in battle, my people were entrusted to watch over his imprisonment." Che-tan's words slowed as he chose them carefully. "My people betrayed Chief Llao when we refused to join him in battle. The escape of Chief Llao would prove disastrous for my people and everyone in Chief Skell's realm."

Tongues loosened and rapid questions fired at Che-tan.

"Uncle Bart was right? It wasn't just a story," Jordan said. "The legends, everything. It's true!"

"Has Chief Llao ever tried to escape?" Allie asked.

Ethan's left eye twitched. "Are there more like you?" he asked.

"One at a time. Let me answer your questions," Che-tan said, overwhelmed by the inquiries.

The kids shuffled backward as they awaited Che-tan's answers.

"Do not fear me. I am your friend. I will answer your questions. First, I do not know 'Uncle Bart' or the legend you refer to, but yes, Chief Llao nearly escaped three thousand years ago. He attempted to build a ship on top of the lake. He intended for it to carry him and his minions away from the reach of Chief Skell, but we stopped him."

"The Phantom Ship," Ethan whispered in disbelief.

Che-tan nodded.

"How did you stop him?" Allie asked.

"When my people discovered his plan, we informed Chief Skell. Chief Skell cursed the ship, turning it into stone."

"So Chief Llao attempted to escape Crater Lake on a boat?" Allie asked.

"Yes."

"That may be the dumbest thing I've ever heard," Ethan said, laughing. "I mean . . . it's a ship in a crater. Where did he think he was going?"

Che-tan shook his head and smiled as he looked down to the Phantom Ship. "It was a desperate plan, for sure," he said with a soft chuckle, "but the ship was not intended to sail on the water. It was meant for the clouds."

"Oh." Allie and Jordan nodded with acceptance, but Ethan was still unconvinced.

"After the escape attempt, the two chiefs developed a treaty for Chief Llao's continued imprisonment. Chief Llao has been silent ever since . . . until now."

"But what does any of this have to do with us—or our parents?" Ethan asked.

Che-tan shook his head. "I cannot answer that question. But it is clear Chief Llao is active again. According to the treaty he made with Chief Skell, he will be destroyed if he attempts to escape, but he is up to something. Perhaps he is building an army of prisoners to battle Chief Skell. Or maybe he is merely making mischief to trick Chief Skell into renegotiating the treaty. It is a mystery." Che-tan paused as he looked into the sky.

"Whatever he is doing, Chief Llao must be stopped."

The air cooled and Jordan shivered at the chill. Jordan, Allie, and Ethan all stood next to Che-tan, watching the horizon in silence as the sun lowered behind the crater's rim.

"Let's pretend we did believe you," Allie began. "What is it you want us to do? I don't understand what we can do to rescue our parents from the prison of a powerful spirit chief? We're just teenagers."

"Yes, you are young, just like me. Because we are young, Chief Llao does not consider us a threat. That is why we were spared imprisonment like your parents. But there is much you can do." Che-tan thought about his words and then corrected himself. "There is much we can do together."

Ethan chewed on his lower lip and sighed. "Che-tan, I think I believe you. If there's anything we can do to save our parents, we'll do it."

"What can we do? Tell us," Jordan pleaded.

Che-tan's head bowed. "The key lies on the Phantom Ship. I am forbidden by treaty from stepping foot on the ship. But you can."

"The key?"

"Yes. The key will unlock the gate to the Prison of the Lost. You must get it tonight."

# - 13 -

# A Long, Cold Night

An orange sliver escaped from underneath the curtained horizon. Ethan watched as Allie sat alone at the corner of the rock alcove, holding her arms as she looked out at the moonlit lake. He followed her gaze. In the shadow of night, the Phantom Ship looked as if its sails would catch the wind and deliver Chief Llao from his prison beneath the lake. Allie shuddered.

Ethan reclined against a flat boulder as Jordan leaned into him. He wrapped his arms around her as he peeked at his watch. Wiggling in his seat, Ethan tried to get comfortable enough to rest, but it was going to be a long three hours until it was time to make the trek to the Phantom Ship.

Despite the body heat from his younger sister, Ethan's muscles quivered. He glanced at Allie. "You doing okay?" The moonlight reflected off the lake, lighting Allie's face.

The high rock walls provided shelter from the western wind but the mountain air cooled rapidly.

"I'll survive." She lifted her knees and rubbed her legs. "What I wouldn't give for a fire."

Ethan's eyes closed and his head rested against the rock. "Yeah, me too."

Rising from her seat, Allie walked out from behind the

sheltering rock as voices wafted down from the lookout high above. Two lights swayed back and forth. "Ethan, Jordan, someone's here."

Waving her arms, Allie hollered back. "We're down here."

"COME UP," Jacob yelled. "WE HAVE FOOD—CLOTHES. WE'LL TAKE YOU BACK TO THE STATION."

Allie paused but only for a moment. "NO. WE'RE STAYING," she hollered back. Allie turned to see Ethan and Jordan standing nearby. "They came back."

"COME DOWN," Ethan yelled, suppressing the chattering of his teeth.

"COME UP!" Brady growled.

"NO!" the three said in unison.

* * *

Brady and Jacob looked at each other with weary disbelief. Jacob shone the flashlight on his face as he turned to Brady. His eyes drooped and his boyish voice lowered, "Let's go get them."

# – 14 –

# Rescue Plan

Jacob's flashlight beamed in Allie's face, forcing her to lower her head and shield her eyes. Turning to Ethan and Jordan, who were once again holding each other for warmth, Jacob sat down on a flat rock, clicked off his light, and then waited for his eyes to adjust to the moonlit darkness. He looked at the kids and then slapped his forehead.

"I'm so sorry. I almost forgot. This is for you," Jacob said, holding out a canvas bag packed full of goodies.

Allie, Jordan, and Ethan remained still, huddled next to each other near a large wind block. Ethan didn't dare move, afraid that the warmth he had captured would vanish.

Standing, Jacob shook out the large fleece blanket that hung over his shoulder, enticing the others with the soft warmth. Allie jumped to her feet, grabbed the blanket, and wrapped herself in a cocoon. As her twirling stopped and her eyes opened, Allie saw the needy look from Ethan and Jordan. She opened the blanket wide, inviting them in. The siblings joined Allie as she wrapped them in warm comfort.

Jacob watched and smiled. "You all hungry? Thirsty?" he asked, reaching into his bag. He felt like Santa Claus on Christmas Eve.

Grabbing a bottle of water, Ethan unscrewed the cap and guzzled half the bottle.

"Just take it easy on the water. We could only carry one bottle for each of us. Here, eat this," Jacob suggested as he handed a bag of Doritos to Allie and a candy bar to Ethan. "Snack up, and then we *really* need to head back to the ranger station for the night."

Ethan moaned with delight as he bit into his candy bar. He hadn't eaten since his unsatisfying peanut butter and honey lunch. He shook his head as he savored the sweetness of the caramel and chocolate.

"Uh-uh. We can't leave," Ethan said, his mouth full of chewy confection. Before finishing what was in his mouth, he shoved in another bite. "We have to stay. There's something we've got to do first."

"What? Freeze?" Jacob looked at the huddled group. Ethan's head poked out, and Allie's eyes gleamed over the top of the blanket; Jordan was hidden underneath. "Guys, you can't be serious. Even with the sweatshirts and blankets I brought, you won't last the night," Jacob said. "We need shelter. We need to go back to the ranger station."

"You brought sweatshirts?" Allie asked. "Where are they?"

"Oh, yeah, they're in Brady's bag." Jacob turned in the direction of the trail and screamed, "Brady! Hurry up!"

A light flashed from around the rocky corner as Brady joined the group, turning the flashlight onto his own face. "I'm right here, relax." With a half wave of his hand, Brady set the bag down. He pulled out a small sweatshirt, and Jordan emerged from underneath the blanket. The other two put their sweatshirts on as well and then donned the stocking caps.

Jordan gave Brady an awkward, sideways hug. "Thank you," she said and then scurried back under the blanket.

"Seriously, guys. Please, let's go back to the ranger station," Jacob pleaded as Brady nodded in agreement.

"No," Allie said. "It could be forty degrees out here, and I still wouldn't go back."

"It might actually be forty degrees," Brady said. "I don't get it. Why do you want to stay out here and freeze?"

"It's the only chance they have!" Jordan hollered, her voice muffled beneath the blanket.

"They?"

"Our parents. They disappeared, and they need our help. It's what Che-tan was trying to tell you, but you wouldn't listen," Allie accused.

"Hmm. Che-tan, huh? Where is your new buddy anyway?"

Allie shook her head. "I don't know. But it doesn't matter."

"Of course not," Brady agreed. "Nice friend, though. He's lounging in his warm house watching TV while you guys are out here freezing . . . But you're right. It doesn't matter."

"Just hold on a minute. Let's all sit down and talk about this like reasonable people," Jacob suggested.

With one brain, the blanket-covered group shifted toward a log that lay next to the wall of rock. Sitting, the threesome leaned back, draping the blanket over them from shoulder to ankle. They sat quietly for a moment, and then Ethan crunched some Doritos.

Pulling out the second blanket, Brady sat close to Jacob and covered them both.

"You're not going to like this," Ethan said, "but everything we're going to tell you is absolutely true. I'd bet my life on it." Ethan paused. "Strange things are happening here at Crater Lake—things we don't fully understand."

"Che-tan doesn't even understand. Not completely," Allie said, glancing at the others.

"Look, you may not believe everything I tell you. I sure wouldn't if I hadn't seen it with my own eyes, but I did, and you need to know." Ethan looked with pity at the two Scouts. "You might be right. We may be stupid staying out here. We may not survive the night, but Che-tan told us how we can save our parents, and we're going to try, no matter what the risk."

"Okay . . . Tell us what happened." Jacob said.

Ethan looked at Allie, then at his little sister. He lowered his eyes to the ground. "Like Che-tan said, our parents were 'devoured' by the earth and sucked into the Prison of the Lost in the Below World. In essence, they were captured by an evil spirit chief and are being held deep inside the mantle of the mountain."

Ethan chuckled as he heard the words leave his mouth. It sounded insane. But then his voice became stern. "They're powerless to escape without our help. Without us, our parents will be lost forever, just like your friends, and leaders, and your dad," he said, staring squarely at Jacob. "We need your help. *They* need your help."

Brady frowned, and his right eyebrow rose as he listened to Ethan and Allie tell about their parents' disappearance. "Whatever. You guys are all cracked." He pulled a can of cola from his bag, popped the top, and gulped before releasing a refreshed sigh. "It's a ghost story—but you forgot the campfire."

Jacob listened to the story as Ethan and Allie retold every detail, from the birds hovering overhead to grasping fingers reaching from the sand. Jacob watched Jordan as she listened; there was no deception in her teary eyes. She looked scared.

"So what is it Che-tan wants you to do? And why tonight? Can't it wait until morning?" Jacob asked before warming his hands with the heat from his breath. Brady perked up, interested in their response.

"Tomorrow is the first official day of summer and the longest day of the year."

"The Summer Solstice," Jacob added.

"Right. For some reason, Chief Llao's powers have been growing stronger the past few weeks. Strange things are happening—dangerous, crazy things." Ethan shook his head. "Summer comes and goes every year, but this year's different. Che-tan is afraid Llao's powers will increase at sunrise of the solstice."

Brady grinned. "Powers? Like laser-beams shooting from his eyes? What kind of powers are we talking about?" Brady asked with a smirk.

"Che-tan doesn't know everything Llao is capable of, or why his powers are increasing, but so far he's been able to control things connected to the mountain, like plants or rocks, or even the ground itself," Ethan said.

"Pretty lame powers, but okay," Brady said with disappointment.

"That's how our parents, and your troop, were sucked under." Ethan adjusted his arm behind Jordan, pulling her close to his chest. He wasn't sure when she had dozed off, but she felt heavy leaning against his body.

Jacob's eyes became thin slits as he looked at Ethan and Allie. "You'd better not be pulling my leg." He studied Allie's expression through his thick glasses. "As freaky as it all sounds, I think I believe you. Getting sucked into a creepy spirit prison makes more sense than my dad leaving us and going home."

Brady's head bobbed forward with frustration as he pulled the stocking cap from his red head.

"What do you need? How can we help?" Jacob asked.

"You're kidding," Brady mumbled, elbowing Jacob underneath the blanket. He tilted his head back to gaze at the stars. "I can't believe I came on this trip."

"You're here now, so get on board. We need you," Jacob said.

"Maybe I should go hang out with Che-tan until we're both ready to help. What do you think?"

Allie glared at Brady, and the group sat in silence.

"Fine, whatever. I'll help."

Ethan's eyes widened. "Thank you. But it may be a little rough. We're going to find the hidden key that unlocks Chief Llao's Prison of the Lost. At least that's what Che-tan called it. Here's what we're going to do."

# - 15 -

# MIDNIGHT SWIM

AT THE APPOINTED TIME, ETHAN ROUSTED THE OTHERS from their semi-restful state. Wearing the sweatshirt and stocking cap Jacob had "purchased" from the gift shop, and huddled with Allie and Jordan underneath the fleece blanket, Ethan stayed warm but still uncomfortable.

Allie removed the blanket and stood, placing her hands into the front pocket of the hoodie. She crowded next to Ethan, Jordan, and Jacob while Brady refused to step out from under his blanket.

Ethan looked at his watch: 11:40 p.m. "Okay, we don't have a lot of time before midnight. You guys ready for this?"

Jacob and Allie nodded, but neither seemed sure.

"NO!" Brady snarled from under the blanket.

Attempting to move Brady into action, Jacob moved next to his fellow Scout and kicked his foot. Brady growled and turned his head away. Jacob kicked and poked again until Brady burst from his seat, towering over Jacob. Jacob stepped back, moving out of the larger boy's reach.

Allie stepped between the boys. "Don't be such a whiner. Let's go," she said, staring Brady down.

Gathering their things, the group moved down the hill, closer to the shoreline. Setting her things next to a stump, Jordan stepped to the lake's edge, leaned over, and tested the water with her hand. She bolted upright with cold shock. "Um, Ethan, I think we need a new plan."

Bending over, Ethan submerged his hand up to the wrist. After a moment, the coldness began to hurt. His mouth tightened as he imagined immersing his entire body in the frigid lake. Even though it wasn't far, swimming to the Phantom Ship no longer seemed like a workable plan. Ethan ran his fingers through his curly hair as he strained to think of another option. There was no alternative.

Ethan closed his eyes and took a deep breath. "Guys, I . . . uh . . . it's worse than I thought. I don't think we can all make it. If we don't cramp up during the swim and drown, we may just freeze to death."

"Or get hypothermia and die slowly," Jacob added. The group was silent, but then, noticing the concern on Jordan's face, Jacob explained. "Hypothermia is serious. It usually happens when you're not dressed warm enough. Your body loses heat faster than you can produce it. In severe stages, a person with hypothermia gets angry and goes a little wacko. You can't think straight, so you make bad decisions, and then your body just shuts down."

Ethan looked at his watch. 11:45 p.m. "There's no time for talking. To see the moon dial on the Phantom Ship at midnight, we have to go now."

Ethan's breathing intensified into fast, shallow breaths as he summoned the courage he needed. Looking nervously at Allie, Ethan began removing his clothing. "Do you mind?" Ethan asked, motioning for Allie to turn around. She was too surprised to heed his request.

"What are you doing?" Jordan asked as Ethan dropped his shirt and sweatshirt to the ground and then began removing his shorts and shoes.

"Cotton holds water. That gets heavy and traps the cold next to the skin. Besides, when I get back, I'm going to need dry clothes to help me warm up," Ethan said.

"You're still going?" Brady asked. "Are you an idiot?"

"Maybe," Ethan admitted with an uncomfortable chuckle.

"I thought we were going to nix that plan," Allie said. "It's too cold."

"You can't make it," Brady added.

"I have to." Ethan glared at Brady, and then, looking at Jordan, his eyes softened. "I'll go, but the rest of you stay here. I'm a good swimmer, and I'll be fast. Just have those blankets ready for me when I get back."

"Come on, Ethan. This is stupid. Why do *we* have to do this? Why can't Che-tan do it himself?" Brady asked. "Seriously . . . if he wants the key from the Phantom Ship, and he knows so much, let him get it."

"He can't," Jordan said.

"Why not?"

"He's forbidden from stepping foot on the Phantom Ship," Allie explained.

"He's forbidden? What's that mean? You just believe everything he tells you, don't you?" Brady said. "That guy's up to something."

"Knock it off. We're out of time," Ethan said. Wearing only his boxer shorts, he took a deep breath, preparing himself for the cold. He strode into the freezing water with a canvas bag hanging from his shoulder. The slimy sediment squished between his toes, and his body convulsed from the shock of the water. After stepping in to mid-thigh, Ethan sprung forward the rest of the way in, careful to keep his hair dry. With his strongest freestyle stroke, Ethan swam as fast as he could toward the Phantom Ship.

"He's not going to make it. It's impossible," Jacob said, listening to the kicking splashes and high-pitched moans as he watched the silhouette of Ethan's arms stretching from the water.

"Shut up!" Jordan said.

Allie placed an arm around Jordan's shoulder.

"I'm just saying, it's too cold," Jacob said.

Brady looked at Jordan; her lip quivered. Running behind a tree, Brady removed his clothing down to his underwear. Folding his sweatshirt around the necklace, Brady tossed the rest of his clothes on top. Racing into the water, he screamed as the sharp stabbing pain in his side nearly froze him in place. With determination, his legs continued to pump high, splashing through the water. After wading in to his chest, Brady began swimming after Ethan.

"Didn't see that one coming," Allie mumbled.

On the shore, Jacob, Allie, and Jordan watched and listened to the strokes and grunts of the boys as they swam.

"How far is the Phantom Ship?" Allie asked.

Jacob shook his head. "Hard to tell. Not far, maybe fifty yards."

"They can make it, can't they?" Jordan asked sheepishly, as if embarrassed she had any doubt.

Jacob paused as the smell of lake water filled his nose. He lied, "Yeah, sure, Jordan. Of course they'll make it."

Walking behind the trees where Brady had undressed, Jacob picked up a flashlight from the ground near the clothes. He handed the light to Allie. "As cold as that water is and as tired as they are, that swim's going to feel more like a mile," he whispered. "They're going to need a lot more than blankets and warm clothes if—I mean, when—they get back. Allie, we need to build a fire."

- 16 -

# The Moon Dial

Rising from the lake, Ethan's trembling hand grabbed onto a blackened rock just above the water line. With his other hand he reached higher and found a handhold and then, with his toes, found a foothold. His muscles tensed as his body emerged from the water. Shadows from one of the large "sails" darkened his path, and his eyes strained to find an adequate grip. Brady remained in the water below Ethan, pushing him upward. Climbing the rocky slope out of the water, Ethan stopped and turned, offering his hand. Brady grabbed it and pulled himself onto the rough shore.

Except for the shadowed areas beneath large rock features, or brief moments when a cloud blocked the moonlight, the full moon lit the island well. Walking across the jagged rocks, Ethan looked at his watch. 11:52 p.m.

"W-w-we d-d-d-on't have much t-t-time," he stuttered through clenched jaw. "F-find the m-m-moon d-dial. C-c-center of island. Get k-k-k-key."

Brady blinked as he walked slowly behind Ethan. His arms contorted and tightened next to his body, and his fingers bent askew. Steam rose from his chest and shoulders, but a slight breeze blew across his wet skin, stealing his body heat away into the bitter air. Brady tried to speak, but only a raspy breath came out.

Navigating up a gentle slope, Ethan led the way toward the island's center, his eyes searching. "Che-tan said the m-moon dial will be f-found between the two largest s-s-sails and will stand th-th-three feet high. It has a round slab and a t-triangle rock at one side," Ethan explained.

Ethan had seen a picture of a sundial before and imagined the moon dial would look similar, but he didn't know how to read a sun or a moon dial. When expressing this concern to Che-tan, Ethan was told to "trust" and "follow the shadow," whatever that meant.

After a few minutes of searching, Ethan spotted the moon dial between the two main "sails." His eyes wandered upward for a moment, taking in the vast height of the narrow rock formations. Brady stopped and waited behind him. The moon overhead shined its light against the moon dial, casting a shadow on the ground toward the south. Ethan looked at his watch. 11:57 p.m. "I g-guess we w-wait."

With his wrist held toward the moonlight, Ethan stared at his watch. His arm shook, making it difficult to tell the time, but he scrutinized his timepiece. 11:58, 11:59—then a cloud floated in front of the moon, casting the watch in shadow.

"W-we have a p-p-problem," Ethan said, his voice rising to match his concern.

"What's wr-wrong?" Brady asked.

"I'm n-no expert, but a s-sun dial n-needs light. I'm guessing the moon dial w-works the s-same w-w-way. N-no light—n-no shadow."

"N-no shadow—no s-sign to the p-prison k-k-key," Brady finished.

"R-right."

Cupping his hand over his wristwatch to darken it even more, Ethan shut his left eye and placed his right eye against his hand, hoping to see the luminescent hands of his timepiece. 12:00 a.m. "It's time."

Ethan looked to the moon, but it was still hidden by clouds.

Then, a narrow beam of light cut through the cloud's core and brightened the moon dial. A pointy shadow inched forward across the ground, meandering as though searching for something.

Ethan watched the shadow change direction. "C-crazy. How is that even p-possible?"

Brady rubbed his eyes, hoping to force them into seeing more clearly. He watched as the moon dial's shadow abandoned the ground, turned west, and moved upward, pointing onto the ship's sail.

The boys hobbled over the rocks and stood next to the sail as the shadow slowed and then stopped. The shadow pointed to a spot on the sail almost ten feet off the ground.

With only a sliver of light cutting through the center of the cloud, the moon dial's shadow faded into the darkened sail. Ethan strained his eyes to see, but it was too high.

Kneeling on all fours next to the sail, Ethan flexed his back. "Brady, you're taller. C-climb on—quick."

Ethan felt his back buckle as Brady stepped on. Jagged rock cut into Ethan's knees and palms. Fortunately, his numb body didn't care.

Tracing the shadowy arrow with his hand, Brady stopped at the tip, where a glass-like stone disrupted the rough feel of the sail. He felt a small indentation just large enough to fit two fingers in the middle of a round stone. Brady reached, but his shaking fingers refused to insert. He pulled his hand back to his body, rubbing it to encourage circulation. He raised his hand again. Sticking his middle and forefinger into the indentation, Brady pulled, but the glassy rock didn't budge. Removing his hand, he examined the rock more closely.

"You almost done?" Ethan moaned.

"Yeah, s-sorry," Brady responded through chattering teeth.

Reaching for the stone again, Brady placed his fingers into the indention and turned clockwise. It budged but didn't turn. With greater force, Brady twisted his wrist. His fingers locked in place like a flat-head screwdriver. The glassy stone ground against the natural rock of the sail. With each twist, the stone unscrewed more easily. After two full rotations, the round rock loosened. Pressing the unusual stone against the sail to keep it from falling, Brady grabbed it with his other hand and held it at his side.

A little larger than a DVD, the opening was too high and dark for Brady to see into. Brady reached his hand into the darkness. His fingers pressed along the interior of the smooth stone cylinder, searching for the key. He felt nothing, so he reached deeper.

"A l-little higher," Brady pleaded.

Ethan arched his back, lifting Brady a few inches higher, allowing him to reach deeper into the capsule.

With the tips of his fingers, Brady could feel multiple items inside the hole, but nothing in the shape of a key. His fingertips moved each item closer to the opening. Pulling the first item out, he dropped it into the canvas bag hanging from his bare shoulder. Then he pulled out the second, third, and fourth items, dropping each into the sack with a heavy clank. When all items were safely stowed, Brady replaced the stone cover and screwed it back into place.

Stepping off Ethan's back, Brady extended his hand to help him rise from the cold ground.

"You g-get it?" Ethan asked, his chest heaving with shallow breaths.

"G-g-got it."

## – 17 –

# FIRE

A PILE OF MIDSIZED STICKS DROPPED FROM ALLIE'S ARMS, then a smaller pile from Jordan landed on top. Allie shined her flashlight on the pile, and she nodded with satisfaction. There were small twigs for kindling, medium sticks to get the fire going, and thicker branches she broke into short pieces to make the fire roar.

Looking over at Jacob's pile a few feet away, Jordan frowned. "His pile's bigger."

"Come on. Let's find some more dead wood," Allie encouraged.

Jacob's pile was complete, but sticks never kept anyone warm. Kneeling in the dirt next to his pile, Jacob built the foundation for his fire. With thin sticks at the bottom, he stacked the firewood in a square, each layer getting a little closer together. Inside the construction, he placed two tight pieces of wadded newspaper he "bought" from the ranger station and then placed a loose wad of newspaper on top. Then, reaching through the crown of his pyramid, he placed twigs on the paper, and then the larger sticks, filling the center. Once the paper lit, the small twigs would catch fire and then spread to the larger pieces. His assembly was complete.

Jacob reached into the fanny pack around his waist and rummaged for his container of waterproof matches. He huffed and grunted when he didn't find them. They were gone. Jacob dropped to his knees and began searching the ground.

Returning with arms full of timber, the girls dumped the wood and watched as Jacob felt along the ground on his hands and knees. Allie spoke, but Jacob didn't hear. He scoured the dirt.

Bending down toward Jacob, Allie snapped her fingers in front of his face. "Jacob, what are you doing? What's wrong?"

"I can't find my matches," he muttered. "They have to be here someplace."

"Do you have a lighter?" Jordan asked.

Jacob stopped his searching and looked at the girl. "Why didn't I think of that? Sure, I'll just use my lighter instead," he said sarcastically. Jacob closed his eyes. "Sorry, Jordan. I'm frustrated. I need something to start the fire. Do either of you have matches or a lighter? Please say yes."

Both girls shook their head in denial. "What about Ethan and Brady? Maybe they have something," Jordan suggested.

Jacob nodded. "Look."

Leaving Jacob to construct the next fire pyramid, Allie and Jordan approached the pile of Ethan's clothes. They searched his shorts pockets and sweatshirt. Nothing. Guiding their steps with the flashlight, Allie walked behind the tree where Brady had disrobed. She fumbled through the front pockets of his shorts but didn't find anything useful. Then she felt a narrow clump in his back pocket. Unsnapping the pocket, Allie reached inside and pulled out a lighter. She held it up. "We've got a lighter!"

Putting the final touches on the second stacked fire pyramid, Jacob looked up as both girls arrived beside him. Accepting the lighter from Allie, he held it to the newspaper at the bottom of the stacked sticks. He flicked the lighter, but there was only a spark. Jacob flicked it again, but still, no flame. Holding his flashlight against the lighter casing, he looked for the shadow of lighter fluid inside. The light caused the red case to glow, but there was no shadow. Jacob lowered his head in defeat.

"What's wrong? Why won't it work?" Allie asked.

Jacob chuckled. "No lighter fluid. It's empty," Jacob said.

"Who keeps an empty lighter in their pocket?" Jordan wondered aloud.

"What are we going to do?" Allie asked.

Jacob shook his head as he prepared to hurl the lighter into the woods. He pulled it back, ready to throw, but then he stopped—and smiled.

"What?"

Opening his fanny pack, Jacob removed his biodegradable toilet paper and tore off a square. Folding the toilet paper in half, Jacob placed his forefinger in the middle, extending half way up the paper, leaving an inch uncovered at the top. Wrapping the paper around his finger, he twisted it at the top, holding the toilet paper together in the shape of a small chalice. Lifting the bottom of his sweatshirt toward his chest, Jacob picked at the soft fuzz on the underside and filled the toilet paper cup.

Jacob glanced at the girls with a silly grin and then dropped onto his stomach near the fire construction. Holding the lighter in his right hand and the cotton-filled, toilet paper cup pinched between the fingers in his left, he took a deep breath. "Here goes nothing."

With the lighter positioned under the cotton fluff, Jacob flicked the lighter. "If we can get the flint in the lighter to spark, we won't need a flame. All we need is something combustible and . . ." Jacob flicked the lighter again. It sparked, and the cotton fluff burst into flame. Holding the toilet paper by the twisted knot and shielding it from the wind with his other hand, Jacob moved the flame to the newspaper sticking out from underneath the wood. The paper caught instantly. Jacob watched with delight as the flame grew, consuming some small twigs and then the larger sticks until it roared. Rolling up a piece of newspaper, Jacob lit it and transported the flame to the second campfire. Within moments both fires burned bright and hot.

Jordan clapped and cheered.

"Awesome!" Allie gave Jacob a tight squeeze as she shrieked with excitement.

They warmed their hands for a few moments and then returned to their work, preparing for the return of Brady and Ethan.

Jacob beamed with confidence. "It's a good start, but we're not done yet."

- 18 -

# BEACONS

WALKING FROM THE MOON DIAL TO THE BORDER OF THE Phantom Ship, Ethan looked over the edge at the glassy water nine feet below. His throbbing feet felt like they had been slapped with a ruler. Ethan could barely feel his extremities, but his fingers felt prickly, achy. A gust of wind caught his back, nudging him closer to the edge, almost causing him to lose his balance. He recovered and then looked at Brady with a tired expression.

Accepting the canvas bag from Brady, Ethan felt the weight of its contents. Stepping closer to the drop, Ethan attempted to jump from the side, but instead of leaping, he fell, flopping hard on his side and sinking into the water. After a brief moment submerged, Ethan reappeared and began a feeble backstroke toward the shore.

Ethan watched as Brady jumped into the water, his arms outstretched to prevent him from sinking past his neck. With a combination of the breast- and sidestroke, Brady caught up to Ethan. Looking ahead, Ethan saw two lights shining like a pair of lighthouses on the shore.

"That's f-f-for us," Ethan stammered.

"Fire!"

After a few minutes of semivigorous swimming, Ethan's kicking became lethargic as he floated on his back. His breathing weakened and his eyes blurred, shutting out the gentle starlight. Closing his eyes felt good, peaceful. The occasional splashes from Brady sounded like distant waves. Even the water felt warmer, like he had somehow been transported from the frigid water of Crater Lake to a calm swimming pool on a Caribbean resort. His body didn't convulse, and he didn't worry about his lost parents. He wanted to shut his eyes and rest, just for a moment. It had been a long day. Ethan relaxed, floating on his back.

With his sight fixed upon the two lights on shore, Brady swam toward land, but, like vertigo's effects, the lights faded further away one moment, and then surged back toward him seconds later.

"How much farther?" Brady asked as his stroke became feebler. "I can't tell."

The lake was peaceful and still—too still.

"Ethan," he called out with a raspy whisper. He heard no response.

Brady turned in the water, facing toward Ethan. He saw Ethan floating on his back with his arms hanging deep in the water. His legs were bent, dangling at the knees. Slowly, Ethan sank.

"Ethan!"

With a surge of energy, Brady raced to his partner, reaching Ethan as his head submerged. Brady's hand shot into the water, grasping for his friend. Feeling a tickling softness on his fingers, Brady tightened his grip, pulling Ethan above water by his hair.

Ethan looked like he was resting peacefully. "Come on, buddy. ETHAN!" he yelled again into Ethan's face, but there was no response.

Brady wrapped his arm under Ethan's neck, holding him above water. He paddled toward land, kicking hard and pulling the water with his only free hand. Brady struggled to swim toward the shore with Ethan in tow.

Brady's eyes focused on the shore lights, but then everything faded. Shaking his head back into consciousness, Brady refocused and continued swimming, his hold on Ethan loosening. The sound of voices drew near, and he paddled harder, but again his vision blurred as his eyes closed. Echoed voices swirled around Brady as his body went limp and his hold on Ethan released.

Ethan drifted away.

– 19 –

# HYPOTHERMIA

THE STEAM ROSE FROM BRADY AND ETHAN LIKE WHITE smoke off the campfire. Except for the occasional twitch, their nearly naked bodies lay motionless, face down on the dirt as Jacob, Allie, and Jordan scurried into action.

Removing his own T-shirt, Jacob pulled the sweatshirt back over his head and kneeled next to Brady. Jacob removed as much moisture as possible from Brady's skin, swabbing the shirt down Brady's back. Jacob then pushed and pulled until Brady was flipped onto his back. Brady's head rolled from side to side as his arms and legs energized into an unconscious flailing.

A couple of feet away, Jordan used Ethan's T-shirt to towel him off while Allie hurried to bring the blankets from their place, toasting near the campfires.

Rubbing Ethan's curly head with the T-shirt, Jordan sopped as much moisture from his hair as she could and placed a stocking cap on his head to trap in the escaping heat. Pushing on his shoulders and then his hips, Jordan tried pushing her brother onto his back, but couldn't. "Jacob, I need help."

Jordan shined the light on Ethan. His lips were blue, and his chest didn't appear to be moving. His mouth was closed, and his nostrils were still. Jordan's breathing raced with panic as she knelt next to her lifeless brother. "Jacob! Allie! I need help!"

Leaving Brady's side, Jacob heaved an exhausted breath as

he turned his attention to Ethan. He helped Jordan push Ethan onto his back, but then Jacob's heart skipped as he looked at Ethan. For Jordan's sake, Jacob tried to keep his expression even and calm.

Unlike Brady's thrashing, Ethan remained still. With his ear next to Ethan's mouth and nose, Jacob held his breath while he listened for the sound of Ethan's breathing. Jacob's heart pounded as he pressed two shaky fingers against the artery in Ethan's neck, hoping to find a pulse. Then he adjusted them and waited. "Yes! I feel it!" Jacob yelled to the others. Jordan gasped with relief as she started to cry. "The pulse is faint but definitely there."

Tilting Ethan's head back and plugging his nose, Jacob opened the airway and began rescue breathing. With his lips sealed around Ethan's, Jacob exhaled into Ethan's mouth and watched as Ethan's chest rose.

Arriving with the blankets, Allie set one next to Ethan and the other near Brady. Wrapping her arms around Jordan, Allie held the young girl's head to her chest and brushed her curly hair with her fingers.

"Allie, I'm going to need your help here," Jacob said.

"Okay, what do you need?"

"Between breaths we're going to roll Ethan onto the blanket. Once he's on, we need to remove his wet boxers and wrap the blanket tight around his legs and waist," Jacob said.

Allie's eyes bulged, and her head shook. "Nuh-uh." Releasing herself from Jordan's clutch, she moved to Ethan's side and spread the blanket. Removing the canvas bag from Ethan's shoulder, Allie looked at Jacob, fearful and nervous, her head still shaking.

"What? Come on, Allie, you have to do it," he said. "It's okay. Its nothing weird, but it could save his life."

"Nope, I'm not gonna . . . you know, take off his . . ."

"Fine." Jacob huffed. "Just be ready to do what I tell you. Jordan, we're going to need you too. We'll help Ethan, but I want you to sit with Brady. Talk to him. Keep him awake. Don't let him fall asleep," Jacob ordered and then looked at Allie. "Ready?"

Allie nodded. Jacob breathed into Ethan and then pushed on his shoulders while Allie pushed on his legs, rolling him into the center of the blanket. Quickly folding the blanket around him, Allie knelt across from Jacob as he continued the rescue breathing.

"Don't you need to push on his chest or something?" Allie asked as she watched.

"No. He has a pulse. He just needs air in his lungs," Jacob said, panting. Laying his ear near Ethan's mouth, he listened, but there was no sound. Jacob closed his eyes and held his breath as he listened again. From Ethan's mouth, the faintest rasp of breath escaped. Placing a hand on Ethan's chest, Jacob felt it rise. Looking at Allie, relief overwhelmed the fatigue of Jacob's expression.

"Jordan, how's Brady doing?" Allie asked.

"He just keeps mumbling. I can't understand him."

"That's okay. Just keep talking to him, Jordan. Good job," Jacob said. "Allie, go up to the fire and see how the water's coming. I'll dress Brady, and then we need to move them."

Jacob finished drying Brady off and then attempted to re-dress him with his shorts and sweatshirt. Lifting and twisting Brady's limp body one limb at a time, Jacob finally got the arms through the armholes and the shorts pulled up. The T-shirt was put on backward and inside out, but it was close enough. Jacob wasn't about to fix it. Breathing heavily, Jacob sat back in the dirt, wiping away the sweat rolling down his temples. Climbing back to his knees, Jacob struggled to roll Brady onto the blanket but eventually succeeded. He wrapped him tight like swaddling a baby, placing the stocking cap and hoodie over his head. Wrapped tight in the blanket, Brady's arms and legs stopped their spastic thrashing.

"Another bottle of water is ready," Allie yelled back from the fire.

"Good. Set it aside and start another. I'll be done dressing Ethan in a couple of minutes, then we need to get these guys next to the fire."

After dressing Ethan, Jacob looked at the stout boy and sighed. "All right, guys. Let's do this."

With Jacob holding onto Ethan's head and shoulders, Allie at his feet, and Jordan in the middle, the three kids shuffled toward the fire until Allie tripped, dropping Ethan's legs into the dirt. Jacob tried to hold his end, but Ethan was too heavy. Jacob and Jordan collapsed to the ground beneath Ethan.

"Guys, come on," Jacob chided.

"He weighs a ton," Jordan complained.

"Okay, everyone get a handle. Let's go. One . . . two . . . three . . . lift!" Jacob directed.

The three kids stood, lifting in unison, and moved Ethan to a spot between the two campfires. Picking up a water bottle that lay on the ground near the fire, Jacob held it to his face.

"It's pretty hot," Allie said.

"But not too hot," Jacob said. "It won't burn. Perfect."

Unwrapping the blanket from around Ethan, Jacob placed the warm bottle inside Ethan's sweatshirt, next to his bare belly. He grabbed a second bottle and placed it between Ethan's legs, and a third heated water bottle he placed inside the hood of Ethan's sweatshirt against his neck. With the warm water bottles in place, Allie rewrapped Ethan, burrito style.

Repeating the process with Brady, minus the dropping, Allie, Jacob, and Jordan situated him next to Ethan between the fires and applied two heated water bottles against his skin before rewrapping him.

Pouring the cold lake water from the last bottle into Brady's empty soda can, Allie set the can on the hot coals to heat. With the top cut off the can, it was easy to fill and pour, and as the only cooking utensil, the empty soda can proved invaluable.

"Excellent." Jacob wiped the sleeve of his sweatshirt across his forehead. "The hot water will warm them up. It'll also make the water safe to drink. Good job, guys."

With the midnight swimmers wrapped next to the fire, Jacob sat down on a rock he had moved close to the blaze. Placing his elbows on his knees, Jacob rested his heavy head in his hands and closed his eyes. The girls sat on the ground next to Jacob's rock and stared into the flame. Raising one hand to pat Jacob's leg, Allie felt his cold, wet shorts. She could see that his sweatshirt was also damp and his body shivered.

"Jacob, you're all wet," Allie commented.

"I'll be fine. I felt how cold that water was when I pulled them out. With the wind blowing, man, I'm freezing. I can't imagine what those two went through," he said as his lips tightened and his brow furrowed in an attempt to hold back tears of exhaustion. "A few minutes by the fire, and I'll be dry and warm. No worries."

"You were amazing, Jacob. Really. Very cool," Jordan said with admiration. "Can I do something for you?"

Jacob looked at the younger girl, and a single tear streamed down his cheek. "Maybe you could get my shoes. I kicked them off before going into the water. I'm not exactly sure where they are."

Jordan stood and grabbed the flashlight from Allie. She started to walk but then stopped. Jordan threw her arms around Jacob and buried her head in his neck. "Thank you for saving my brother," she whispered and then raced off with light in hand to find Jacob's shoes and socks.

Jacob didn't respond—he couldn't.

"You really did great," Allie complimented as she stared into the flickering fire.

"It was a team effort," Jacob said, removing his glasses and rubbing his eyes before wiping the sweat and tears from his face.

"Yes, but you led the team. You knew what to do. You saved Ethan and Brady. You were incredible. I'm so glad you're here."

Jacob looked at the boys resting on the ground next to the

fire, wrapped in their blankets. "Once their body temperatures rise to normal levels, they should be as good as new."

Allie nodded.

Returning with Jacob's shoes and socks, Jordan set them on the ground next to Jacob's feet. "Guess what we forgot," Jordan said playfully. She waited for a moment, but no one bothered to guess. From behind her back, Jordan pulled the dripping canvas sack that Ethan had carried to the Phantom Ship. She held it high and smiled. "There's something in it," she said in a sing-song tone.

Allie's eyes widened with excitement, and Jacob reached for the bag, but Jordan pulled it back. Cocking his head, Jacob glared at Jordan. She took the hint.

Setting the bag on the ground in front of Jacob, Jordan huddled close to Allie. Tipping the bag, Jacob poured the contents onto the dirt. They all stared with wonder and a little disappointment.

"Interesting."

## – 20 –

# The Prison Key

FOUR ARTIFACTS LAY ON THE GROUND IN FRONT OF THE huddled group, but none of the items looked like a key. Running her hands across the items, flipping them over, pushing and separating them, Allie's hope of freeing her parents faded with her failure to locate a key. She sighed with disappointment as she leaned back.

"Is this it? Did Brady and Ethan risk their lives for this? Some stupid museum pieces?" Allie said.

"How can we save our families with this stuff?" Jordan asked.

Allie shook her head in disbelief.

Unlike Allie and Jordan, Jacob's eyes brightened as he looked at the treasures in front of him. Although he didn't see anything resembling a key, the artifacts seemed special. Anything that old must be valuable.

"There has to be a reason why these items were hidden so well," Jacob suggested. "Maybe we can find a use for this stuff."

"And maybe Che-tan will know more about them," Jordan added.

"Yeah, maybe . . ." Jacob started, but his attention focused on one of the artifacts, a dagger that butted against his right foot. Leaning down, he picked up the short weapon and held it in front of his face. The dagger's hilt was white and hard, and the leather scabbard was caramel brown and firm, almost petrified. Grasping the hilt, Jacob eased the dagger from the scabbard.

Even Allie's disappointment couldn't keep her from beholding the dagger with admiration. Outside of its leather casing, they could see that the blade was chiseled midnight glass, the tip needle sharp.

Jacob rotated his wrist and turned the dagger in his hand, examining it from every angle. The thick grip was wrapped in leather strapping with three colorful beads dangling from the leather. The dagger felt natural in his hand, light and well-balanced. Although the hilt looked like stone, the feel was warmer and lighter than stone. Was it carved bone? Jacob looked and then held it to his nose and sniffed, not that he knew what bone smelled like. Still unsure, Jacob pressed his tongue against the hilt. It *was* bone.

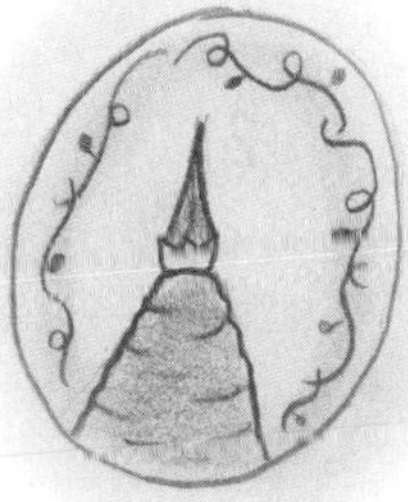

Engraved into the bottom of the hilt, intertwining vines encircled a thin pine tree on a hill. Turning the dagger so the sharp tip pointed to the ground, Jacob showed the symbol to Allie and Jordan.

"Do either of you recognize this?" Jacob asked, pointing to the emblem. Both girls shook their heads.

At the top of the hilt, where the blade extended from the grip, three carved points reached up the nine-inch blade. Jacob figured the bone points served a dual purpose of holding the blade tight into the hilt and making the dagger look really tough. He smiled as he savored the idea of holding an ancient dagger in his hand. *Nice!* Placing the dagger between his knees with the blade facing up, Jacob hovered his finger just above the sharp tip, slowly inching it to the blade to test its sharpness.

"That doesn't seem very smart," Jordan warned.

Pulling his finger back, Jacob winced and then watched as thick drops of blood formed on his fingertip before dripping onto the dirt. It didn't look like his finger had even made contact with the black blade, but it must have. The test was complete. The dagger was definitely sharp, and Jacob looked like a fool for piercing it into his flesh. Placing his finger in his mouth, Jacob sucked the blood and spat. He looked at the small incision on his fingertip. The blood continued to ooze from the wound. Opening his fanny pack, Jacob pulled out a small plastic box and opened it with one hand. He pulled out a bandage, peeled back the paper, and applied the bandage. Re-sheathing the dagger, Jacob laid it in the dirt with a minor scowl.

Opening her mouth as if to say, "I told you so," Jordan closed it when she noticed Jacob's weary glare.

"Someone got grumpy," Jordan said.

Jacob flashed a horsy smile to refute her claim, but it looked more like he was showing off to the dentist.

Allie smiled as she watched the two new friends interact like siblings.

She held, cupped in her hands, a heavy stone bowl with a rounded, egg-shaped bottom. She traced the ridges on the bowl's exterior and rubbed her hand across the narrow base. Setting the bowl upright on the dirt, she watched. Sure enough, it toppled onto its side.

"Kind of a dumb bowl," Allie commented. Picking it up again, she examined the rough ridges. There were no markings on the bowl, no color. Just plain old stone. She reached for the next item.

Since Jordan already held the item she wanted to look at, Allie picked up the only remaining relic. Jacob didn't fight her for it because he was still fixated on the dagger that lay near his foot.

Allie looked at her item. "Another rock. Big wow," she mumbled.

The rectangular stone was polished black and smooth, the size of a dollar bill but thicker, perhaps half an inch. In the center was a round hole the size of a quarter. At first glance it looked like a sleek cell phone. Like the bowl, there were no distinguishing symbols or colors—just solid and plain.

"What do you have there?" Jacob asked.

"A rock," Allie responded, tossing it back to the ground.

"Well, look at this," Jordan prompted, holding a hollowed out stick. The thin pipe tapered at one end. Longer than the dagger, it was covered in bright stripes of indigo, cranberry, white, and mustard. Two narrow handles stuck out wide from the sides. Jordan placed one hand through each handle and held the stick to her eye, peeking through the shaft at the boys lying in front of the fire.

"Does it make any noise if you blow on it?" Jacob asked.

Holding the flute to her lips, Jordan took a deep breath and blew, but it only sounded like a gentle breeze passing through a hollow tube. Turning toward Jacob, Jordan puckered her lips and blew again, casting a forceful rain of spit onto his face, but still, no sound. With the sleeve of his sweatshirt, Jacob wiped the spit from his face and cleaned his glasses. Jordan tucked some long curls behind her ear and averted her eyes in embarrassment.

"May I?" Allie asked, extending her hand. Jordan handed her the flute. Instead of placing her hands through the narrow handles, Allie held them with her fingertips, the pinky on each hand extended outward.

"Very dainty," Jacob teased.

Allie blew. There was nothing but the sound of silence. Turning the flute in her hand, she held it up to the moonlight and looked through the open end. She gazed down the hollowed interior, noting the round beams of moonlight that decorated the inner shaft. Looking again at the exterior, she noticed round holes amid the various colored stripes.

"Hmm. It's definitely a flute of some kind," Allie suggested.

Putting her hands through the grips, her fingers were in position to cover the holes. Choosing one opening near the blowhole, Allie stood, covered the hole, puckered her lips, and blew. A gust of wind encircled the camp as a beam of semi-frozen water vapor shot from the flute and suffocated the fire, extinguishing the flames instantly as inches of thick ice smothered the firewood.

"Whoa!" Jacob said, stumbling to his feet and gaping at the frozen firewood that had been burning hot just seconds before.

Removing the flute from her mouth, Allie held it outstretched in the palm of her hands. Her eyes were wide with shock. "I-I'm sorry?" she said, confused about what had just happened. She passed the flute carefully to Jacob.

"I think we have more here than we realize," Jacob said.

Jordan chuckled. "Duh."

Allie, Jacob, and Jordan sat in silence for a moment, staring at the flute as they considered the artifact's unusual power.

"That was AWESOME!" Allie said, unable to hide her enthusiasm.

Jordan's head nodded. "Do it again," she tempted softly.

Allie licked her lips. Her eyebrows rose and her head tilted as she looked at Jacob. He handed the flute back to her, a large smile crossing his face.

Placing the flute to her mouth, Allie prepared to blow.

"Let's try not to put out the other fire this time," Jacob cautioned.

With the flute still in the ready position, Allie turned toward Jacob with a sour grin. Covering his head, Jacob ducked as the flute pointed directly at him. "Hey, I don't want to have my brain frozen," Jacob said.

"Who would notice?" Jordan quipped to her own amusement.

Lowering the flute, Allie winced with an exaggerated frown. "Sorry, Jacob." Stepping away from the group and the campfire, Allie raised the flute again and took aim at a sickly pine tree. Placing her index finger over the same hole, she blew. Again, the wind gusted around the group as frost exploded from the flute, hitting the tree and turning it into an instant Popsicle.

Crowding near Allie, Jacob looked at the new toy with envy. "What else can that thing do? How many holes does it have?"

Allie examined the flute, looking for additional holes.

Running her fingers over the exterior like she was reading Braille, she felt for indentations and holes hidden among the brightly colored stripes.

"I'm finding four holes," she said. "You want to see what they do?" she asked.

"Of course!"

Locating a hole one inch down the flute, Allie positioned her finger, raised the flute to her mouth, and prepared to blow. She took a deep breath but then removed the flute from her mouth as her head cranked to the left.

"What was that?" Allie asked. Her eyes followed a fleeting shadow into the trees.

"What?"

"Jacob, did you see that?" Allie asked.

Jacob shrugged.

Turning, Allie looked near the fire. Both Ethan and Brady remained still, wrapped in their blankets. They couldn't have moved enough to create any kind of shadowy movement.

"What is it?" Jordan asked again.

"It's nothing," Allie said as she shook her head.

Returning her attention to the flute, Allie stood straight, holding the instrument in her mouth like she was preparing to play an emotional aria at the symphony. Placing her finger over the second hole, Allie took aim at the same tree, which was now covered with ice. She blew.

Instead of frost and ice, flames blazed from the open end of the flute, shooting at the iced tree, causing it to burst into flames. Allie's eyes widened with fear at the burning inferno just fifteen yards away.

Jacob shielded his eyes. "Put it out! Put it out!" he hollered.

Placing her finger back over the first hole, Allie took aim and blew, shooting a frozen mixture toward the fiery tree. The ice landed but didn't fully quench the fire. Taking another deep breath, Allie propelled a greater spray of ice that extinguished the blaze.

"That is the coolest thing I've ever seen," Jordan said in a shocked monotone. Allie and Jacob couldn't disagree.

"Yeah, it's cool, but maybe we should put that thing away before we catch the entire forest on fire or destroy something we can't fix," Jacob suggested.

"Come on. We ought to at least know what it can do." Jordan countered.

Jacob and Jordan both looked at Allie, waiting for her vote to settle the matter. "Well, I'd like to know what the flute is capable of. It could come in handy," she began as Jordan's head bobbed, "but I don't want to accidentally obliterate Crater Lake either."

"So . . . ?"

"Let's put the flute away for now, and we can test it out in the daylight," Allie suggested. Surprisingly, both Jacob and Jordan found the compromise acceptable.

"But let's restart that fire first," Jacob suggested.

"Agreed."

Returning to the ice-covered fire pit, Allie restarted the fire with her personal flamethrower. Despite being covered with ice, the wood exploded into flame.

After adding wood to the fire, the kids sat and warmed themselves.

Allie placed the flute on the ground with the other artifacts, but her eyes couldn't let go. She gazed upon the flute, eager to test it further.

## - 21 -

# The Mist of Darkness

Jordan leaned against Jacob. Her eyes grew heavy, and she quickly fell asleep with her arm wrapped around her new friend. Allie smiled as Jacob made a goofy face, embarrassed by the girl cuddled against him.

"Allie," Jacob whispered, "do we have any water I can drink?"

Allie looked to the fire where she had been heating water in the soda can, but the can was lying on its side, crumpled in the coals. "Ah, well . . . I don't think the can appreciated the fire and ice treatment. I think it's dead. I can get one of the bottles out from Ethan's or Brady's blanket," she suggested.

"No. They need the warmth. I'll be okay for now. Let's try to get a little rest."

Allie agreed. She closed her eyes, but despite her exhaustion, she didn't feel sleepy. There were too many thoughts tumbling around in her mind: her parents, the flute, the evil Chief Llao, her new friends, Che-tan, the near deaths of Ethan and Brady, the Prison of the Lost. And why did she and her young friends avoid Chief Llao's imprisonment? What was so special about the age of sixteen? Do you lose your innocence with age? She didn't think so. With so much to think about, how could she sleep?

Opening her eyes, Allie began speaking as she turned to look at Jordan and Jacob. Jordan clung tight against Jacob, who seemed to rest in relative comfort. Except for his head cocked backward with his mouth wide open, he looked peaceful.

Listening to the crackle, Allie enjoyed the smell of the campfire. It reminded her of camping with her mom and dad. Even though she complained every time the family went camping, she secretly liked it. If the earth hadn't devoured her family, forcing her into a potential battle against an evil spirit chief, this would be a nice night—definitely memorable. Feeling the uncomfortable heat from the fire against her bare legs, Allie stood and turned, letting the fire warm the back of her legs as well. After a moment, she stepped away to a more comfortable distance and turned back to the fire with her hands outstretched. She watched as the flames licked the air and small pieces of ash floated out of sight.

Running her tongue across her lips, Allie realized that like Jacob, she too needed a drink. She thought about grabbing a water bottle from one of the boys' blankets but then decided against it. She knew Brady and Ethan needed the heat more than she needed a drink.

She examined the artifacts on the ground and then picked up the bowl. With bowl in hand, she walked toward the lakeshore, leaving the rest of the group resting next to the campfires. The temperature away from the fire felt cool but pleasant, and the moon provided ample light for her to see. Dipping the bowl into the moonlit lake, Allie filled it to the brim and walked back to camp.

Allie watched each step as she held the bowl at arm's length. Despite her best efforts, the water sloshed over the edge and onto her hands, causing her to shiver. For a moment, her eyes rose from her feet and gazed at the camp a short distance ahead, but then her attention turned to the woods. A shadow raced across her peripheral view. Her head swiveled as her feet halted. Allie searched for the shadow hiding in the darkness but then stopped.

"Relax, Allie," she told herself.

Shaking her head, she shrugged off her paranoia and continued walking. *Tree branches move in the wind. Bats fly in front of the moon. Things move in the woods at night*, she thought. "Get over it," she mumbled.

As soon as the words crossed her lips, she halted again. This time, there was movement to her right. Her eyes darted toward the shadow, and then she twisted back in the other direction. Nothing was there.

Then, above her, the night sky blackened further as a mist of darkness traversed the sky from east to west. The stars disappeared in a wave of black but then returned as the void passed. Allie shuddered and quickened her pace, unconcerned about the water splashing from the bowl. Then, from the woods, a silhouette drifted from the trees between Allie and the camp.

With the specter hovering above the path, the light from the fire dimmed, its light blocked by the shady haze. Allie took a step back and then turned, but twirling in place, she saw the translucent mist everywhere. The mist of darkness stole every speck of light the night offered like octopus ink in water, expanding in every direction until it surrounded her.

Allie gasped. She considered running through the fog, back to her friends by the fire, but her feet were glued to the ground. She wanted to scream, but her dry mouth locked shut. With the stone bowl still in her hand, Allie stood like a statue as the ominous mist pressed closer against her.

Dropping to both knees, Allie lowered her head. She felt pain and sadness, fear and loathing, but the feelings were not her own. She waited for the darkness to devour her like the ground had devoured her parents.

Allie squeezed her eyes shut, and her body tensed as she hunched over the bowl. The weight of the surrounding haze crushed her into the dirt, but then, a flash of stunning white burrowed into her closed eyes, causing her to swoon.

As the light faded, Allie's eyes reopened. Compared to the brilliance of the light, the night seemed even darker, but the weight and gloom she had felt were gone. Allie blinked and then kept her eyes closed, allowing them to recover from the radiance that had sent the gloomy mist bolting into the woods. Spots of twinkling bright white dappled her vision. Sitting still for a moment to allow her sight to adjust, Allie saw a figure walk toward her from the campfire.

"Jacob!" she called out, but there was no answer. "Jordan, Ethan, Brady! Who's there?" she cried out, her vision still impaired. She listened to the silence, then a figure stepped into view.

"Che-tan? Is that you?"

# - 22 -

# THE HAWK

THE FIGURE MOVED TOWARD ALLIE AND THEN HALTED, standing above her. Allie's eyes struggled to adjust from the blinding white and splotchy spots that still littered her vision. With the mist expelled, the moonlight returned and the stars twinkled. Squinting, she looked at the figure before her. Allie rose high on her knees, preparing to stand.

"Che-tan, is that you?" she asked again, still unable to see him clearly.

Che-tan looked more like a medieval monk than a teenager. Instead of blue jeans, boots, and flannel, he wore a flowing brown robe, cinched at the waist with a thin leather strap that attached to a pocket-sized purse hanging to the side. Only his eyes and nose could be seen from underneath the oversized hood. The robe brushed the ground and the sleeves hung long, covering his hands down to his fingertips. He held the ancient flute.

Pushing back the hood, Che-tan uncovered his head and reached toward Allie with one hand. She felt relief as she recognized Che-tan and grabbed his hand, allowing him to pull her from the dirt.

Dusting herself off, Allie brushed back the blonde hair hanging in her eyes. Standing next to the robed teen, Allie's relief fled as she scrutinized Che-tan. "Why didn't you answer me? When I called out to you, why didn't you say something?" Allie asked. "You scared me."

"I apologize. Your friends are sleeping, and I did not want to disturb them. You have all had a long night, and they need the rest," Che-tan explained.

Allie's head cocked as she leaned around Che-tan, peering at her friends back at the fire. The incredible flash of light had not disturbed them. "Okay, but what's with the spooky robe? At first I could . . ." Allie thought for a moment and then continued. "I could see through you like you were a ghost. Was that you?"

Che-tan's stern face brightened with a smile. "Yes, that was I, but I am no ghost."

Allie's forehead crinkled.

"Perhaps your eyes deceived you," Che-tan suggested.

"What was that bright light? And what was that blackness that surrounded me? It was so heavy. It made me feel so . . . so . . . lost. So desperate."

"Your friends have done very well tonight," Che-tan said, holding up the flute.

"Yes, they have," Allie agreed. She held out her hand and waited for Che-tan to return the flute.

"I have been watching. You have learned some of the instrument's powers. Well done. The darkness that surrounded you was a slave force sent from Chief Llao. Judging by their quick retreat, the slaves were only meant to frighten you."

"It worked," Allie said, her voice wobbling.

"I startled the slaves with the power of the flute, casting them back to a more comfortable darkness." Che-tan shook his head. "They have no loyalty to Chief Llao, but he is their warden, and they must obey," Che-tan explained. "Their will is not their own. They are mere instruments to be acted upon and controlled. It is very sad." His head lowered, and his eyes closed in pitied reverence.

Extending her hand again with a gentle jab toward Che-tan,

Allie waited for the return of the flute. "My friends almost died trying to get these artifacts because you said there would be a key, a key that unlocks the prison. I don't see a key, Che-tan. Where's the key?"

Che-tan remained silent.

"The stuff they brought back may be interesting, powerful, but I don't see a key. Che-tan, I want the key."

"Do not be so quick to judge. Things often have a dual purpose," Che-tan said. He hesitated but then placed the flute in Allie's hand.

"So we do have the key, or keys?" Allie asked. "I don't understand. How can these artifacts free my parents?"

"I do not know. But I have to believe there is a reason why the artifacts were hidden on the Phantom Ship. Our legends tell us about these artifacts and their supernatural powers, but I do not understand their capabilities. Not fully."

"It sounds like you know just enough to give us false hope and get us killed," Allie accused as her voice faltered. "Do you know how close my friends were to dying?"

Che-tan shook his head.

"They swam out to the Phantom Ship in ice-cold water because they trusted you. But you don't even know what you're talking about. Do you?" Allie charged.

Allie could hear Che-tan's knuckles crack as his fists clenched underneath his robe. She watched as his grin turned to a pallid glare. "I am here to help you," Che-tan repeated.

"I don't believe you, and I don't want your help," Allie said. "We can figure out the artifacts ourselves. You are no help to us. Why don't you just go away?"

Che-tan's eyelashes fluttered, and his mouth opened. "You do not want my help?"

"No."

"Without me, would you have found the magical artifacts that will help you in the quest to free your parents? Certainly not. Would you still be cowering on the ground as the dark shadows overtook you? Indeed. You need my help, and you *will* do what I tell you," Che-tan blustered.

Allie stepped backward, tripping over the stone bowl that still lay on the ground. She stumbled but then planted her feet, her eyes widening with liberating hope.

Che-tan took a step toward her but stopped when he felt a sharp poke into the back of his robe. He began to turn, but the pointed pressure became firmer.

"No. I don't think anyone will be taking orders from you," Brady said, holding the dagger against Che-tan. With the thick blanket still wrapped around his shoulders, Brady held the deadly weapon while the other hand gripped the blanket together, tight around his neck.

"Brady, I can't believe it. You're okay?" Allie asked.

"Yeah, I'll be fine. You?"

"I'm good now, thanks," Allie replied with a smile, amazed by Brady's recovery.

"Now, Mr. Che-tan," Brady enunciated as he raised one red eyebrow. "Get lost."

Che-tan placed the hood back over his head and bowed. "I cannot leave you alone. You are not the only ones trying to free your loved ones. I need you, and you need me."

"You don't listen so well, do you, Che-tan?" Brady said.

"I will tell you everything I know about the legends and powers of Crater Lake. Please, let us work together."

"No deal, buddy," Brady said, pressing the dagger against the robed teen's back. Allie nodded to Brady for encouragement.

"You *will* help me." Without further warning, Che-tan raised his arms straight from his side and mumbled an incomprehensible phrase. Suddenly, Che-tan's body burst into pieces as four large birds took flight. Not even Che-tan's brown robe remained. He was gone.

Following the course of the birds as they flew in line, Brady stared in disbelief. His eyes rose and fell with the flight of the birds and then around as the birds circled him near the ground.

Allie recognized the fleeting shadows as they raced from side to side, up and down, casting gloom and darkness on the otherwise well-lit night. Rising high, the birds circled but then dove toward the watching kids. Allie and Brady spun in place as they attempted to keep an eye on the circling birds. Then, the birds lofted upward.

"What in the world is—?" Brady began asking but stopped the instant he noticed the birds diving again. This time they dove directly at him. He stepped to the side, but the birds adjusted, maintaining a collision course. Turning, Brady began to run back to the fire, but the birds were too fast. Flying over his head and past the fire, they hurtled back toward him, single file.

Speechless, Allie watched as the birds prepared to attack.

Rushing back to Allie's side, Brady tensed as the birds plunged toward him like heat-seeking missiles. He tensed his body and flexed his muscles, preparing to have four large birds crash into him at full speed. He cringed as he awaited impact.

He puffed out his chest as the birds quickly approached. He tried to avert his eyes, but he had to watch. Shooting at Brady, the birds moved out of line and flew two astride. Their wings expanded as they pulled up, extending their talons at Brady's face and chest. Then in an instant, they had reassembled into one large bird with a massive wingspan that seemed to smother Brady in approaching darkness.

Brady's eyes squeezed tight. He waited for the collision, but there was nothing except the odor of warm breath. Opening one eye, Brady found himself nose to nose, staring into the hooded face of Che-tan.

"W-what are you?" Brady blurted.

"I am Che-tan—the Hawk."

Brady took a step back and turned to Allie, who was watching in stunned silence a short distance away. Brady nodded. "Okay then. Why didn't you just say so?" he asked with a nervous chuckle.

Che-tan ignored Brady and turned to Allie. "Chief Llao's powers are growing stronger. We must combine our forces without delay. Daylight will soon be upon us."

"We already got the artifacts. Like you said, our friends are sleeping, and I doubt Ethan recovers from his hypothermia as fast as Brady did. What else can we do?" Allie asked.

"You have proven to be very resourceful and determined. We must use this in locating the entrance to the Prison of the Lost. Only when we find the gateway will we know how it is to be unlocked. We must find the gate and release the many slaves of Chief Llao."

Brady stared, but Allie bobbed her head in agreement. She absorbed Che-tan's words. "Okay, okay, we need to find the gateway. We can do that. Yeah, we can definitely do that."

"Then we are in agreement?" Che-tan asked. "We will work together?"

Allie's head continued to nod. "My parents need me. What choice do I have? I'm in."

Brady huddled in his blanket. "If I don't agree, you'll probably eat me like a fat, juicy worm."

Che-tan's face remained resolute.

"I have one demand," Brady mentioned, his voice wavering. "Well, it's more of a request really: no more freak show, okay? You'll keep that whole crazy bird thing under wraps. Please," he pleaded.

Che-tan nodded in agreement. "Good, it is settled. Grab your things, and we will go."

"Whoa, wait a minute. We need to get the others," Allie said.

"And you said we need to find the gateway. How are we going to do that?" Brady asked.

"Your friends must stay behind. I am sorry, but they are not ready, and we cannot wait. They can catch up later when they are rested. Daylight will be here soon, and Chief Llao's powers will be even more potent. Everything we need, you retrieved from the Phantom Ship. It is a puzzle. We have all the pieces, but we must learn how they fit together. As for our next destination, I believe I know where to find the answer."

"Che-tan, we can't leave the others behind. They're in this with us. We're stronger together," Allie said.

Che-tan shook his head, his ponytail waving. "No. We cannot wait."

Brady stepped forward with a surge of confidence. "We are a team. No one person, or *thing*, commands the others. With everything we do, we'll vote. Majority rules."

"There is no time to vote. We must go," Che-tan urged in his mild accent.

Allie folded her arms and stood next to Brady in solidarity. "We vote as a team, or there is no team," she said. "We are not your servants."

"Fine. Enough. I vote we move now before Chief Llao gains greater power. I vote that we leave your friends to rest and recover so they can join us later. That is my vote," Che-tan said.

"I vote 'no' to all of that," Brady said with a smirk.

Both boys looked at Allie. She considered her options. "If Che-tan can show us where we are supposed to go, I will vote with him." Seeing Brady prepare to argue, Allie pulled him aside, whispering in his ear.

Brady nodded. "All right, Mr. Che-tan Smarty Pants, I'll play along. Tell me, where are we going?"

## – 23 –

# ARTIFACT

"COME ON, CHE-TAN," BRADY TAUNTED. "WHERE ARE WE going?"

Bending over, Che-tan grasped the stone bowl and lifted it from the dirt. "I believe the answer is in the bowl."

Grabbing the heavy dish from Che-tan's hand, Brady examined the bowl, inside and out, rubbing his fingers across it. "He's nuts. There's nothing in the bowl. It's plain old stone," Brady said, handing the artifact to Allie before challenging Che-tan with a hostile glare.

"You are a strange one, Brady. At moments you are noble, courageous. Other times you are a selfish, cowardly child. What gives you the confidence to be brave right now? Are you showing off for a pretty girl? Or do you feel threatened? Do you have to assert your own power?" Che-tan questioned.

Grabbing Che-tan by the scruff of his robe, Brady pulled him close, their noses touching. "How do you like that, Che-tan?"

Che-tan smiled and then his face morphed into an angry bird with yellow eyes and a sharp beak. Brady let go of Che-tan's cloak and backed away, his chest heaving with shallow breaths.

Che-tan's face returned to human form. "We will need the bowl and water from the lake, and there should be some kind of translator," Che-tan said.

"Translator? What do you mean?" Allie asked.

"It could be a piece of wood, or leather, maybe even a thick cloth. There will be a hole in the material through which we can read the ancient writing on the bowl," Che-tan said.

"But there's nothing on the bowl. There's no ancient writing," Brady argued, earning a cold stare from Che-tan.

Recognition flashed in Allie's eyes. Racing to the fireside, she picked up the sleek black stone with the quarter-sized hole in the center. She glanced at Ethan wrapped tight in his blanket next to the fire. Jordan and Jacob slept cuddled together on the log near the flames. Grabbing a water bottle from the dirt near Brady's resting area, Allie tiptoed from the campsite and returned to Che-tan and Brady, who continued their infantile staring contest. Neither flinched.

"Knock it off," Allie said, unimpressed with the struggle for dominance. "Let's focus. I believe this is what you were asking for," Allie said, extending the black stone to Che-tan.

Che-tan's eyes enlarged as he beheld the polished rectangular stone. He held it in both hands with admiration. "I have never seen a translator like this before. I have never even heard of one like this," he said, caressing the stone. He rubbed it between his hands, feeling its cool smoothness. His eyes gleamed like he was holding a bar of gold.

"And here is some lake water," Allie said, holding out the water bottle.

Holding the bowl in one hand, Che-tan's eyes beamed. He raised the translator above the bowl. "Allie, water . . . please."

Unscrewing the cap, Allie poured the contents of the bottle into the bowl. She watched Che-tan peer through the hole as he moved the translator over the water. Confusion replaced Che-tan's giddiness.

"What's wrong?" Allie asked.

Brady laughed. "I don't think it's working. Could it be Che-tan doesn't have a clue what he's talking about?"

Allie held up one finger. "Shut it, Brady."

"I do not understand." Che-tan tugged his ear. "This is a

translator, and this is its motivator," he said, looking at both artifacts. "What am I doing wrong?" he wondered aloud as he continued gliding the stone over the deep dish.

"What's a motivator?" Brady asked. Allie's attention snapped to Brady, surprised to hear the first non-confrontational words escape his mouth since waking up.

Che-tan's disappointment in the failure of the artifacts overrode his interest in Brady's change of heart. "Some people call it a seer basin, but . . . wait a minute."

"Oh, sure, a seer basin. Why didn't you say so," Brady mocked.

"Look, this translator is different than others, so it would make sense that it works differently, no?"

Allie shrugged.

Kneeling, Che-tan placed the translator on a flat area of ground and set the bowl with the egg shaped tip in the hole. He positioned it with both hands, making minor adjustments, and then let go. It balanced. With the translator cradling the motivator, Che-tan peered into the water filled bowl. His white teeth gleamed with satisfaction.

"Let me see," Brady said, nudging himself closer to the bowl. Gentle waves rippled across the water. He concentrated. With only the moonlight to brighten the bottom of the dish, Brady had difficulty seeing anything at all. Then, like staring at a puzzle picture, the wavy pattern faded into the background and the true image became clear. Starting at the top of the deep bowl, the words wound downward, counter clockwise, until they covered the bottom of the dish.

"I see it!" Brady exclaimed, matching Che-tan's broad grin.

"Well?" Allie asked. "What does it say?"

Che-tan and Brady began deciphering the words, but reading backwards in a swirling motion proved to be difficult. Brady traced along the words with his finger as he read slowly. "Invade the conjurer's home and stab him through the eye. Listen to him scream and watch him perish. His inheritance will become yours." Contorting his face with disgust, Brady looked at Allie and Che-tan. They looked equally grossed out by the mental image of a dagger plunging into an eyeball.

"It said all that in English?" Allie asked.

Brady nodded. Che-tan shook his head. They looked at each other. "Mine was English," Brady said. "Yours?"

"No." Both boys shrugged and turned back to Allie.

"So this bowl says we have to stab a conjurer through the eye and watch him die, so we can steal his inheritance?" Allie asked. "That's not literal, right, Che-tan?"

Che-tan's eyes bulged.

"I mean, it sounds so, so violent . . . disgusting," Allie said. "Brady?"

"Well, we already pillaged the Phantom Ship by stealing the artifacts. It sounds like it's time to rob an old man," Brady surmised with an uncomfortable chuckle.

"I'm not doing it," Allie said. "I'm not a thief, and I'm certainly not a murderer."

Che-tan watched Allie as her hands fidgeted and her eyelashes fluttered. "Of course you are not those things, Allie, but what if the conjurer is Chief Llao? Is it theft and murder to stop a bad man from hurting your family?" Che-tan asked.

Allie didn't have an answer. She thought for a moment and then sat on the ground next to the stone bowl and translator. She peered into the water herself and reread the words, hoping the boys had made an error. They hadn't.

"Yeah, I actually agree with Che-tan," Brady said. "When the police rescue a hostage, are they doing something wrong when they break in and shoot the bad guys? I don't think so. In fact, if they didn't stage a rescue, that would be wrong. So in a way, it's our duty. It's the right thing for us to rescue the others, even if it means killing a bad conjurer and claiming his inheritance." Brady looked at Che-tan. "Right?"

Che-tan lowered his head, nodding in agreement.

Running a hand through her hair, Allie took a deep breath

and exhaled. "I agree with you—I guess. But if I have to stab someone in the eye, seriously, I think I'll puke."

"Don't worry Allie, Che-tan will stab the conjurer for us. Right, Che-tan? You're a brave Indian," Brady said as he adjusted the dagger in his hand.

Che-tan glowered at Brady.

"What? It was a compliment."

"Because I am a Native American, you think I do not mind stabbing someone in the eye?" Che-tan asked.

Allie nodded. "It's a little racist," she agreed, smirking at Brady.

"Fine, sorry. I didn't mean it that way. I just thought . . . never mind. In any case, Allie, we'll take care of it. We don't expect a girl to stab someone anyway."

It was Allie's turn to glare at Brady. "Now you're being sexist. You don't think I'm capable because I'm a girl?"

Brady looked at Che-tan and Allie. "But you said . . . I . . . I'm just going to stop talking now," he said, shaking his head in defeat.

"Good idea," Allie agreed, flashing a sneaky smile at Che-tan. "So we know what we need to do, but where do we need to go?" Allie asked. "Where will we find the conjurer?"

"That is easy," Che-tan said. "Wizard Island."

# - 24 -

# Gassing Up

Ethan's eyes shot open, staring into the dark sky overhead. He lay on his back, wrapped tight in his blanket between the two campfires; next to him, a mess in the dirt indicated where Brady had been.

The warmth of the waning fire and hot coals was uncomfortable against Ethan's face. Turning his head away, his neck creaked, and he felt a sore pressure between his knees. Ignoring the dull, throbbing pain that consumed his entire body, Ethan sat up and then stretched his arm under the blanket as far as he could. Reaching to his knees, he grabbed a water bottle that had been placed against his skin for warmth. Gripping the bottle, Ethan searched his mind, but his memories were a vague dream. Sucking a small amount of spit in his dry mouth, Ethan licked his lips and scratched them together while still holding the bottled water.

Attempting to sit up fully, the blanket loosened around Ethan's shoulders, allowing cold air to seep into his toasty cocoon. The heated water bottle near his neck fell down his sweatshirt and lodged against his back. Shimmying until the bottle rested in a comfortable position at his side, Ethan lay back, returning his gaze to the sky. He accepted the cold air into his lungs.

The moon had fallen low on the horizon, and the stars had

dimmed. Searching for his companions, Ethan turned his head and looked at his sleeping sister, cuddled close with Jacob. He licked his parched lips again, but his tongue offered no moisture. He tried to sit, but his aching body wouldn't allow it. Ethan's toes and knees, his shoulders and arms, his fingertips—everything hurt. The muscles in his legs burned, at times quivering with uncontrolled spasms. Even the muscles in his ears seemed to hurt, although Ethan couldn't understand how that was possible. Do ears even have muscles?

Ethan unscrewed the cap from the bottle and drizzled water into his mouth, a small amount sliding from the corner down the side of his cheek. The water hydrated his lips and tongue like a sponge, inflating them to their proper levels. Pouring more water into his mouth, Ethan closed his eyes to savor the feel, and then, screwing the cap back on, he tucked the blanket around him and lay back onto the dirt. Gazing at his little sister, Ethan smiled as Jordan's eyes opened and returned his stare.

"How are you feeling?" Jordan whispered.

Ethan thought for a moment and then responded in a weak voice. "I don't know. It feels like I went skydiving without a parachute. I hurt and I'm exhausted and cold. So not too great, I guess." Ethan paused and inhaled through his nose as his eyes closed. "I feel really weird."

Jordan smiled in recognition of her brother's usual complaining. "Whiner," she said, moving herself away from Jacob and kneeling next to Ethan. Her eyes grew wide with excitement as she prepared to tell him about the ancient dagger and magical flute he had recovered from the Phantom Ship, but she stopped when she noticed Ethan's attention wane. "Ethan . . ."

Ethan could hear the mumble of words in his ears, but he couldn't comprehend them, and he didn't have the energy to focus. Facing his sister, Ethan became still, and his eyes glazed over. Placing a hand on his forehead, Jordan felt the extreme heat of his body temperature and removed her hand. Ethan's eyes fluttered as he gasped for breath. Then his eyes rolled back in his head, exposing only the whites, as his body began to convulse.

Grabbing Ethan's shaking body, Jordan looked around for help. "Jacob!" she screamed. "Wake up! I need you. Help!"

Shaking the fog from his mind, Jacob opened his eyes and stood with a slight wobble. Seeing Ethan, Jacob set his bare knee on the dirt and placed one hand on Jordan's shoulder as he peered into the whites of Ethan's eyes. Ethan's body shook as Jordan attempted to hold him still.

"Jordan, just back away for a minute," Jacob instructed. Jordan didn't listen. "Jordan, seriously, give him some space. If you try to hold him down, you could hurt him, and he could hurt you. Move away."

Looking up at Jacob, Jordan removed her hands from her brother and left them hovering just above him in a ready position. "What's wrong with him?" Jordan asked between muffled sobs. "Is he going to die?"

"He's not going to die," Jacob said, "but you need to stay calm. You can do it," he encouraged.

"Do what? What should I do?"

Jacob scratched his head. "Um . . ." Jacob was a fourteen-year-old freshman in high school with basic first aid skills, not a doctor.

At first, Ethan's body merely pulsed inside his blanket, but then his seizure turned violent as his arms began to thrash and his legs kicked at the restricting blanket. Jordan moved closer, preparing to throw her body on top of his, but Jacob grabbed her wrist and pulled her away. Jordan's eyes welled with tears as she looked at Jacob.

"Let's think about this," Jacob suggested. Jordan watched his mouth move, but she wasn't listening. "We know he's hypothermic. So what does that mean?" Jacob questioned as he started pacing. "It means his body temperature dropped quickly and remained low. Okay—so we heated him up. What else? What else?" Jacob asked, quizzing himself. "When the body gets cold, it tries to warm itself by creating body heat. It shivers. Yeah, that's right, the body shivers, which is actually rapid contractions of the muscles. The muscles move quickly, almost vibrating, expending energy, which warms the body," Jacob said to himself.

Jordan looked up at the pacing boy, unsure how any of this babbling would help her brother.

Jacob remained focused in his thoughts. "So what does a body need when it uses lots of energy? It needs more energy and rest. So how do you replace energy fast? Food—food that the body can break down and convert into fast energy. Sugary food." Jacob stopped pacing. Looking around, he saw the stone bowl sitting near the fire, and it had water in it. "Perfect."

"What?" Jordan asked, noticing the smile on Jacob's face. "You have an idea?"

"Yeah, I think I do. Jordan, we need to get some energy into Ethan. We need to feed him. His body's trying to recover, but it has no fuel. We need to gas him up," Jacob said.

"Gas him up?"

"Yeah. See if you can find me one of the candy bars I brought from the ranger station. I think there's at least one left. And let's get this water heated up," Jacob said. Noticing the bottom of the bowl balanced on top of the rectangular stone, Jacob shrugged, "Good idea."

Moving the rectangular stone with the hole at the center, he brushed away some coals in the fire and set the stone down. Careful to balance the bowl just right, he set the eggy tip into the hole and then pushed red coals around the dish with a stick.

"I found some chocolate in the bag," Jordan said, handing it to Jacob.

"Great." Jacob watched the bowl, hoping it wouldn't topple.

"What are you doing?" Jordan asked, her sobbing now under control. Hope radiated from her eyes as she watched Jacob.

"Chocolate is perfect, high in sugar, and very meltable," Jacob said, taking the bar from Jordan. "Meltable? Is meltable a word?" Jacob wondered aloud but then refocused as he caught Jordan's impatient gaze. "Sorry. We're going to make hot chocolate. If we can get Ethan to drink some it might calm his body by restoring some heat and energy. It will also help hydrate him. We're going to gas him up," Jacob explained. "We just need to heat the water, so it will melt the chocolate."

Jordan smiled. It sounded logical, kind of, and she figured it wouldn't hurt to get nourishment into her brother; besides, she liked the idea that chocolate was nourishing.

After a few minutes, Ethan's body came to rest. He lay in the dirt, uncovered, curled in the fetal position. Spreading the blanket on the ground near Ethan, Jordan rolled him on top and then retucked the blanket around him.

Surrounded by hot coals, the water in the stone bowl began steaming. Breaking off a square of chocolate, Jacob broke it into smaller pieces and dropped it into the water, watching as the pieces of chocolate sank to the bottom; it was impossible to tell if it was melting or not. Grabbing the pocketknife from his fanny pack, Jacob extended the longest blade and dipped it into the water, stirring gently. Pulling it out, he looked at the tip; soft brown chocolate covered the thin blade.

"It's working." Tearing off additional squares, Jacob added small chunks of chocolate to the hot water and stirred until it became muddy. Dipping his finger into the bowl, Jacob held it in place to test the heat and then licked his finger to taste the hot chocolate.

"How is it?" Jordan asked.

Jacob made a face. "Well, it's nothing to get excited about, but I think it will do the trick." Scooting behind Ethan, Jacob propped Ethan's back against his chest and held Ethan in a sitting position. "I'll hold him up," Jacob said. "Give him the water—slowly."

Pulling the sleeves of her sweatshirt over her hands like oven mitts, Jordan picked up the stone bowl and knelt next to Ethan. She first placed the rim of the bowl to her own lips, worried that it might be too hot, but finding the temperature on top of the bowl comfortable, she raised it to Ethan's lips and began to tip it. "Jacob, can you open his mouth a little?"

Reaching with one hand, Jacob pulled down on Ethan's chin, creating a narrow opening. "Best I can do," he said.

Returning the bowl to Ethan's mouth, Jordan placed the rim against her brother's lower lip, pushed down, and then tipped the bowl. The muddy water moved toward Ethan's mouth but stopped just short. Adjusting the bowl in her hands, Jordan raised it higher and tipped it at a steeper angle. The water touched Ethan's lips and drained over his teeth and into his mouth. A small amount trickled down his chin, but Jordan continued to pour. After some of the hot liquid emptied into Ethan's mouth, Jordan removed the bowl.

Pushing up on the chin, Jacob closed Ethan's mouth and tilted his head back. Jordan waited in breathless anticipation. Ethan's Adam's apple jumped as he gulped down the liquid.

Repeating the process, Jordan again placed the bowl's rim at Ethan's lips to give him another drink. As the stone touched his lips, Ethan's eyes opened wide. He stared into the stone container. From underneath the blanket, Ethan's hands reached out and grabbed the bowl, tilting it high as he guzzled the remaining contents. Ethan leaned back against Jacob and then jumped to his feet.

"That's good stuff!" Ethan shouted as he hopped up and down like he was skipping rope. Still kneeling, Jordan's mouth opened and her forehead crinkled. Jacob also watched with amazement, still holding Ethan's blanket against his body. Jacob tried to speak, but he could only manage to stutter incoherently.

Rising to her feet, Jordan gave her big brother a hug. "You're okay. I mean, really?" Jordan asked.

Ethan couldn't control his enthusiasm. "I feel fantastic. In fact, I've never felt this good . . . ever," he said before breaking into boisterous laughter. "I feel . . . what's the word? Perfect!"

Picking up the stone bowl from where Ethan had dropped

it, Jacob examined it. Faint remnants of chocolate clung to the bottom of the bowl and the rim where Ethan had taken his drink. "Hmm."

Giving his sister another squeeze, Ethan looked around the makeshift camp, taking in the scene of the fires and blankets. "So where'd everyone go?" he asked.

Jordan and Jacob looked. Their eyes darted around the camp and into the woods, then near the water, looking for Allie and Brady. For the first time, they realized their friends were gone. Jacob's face tightened and his head lowered as an almost inaudible growl of displeasure escaped his lips. "Brady."

- 25 -

# FOLLOWED

A DEEP CRIMSON GLOW EMERGED ON THE EASTERN HORIzon as Allie, Brady, and Che-tan hiked around the western border of Crater Lake toward Wizard Island. Between the peeking sun and the black night sky, muted grays and purples blurred the line between the hours of darkness and morning. Hiking at the front of the group, Che-tan moved swiftly, glancing back and slowing his pace with some annoyance. As soon as Allie and Brady caught up and prepared to rest, Che-tan pushed forward, again broadening his lead.

Allie and Brady looked at each other and shook their heads with irritation at their self-proclaimed leader. Allie didn't like it, but what choice did she have? She had to keep up. Even though the sun had not yet risen, the biting mountain air mellowed as she trudged forward.

After climbing atop the rim of the crater, the group had acquired a path across a rocky plateau. Allie couldn't see an actual path, but Che-tan said it was there, so she followed him. They hiked between car-sized boulders, watching each step, fearful of stepping into a crevasse, but the early morning hike was uneventful.

The sparse grass and trees were lonely. Allie felt like she was at the top of the world. She imagined reaching with her hand into outer space and plucking a star like she would an apple from a tree. The sky was so vast, and she felt so small. She knew it was silly, but even though she was with Che-tan and Brady, she felt alone. She missed her parents.

The group hiked toward Wizard Island, at least that's what Che-tan said, and Allie believed him. Of course she had never been there, and her night vision didn't allow her to verify her final destination, but why would he lie? Allie considered the possible answers to that question, but she didn't like any of them. Maybe Che-tan was a psychopath luring her and Brady to their deaths, or maybe he was an agent of Chief Llao, walking them to a prisoner exchange, or maybe he was taking them to be sacrificed to the evil spirit chief in exchange for some mystical favor. Allie blocked the worrisome thoughts from her mind. She trusted Che-tan. She had to.

Allie looked at Brady, who walked a few paces behind. He wiped the cool sweat from his forehead with a shaky hand. Her head shook as she noticed him both shivering and sweating. Allie knew Brady was pushing his body harder than he should, but what choice was there? They couldn't give up now—in the middle of nowhere—in the dark.

Allie focused on the sliver of sun rising on the distant horizon. She chose a marker up ahead and convinced herself she could make it at least that far before giving up. When she reached the marker, she chose another: a twisted tree, a rock shaped like a piano, an indentation in the rim of the crater like a chip in a teacup.

"How are you doing, Brady? Do you need to rest?"

Brady kept his feet moving. "If I stop, I think I'll just die. It kind of sounds good right now."

Che-tan stopped. With the coarse fabric hood hanging at his back, he bent over and lifted the brown cloak over his head, revealing his usual boots and faded jeans, and a sleeveless flannel shirt. The cloak dropped to the ground in a brown heap next to his feet as Che-tan looked at his beleaguered companions pulling up the rear. With a gentle kick of his foot, the cloak sprouted wiry legs underneath a misshapen pile of feathers. It waddled a short distance and then lifted into the air, making a home at the base of a white pine before dissolving into the dirt and needles.

"We must hurry," Che-tan said, calling back to the others. "The sun is rising. Chief Llao's powers are growing strong."

Allie leaned forward, placing her hands on her knees as she stared at the ground.

As Brady approached, his eyes rose to meet Che-tan's. Panting, he passed Che-tan and Allie and continued slogging ahead.

"We are close," Che-tan said, pointing to Wizard Island below.

The rising sun radiated orange and red, but inside the crater, a blue haze hovered around Wizard Island.

"How do we get down there?" Allie asked.

"The path will lead us away from the rim for a short while. When we enter the forest, we will begin a gentle descent to the lake. Then the final trek to the shore will be steep. Many loose rocks. We must be careful," Che-tan warned.

Che-tan's eyes glanced at the flute Allie carried at her side. His stare lingered for just a moment, but Allie noticed. Uncomfortable with Che-tan's interest in her flute, Allie concealed the instrument behind her back.

"I must warn you, the forest is dark. I fear Chief Llao has watchful eyes inside. We must stay close. You cannot fall behind," he said, calling to Brady, who continued walking ahead.

Brady didn't respond.

"Let's go," Allie said. She gripped the flute tight in her palm and continued hiking.

Che-tan followed, but his eyes wandered into the trees. He watched and listened. Someone, or something, lurked in the shadows.

# – 26 –

# LEFT BEHIND

CRADLING THE STONE BOWL IN HER PALMS AS SHE RINSED it in the water, Jordan paused for a moment. A slice of the rising sun reflected off the lake. Above the rim of the crater, the colors of daybreak muted as they fell into the crater's soupy haze. Not quite fog but more than a mist, the haze hovered above the water, framing the Phantom Ship with an eerie pall. Placing the bowl into the cold lake, Jordan scooped the water, stood, and then hurried to her friends near the campfire.

Sitting on his rock, Jacob remained in a bitter daze; his head leaned forward in his hands. "How could they leave *me* behind?" he muttered under his breath.

Tugging at the string straps hanging from his hat, Jacob glanced at Jordan and her "invalid" brother. Jacob wished he felt that good. He removed his glasses and rubbed his eyes.

"Ethan!" Jacob called.

Ethan placed a bundle of sticks on the fire. "What?"

"We're leaving soon. Why are you building up the fire?"

"I'm glad you asked," Ethan said. "Drinking the water from the stone bowl saved my life. Maybe I'm exaggerating, but I don't think so."

"What's your point?" Jacob asked.

"Well, if drinking from the bowl makes me feel this good, after being comatose for hours, I just thought you and Jordan would like to have some as well," Ethan explained. "Maybe it will give you an extra boost."

"Your healing was miraculous, there's no question, but you think it's because you drank chocolate water from a stone bowl? I think you're getting a little loopy."

Ethan looked at Jacob with surprise. "Why would you even question? You told me about the flute and its magical power of blowing ice and fire. Why is it hard to believe the other artifacts might also have magical powers?"

Jacob considered the question as Jordan stepped next to the fire holding the bowl of water. His head shook. "Well, I guess it wouldn't hurt to take a drink. It's only water," Jacob admitted. "What harm could it do?"

Ethan smiled. "Yes!"

Raising the rim of the bowl to her lips, Jordan prepared to drink but stopped as both Ethan and Brady raised their hands, signaling for her to wait. "What?" she asked. "You just said it couldn't hurt."

"Look, I don't know if the bowl is magical, or if the water is magical, or if it's a combination of the two," Ethan said. "But either way, I think we should purify the water before we drink it. The last thing I want today is explosive diarrhea."

Jordan laughed, but Jacob nodded in agreement. "The water could have parasites, like giardia, which would make us crazy sick. Let's boil it, and then we'll drink," Jacob agreed.

Taking the smooth black rectangle from his pocket, Ethan set it near the fire, surrounding it with red-hot coals. He took the bowl from Jordan and positioned the tip over the quarter-sized hole. Staring down, he attempted to balance the bowl but then pulled his hands away as he smelled burning hair. He winced, rubbing his hands together.

The bowl remained upright, but something else was happening. Peering into the center of the bowl, Ethan watched as the water swirled in a counter clockwise direction. His eyes blinked as he focused, and then he saw it.

"Hey, guys, tell me I'm not crazy," he said, pointing to the center of the bowl. "Are you seeing this?"

Positioning themselves near the stone container, Jacob and Jordan looked inside. Jacob's eyes widened. "You're not crazy. I see it too. Letters? They weren't there before."

"It looks like gibberish. What's it say?" Ethan asked.

Bending down to get a closer look, Jordan began to read. "Invade the conjurer's home. Stab him through the eye. Listen to him scream. Watch him perish. His inheritance will become yours."

"How does it say that?" Jacob asked. "I don't see that. Where does it say that?"

"Read it backwards, right to left, as it curls down the bowl," Jordan instructed, a hint of condescension in her voice.

Ethan attempted to read. "You're right."

The letters formed words, but backwards, and without spaces. The boys read slower than Jordan, but finally, after a full minute of staring, Jacob finished reading. "I think I got it," Jacob said.

"Yeah, me too," Ethan confirmed, but he sounded less confident.

Jordan's smile signaled victory, just like when she beat her dad at a game of chess.

"Okay, now that we know what it says, what the heck does it mean?" Jacob asked.

"It's a clue. It's telling us where we should go next," Jordan said.

"But can you make sense of it? What does it mean to 'invade the conjurer's home and stab him in the eye'?" Ethan questioned.

"I don't know what it means, but I know where we should go," Jordan said.

"You do?" Jacob asked with astonishment.

"Sure. Uncle Bart told me all about the conjurer's home." Jordan looked at Ethan, hoping for a look of recognition, but his face was blank. "I think the others are already on their way.

They must have left us, knowing Ethan was too weak to travel. But they left us the clue so we could find them."

"So where do we go?" Ethan blurted.

Jordan didn't answer. "What's that?" she asked, pointing to the side of the bowl.

"I don't see anything."

Picking up the bowl, Jordan held it close to her eyes but the writing on the side disappeared. She cocked her head, and her eyes squinted with concentration. Nothing. Balancing the bowl back on its stone base, she looked again and the writing reappeared on the side of the bowl above one of the ridges. Leaning low, near the coals, Jordan held back her curly hair and read the message. "Hurry! Without you, your friends will be destroyed."

"It doesn't say that," Ethan challenged.

Jordan's head bobbed.

"What does it mean?" Jacob asked.

Jordan thought for a moment. "It means we need to get to Wizard Island—fast."

- 27 -

# Losing Jordan

Stratified clouds caught the rising sunlight, refracting a myriad of golden hues; stacks of oranges and yellows rose in the eastern sky. Despite the grandeur of the sunrise, Ethan and Jacob concentrated on the fire in front of them.

The crisp mountain air was already warming, but the boys sat close to the fire for warmth. The flames had died down, but the red and white coals warmed their legs and caused the contents of the stone bowl to bubble into a slow roll.

"Water's ready," Jacob announced.

With his sleeves covering his hands, Jacob lifted the container and waited a moment for it to cool. Then he placed his lips on the stone bowl. The warmth of the stone felt good on Jacob's mouth; he sipped the contents, then, after adjusting to the heat of the liquid, he took two deep gulps. Jacob took a deep breath and prepared for another drink but was stopped as Ethan placed a hand on his arm.

"The rest is for Jordan," Ethan reminded.

Jacob nodded and handed over the bowl for Ethan's safekeeping.

"One more sip," Jacob begged, pinching his fingers close together, indicating how small the sip would be. "Where is Jordan, anyway?"

Ethan held the bowl in his lap. Turning, he scanned the

area, looking for his sister. "Maybe she's going to the bathroom or something," Ethan suggested. "Jordan! Water's ready!" he screamed.

Ethan listened, expecting an echo to reverberate off the rock and water or his sister to answer, but the morning air absorbed his voice. "Hmm. We'll give her a couple more minutes," he said, placing the bowl back on its base atop the coals.

"Do you think she's still mad?" Jacob asked, raising his eyes from the fire to make sure Jordan wasn't lurking nearby. "She was kind of ticked when we decided to wait for the water to heat up, like we were ignoring her or something. I mean, I know we need to get to Wizard Island fast, but . . ."

"Nah, she's fine," Ethan said, and then, catching Jacob's unbelieving look, added with a smirk, "Well, at least she'll get over it. We all want to get to Wizard Island, but it only makes sense to be prepared. If this water does for you what it did for me, I think it's fifteen minutes well spent." Looking down at his wristwatch, Ethan noticed it had stopped; the midnight swim broke the watch like it had almost broken him.

A broad smile covered Jacob's face. He jumped from his place on the log, his eyes wide with enthusiasm.

"How you feeling, big guy? The magic water kicking in?" Ethan asked, but he already knew the answer.

Looking like he would explode with vigor, Jacob suppressed his limbs' desire for perpetual motion as he struggled to stand still and remain calm. Then he answered, "I feel good."

"Ha!" Ethan laughed at the understated response. "I'm impressed, Jacob."

Jacob couldn't resist. "It's incredible! I feel like running a marathon . . . or two." Jacob laughed. "I'm not tired. My body doesn't hurt at all. This is AWESOME!"

Ethan smiled, and then his eyes rose high on the hill and then down near the water and into the trees as he looked for Jordan. "Where in the world can she be? I thought she was in a big hurry," Ethan mumbled. "Jordan! Where are you?" Ethan's eyes continued to scan the area. "Come on, let's find her and get going."

They split up, and Jacob followed the path up the hill, looking throughout the splotchy groves. Low on the slope, Ethan approached the water and looked each direction along the shoreline. To his right, the ground flattened with occasional boulders and trees, while to his left, the shore was rocky and the steep mountain rose to the crater's rim. *A normal person would explore the easier path*, Ethan thought and then chose the difficult path, climbing a large boulder to start his search. Jordan wasn't normal.

After searching around rock formations and behind trees, Jacob stopped calling out for Jordan and instead hollered for Ethan. He hadn't heard Ethan yelling for a while and didn't want to get separated. Abandoning his search high on the slope, Jacob jogged toward the water, where he had last seen Ethan.

"Ethan? ETHAN!"

## - 28 -

# The Necklace

NESTLED AGAINST A WHITE ASPEN, JORDAN HELD THREE interlocking stones in her hands. She stared as if in a trance, unwilling or unable to respond to the approaching calls of her brother.

"Jordan, we've been looking all over for you," Ethan said as he hopped from a flat rock to the ground near his sister. She remained silent, engrossed with the necklace cupped in her hands. "Jordan, did you hear me? What are you doing? Let's get going."

Looking up at her brother, Jordan laid the necklace across her lap as the clear, blue, and red stones pulsed like the lights on a police car.

Ethan watched with intense interest, transfixed on the same necklace that commanded his attention at the ranger station. At the station, the stone necklace didn't emit light or pulse; it had just looked like an old necklace, but even then it had demanded his attention. "Where'd you get that?"

Lifting the necklace from her lap, Jordan lowered her head and placed the thin leather strap around her neck. The light from the stones dimmed as the necklace hung against Jordan's chest, a couple of inches lower than the imitation necklace Uncle Bart had given her. She shook her head and looked at her brother. Her trance was broken.

"It was in the woods," she muttered.

"In the woods? How? Where?" he asked.

"Last night when you and Brady got back from the Phantom Ship, we had to put your dry clothes back on you. My job was to gather the clothes."

"Yeah, so?"

"When I picked up Brady's sweatshirt, this fell out. I was in a hurry, so I picked it up and put it in my pocket. I forgot all about it until a few minutes ago when I felt the bulge. I took it out and looked at it, and . . ."

"And what?" Ethan asked.

Jordan looked around, a lost look in her eyes. "Where are we?"

"Ethan! Jordan! Can you hear me?"

Ethan barely heard Jacob's faint call. Jumping onto the flat rock and then upon a higher, oval boulder, Ethan looked in the direction of the call, then, spotting Jacob a short distance away, waved his hands. "We're here," he yelled.

They were back together at last . . . almost.

Ethan turned back to the spot where Jordan had been sitting. "Jordan? Jordan!" Training his eyes along the boulders of the shoreline, Ethan spotted her, hopping and climbing. "Jordan!" She didn't respond.

"Ethan, what's going on?" Jacob hollered from his perch atop a nearby rock.

Glancing quickly at Jacob, Ethan tried to keep an eye on his sister. He turned back at Jacob. "She's gone loopy!" he yelled.

Jacob nodded.

"Get the stuff from camp. Put the water in a bottle. Bring the bowl and the base and anything else you can find. I'll keep following Jordan." Not waiting for a response, Ethan turned and started after his sister.

Jacob waved in agreement and then bounded across the boulders and along the narrow passageways on his way to retrieve the purified water and stone artifacts.

# – 29 –

# Abandoned

Hidden in the shadows where sunlight couldn't penetrate, watchers glowered, their heavy breathing masked by a gentle breeze blowing through the evergreen boughs.

Multiple layers of shrubs and evergreens hid the spotless blue sky outside the forest. Tree roots poked from the ground, and tangled vines hung low, brushing against the hikers' faces. Brady ducked to avoid contact, but as the obstacles became more frequent, he gave up. He strode through, letting the moist plant flesh wisp across his skin.

He trudged along at the front of the pack, and Che-tan followed close behind. Pulling up the rear, Allie struggled to stay within three arm's lengths of Che-tan. Other than her regular glances down at the path, Allie kept her eyes straight ahead on Che-tan's back. Then she noticed his attention diverting into the woods. Allie followed his gaze but saw nothing, so she refocused on his back and worked to control her labored breathing.

Che-tan's pace slackened. His eyes scanned the woods frantically.

Stepping closer, Allie placed one hand on his shoulder. "What's wrong?" she asked.

"Shhh. Listen."

Allie listened. "I don't hear anything," she whispered.

"Exactly."

With her hand still on Che-tan's shoulder, Allie listened again. He was right. With the exception of Brady's footsteps, she didn't hear a thing. No birds chirping or insects buzzing around. The breeze had even calmed into dead quiet.

Allie leaned close, her mouth near Che-tan's ear, ready to ask another question, but Che-tan raised his hand to silence her. Then, without warning, he burst into pieces. Four large hawks exploded from his body. The birds lofted upward, dodging the dangling vines and evading thick branches. Tree limbs slanted and bent, leaning into the birds' path as if attempting to trap them inside a cage, but the birds maneuvered, changing course as they flew through the upper canopy and into the clear sky.

With her mouth hanging open, Allie kept her hand raised as if still positioned on Che-tan's shoulder, but the shoulder was gone. Che-tan was gone.

## – 30 –

# THE MOUTH

RACING TO KEEP UP WITH HIS LITTLE SISTER, ETHAN LEAPT from boulder to boulder as though they were giant stepping-stones across a creek. No matter how fast he moved, Jordan managed to stay a couple of paces ahead. Even with his renewed energy from drinking the lake water, Ethan gasped for air. Stopping for a moment to regain his breath, Ethan placed his hands on his knees. Below him and to his left, a small fissure in the rock caught his eye. He looked deep into the crevasse and then looked up to find his sister.

"Jordan! Stop!" he screamed, but Jordan kept going.

Ethan's brief rest had allowed Jordan to lengthen the gap, so he resumed his chase, running and jumping along the rocky corridors and boulders around the lower rim of the lake. Looking ahead, Ethan could see Wizard Island in the distance. "At least—we're going—in the right direction," he said.

Ethan watched as his sister navigated the rocky terrain with the expertise of a world-class mountain climber. Then she dropped down from a tall rock formation to the ground, out of sight. He waited for her to reappear, but she didn't. "Jordan?"

Making a long leap onto the tall rock where he had last seen Jordan, Ethan searched. He circled the tall rock and then dropped to his hands and knees as he looked to the ground below the boulders.

"JORDAN! Where are you?"

Tall boulders surrounded the ground in every direction, forming a cup. Ethan scratched his head. "Jordan!" he screamed, gripping his hair.

"She's not there," Jacob said, standing on the rock opposite Ethan. He peered into the same hole.

Ethan looked up, surprised to see Jacob standing there. "Where'd you come from?"

Jacob tied his sweatshirt around his waist and hung the canvas bag over his shoulder. "I've been following you for a while. You didn't hear me calling you?"

Ethan shrugged. "Did you see Jordan drop down from this rock?"

"Yep."

"Where'd she go?" Ethan asked, throwing his hands into the air. "What's going on here?"

"Come over here," Jacob said.

Ethan didn't budge.

"Ethan, come on," Jacob urged again, motioning with his hand.

Ethan hopped across the divide and stood next to Jacob. "What?"

Jacob pointed to the base of the rock Ethan had been standing on. "She went down."

Dropping to his stomach, Ethan held his hand above his eyes to block the sunlight as he squinted into the shadow. Sure enough, at the base of the boulder was a narrow fissure.

Dropping off the boulder, Ethan knelt next to the opening. "You're saying she went down there?"

Raising his hands as if to shield himself from the attack, Jacob responded, "You have a better idea?"

Ethan didn't even have a worse idea.

The jagged opening was thin, only a couple of feet wide and a few feet long. Ethan turned his head and poked it through the hole, peering into the blackness.

"What do you see?"

"Not a thing. I'm going to kill that girl when I catch her," Ethan said.

"What are you going to do now?"

Ethan considered his options.

"Ethan?"

Ethan's chest heaved. "I'm going in." Turning around, Ethan flopped onto his stomach and scooted backwards, his feet entering the narrow opening first.

"I don't think you'll fit," Jacob said with an uncomfortable chuckle.

Ethan persisted, squeezing into the fissure.

"Do I really need to tell you what a bad idea that is? Seriously?" Jacob challenged. "Have you forgotten that your parents were eaten by the earth? And you're going to lower yourself into that . . . that . . . mouth? Come on, Ethan. Let's think about this for a second."

Ethan stopped lowering himself and looked up at his friend. "I have to go after her. She's all I've got."

Jacob nodded.

Scooting himself backward again into the opening, Ethan was in up to his waist when he suddenly stopped. His eyes bulged and his body writhed. "AAGH! NO! AAGH! OH HELP!!"

Jacob jumped from the edge of the boulder, his feet hitting the ground near Ethan's head. He extended his hand, and Ethan grabbed it before breaking into a toothy grin.

"You big jerk!" Jacob said as he removed his hat and scratched his head. Looking into the sky, he held the back of his neck and sighed.

"I'm sorry, Jacob. I just wanted to lighten things up a bit. Wish me luck."

"Seriously, you can fit down there? I don't want to have to pry you out."

"I guess we'll find out," Ethan said, lowering himself deeper into the hole. From his chest up, he stuck out of the fissure.

Ethan turned his head sideways and lowered the rest of the way down.

Jacob stuck his head through the opening. "Whoa, you weren't kidding. I can't see a thing down there. Are you okay?"

"Yeah. My feet can touch, but it's kind of slippery. It goes deeper into some kind of a cavern, but I can't see that well." Ethan released his grip with his first hand, leaving one set of fingertips on the exterior of the crevasse. His feet searched and eventually found a stable hold on the slippery rocks. He released his second hand. "My eyes are still trying to adjust to the—"

Cascading rocks and pained screams echoed upward into Jacob's ears. "Ethan?" The sound of additional falling rocks continued to trickle. "Ethan?"

"I'm okay—kind of," came the response from deep inside. "The good news is, I made it to the bottom."

Tasting blood in his mouth, Ethan spat.

"Do you see Jordan?"

Ethan moaned in pain. "No. But my eyes are starting to adjust. There's quite a bit of light coming through that hole."

"Really?"

"No. But there would be if you'd get out of the way." Ethan looked around the cavern and then climbed a short way back up to the opening. "Moss. I slipped on moss?"

Next to the footprint where he had slipped, Ethan could see a smaller set of controlled footprints. "She definitely came down here."

"Then where is she?"

Reaching up to his throbbing head, Ethan's hand felt sticky goo running down his temple. "I think I'm bleeding!"

"You don't need to yell. I'm right here," Jacob said as he lowered himself through the opening. "Here, take this." Extended in his hand was the canvas bag, weighted with the stone bowl, the stone rectangular base, and some other sundry items, including a couple of bottles of purified lake water.

Grabbing the bag from Jacob's hand, Ethan climbed down

to the cavern floor. He watched as Jacob gracefully navigated the mossy rocks.

"That wasn't so bad," Jacob said.

"Show off," Ethan said with a smirk, followed by a wince as he felt another sharp pain on the side of his head.

Feeling for Ethan's hand, Jacob knelt on the ground and rummaged through the canvas bag. Pulling the stone bowl and a bottle of water from the bag, Jacob poured a small amount into the bowl. "Drink this."

Holding the bowl to his lips, Ethan drank. Within seconds, the pain in his head vanished and the taste of blood disappeared from his mouth. He felt near his temple, but the blood was gone from his face. "We need to market this stuff. We'll make gazillions," Ethan said, only partly in jest.

"So you feel better?"

"Good as new. Even better." With his eyes adjusted to the darkness, Ethan saw a slender beam of light entering through the mouth, illuminating the mossy rocks near the top of the entrance. At the far end of the cavern, he saw increased blackness.

At the edge of the darkness, an archway was cut in the stone. The cave continued, tunneling deeper underground. They stood at the tunnel entrance, afraid to move.

Ethan looked at Jacob. "I think I know where Jordan went."

"Duh."

## - 31 -

# Lava Tunnel

The air inside the cavern was cool, yet a musty odor assaulted Ethan's nostrils as he stood near the tunnel archway. Rising fifteen feet from floor to apex, the towering tunnel walls were coarse to the touch. With his fists clenched tight, Ethan stared into the oblivion of the pure black tunnel and nearly choked on his spit.

Fumbling through the canvas bag, Jacob found what he was looking for. Glancing back to the soft light that entered the cavern through the lips of the narrow entrance, he turned back to face the tunnel. He gripped the round handle of the flashlight and pressed the button. An audible sigh of relief escaped his lips as the flashlight's beam brightened the cavern. Jacob looked to see if Ethan had heard. If he had, he didn't show it.

He pointed the beam of the flashlight into the abyss. Ethan stood beside him at the center of the archway. The light seemed glorious against the utter gloom they had faced, even though the light only brightened a diameter of twenty feet and imposed just a few yards into the tunnel. The rock walls were white from the glow, but Jacob's pulse quickened as he noticed the tunnel aim sharply downward.

An aggressive gloom pressed against the boys from all sides, buffered only by the flashlight's fluorescent beam—hardly a dependable protection against anxiety and dread.

Cupping his hands to his mouth, Ethan screamed loud enough to make his throat hurt. "JORDAN!"

He listened as the echo raced down the stone tube before fading into silence. Turning his body, Ethan leaned toward the tunnel, listening for a response. Nothing. Looking at Jacob, Ethan grimaced with worry for his parents and anxiety about Jordan, but he was mostly afraid of stepping into the darkness of the lava tunnel.

Concentrating to maintain his normal breathing, Ethan looked back at the cavern entrance, the dim light barely perceptible when compared to the brightness of the flashlight. Then glancing around the main cavern, he realized he was in the wide cavity of an earthen mouth. Looking ahead into the tunnel, he could see the narrow gullet he would pass through on his way into the bowels of the mountain. Ethan wondered if he was offering himself as dinner to appease the appetite of Crater Lake.

The boys remained still in front of the lighted archway, unable to move. They stared straight ahead. If only the water from the bowl had provided courage instead of energy. *That would be much better*, Ethan thought. At this moment Ethan would be happy to trade his vigor for even a little bit of bravery.

Ethan placed a shaky hand on Jacob's shoulder. Together they took a step into the lava tunnel.

# - 32 -

# *SHHH!*

Shhh!" Brady whispered. He stopped midstep, careful not to make a single sound. He listened.

*Crack!* Allie glared at the twig beneath her foot and swore through clenched teeth.

Allie was beyond grumpy, and she knew it, but what could she do? Her hair felt crusty, her legs hurt, her clothes were filthy, and she had a horrible taste in her mouth, like she hadn't brushed her teeth for a week. Just thinking about being grumpy made her even grumpier.

The last twenty-four hours had been the worst of her life, and everything bugged her. Like a small pebble in the toe of a shoe, each minor annoyance grew into a larger pain as time passed. Right now, Brady was that pebble.

One thing was certain, Allie didn't like being "shhh'd." She had been hushed just an hour earlier, right before Che-tan abandoned her, bursting into a flock of birds and flying away to hide from the encroaching evil. "I'm going to smack the next person that shushes me," she muttered. At least Brady couldn't fly away and abandon her like Che-tan did.

Eerie silence.

Dark mist wrapped around the hikers like a noose around the neck. In the predawn morning, Allie had felt the same smothering evil and hopelessness. The fear had been overwhelming;

the uncertainty of danger and the knowledge of her weakness had caused her to despair. Was the black mist a deadly toxin that would melt off her face? Or was it a suffocating fog that would suck her into the Below World, dooming her to eternal torment? No. After her experience last night, Allie knew the mist was a gathering of disembodied slaves, sent to scare her. Allie's jaw clenched. The thought made her mad.

Brady looked deep into the woods as the mist engulfed him. His shoulders rose and fell with each rapid breath.

Allie could hear Brady's breathing quicken as the mist pressed against him. She knew what he was feeling but refused to give in to the fear. Then insipid eyes floated by, staring. At first, Allie didn't know what the thin ovals were, but then they blinked. For just a moment, the creamy eyes with thin red pupils were camouflaged in the shadows of the mist. The image caused Allie to shudder.

From every angle, the mist approached boldly. Looking up, Brady saw the darkness lowering upon him, attempting to crush him. His eyes closed tight and his fists clenched. Crouching in place with his eyes glued shut, Brady's heart pounded.

"Cover your eyes," Allie said.

Brady obeyed.

With her finger placed over the fourth hole of the flute, Allie squeezed her eyes shut and blew all the air from her lungs through the colorful instrument. The burst of brilliance was like a nuclear explosion. Even with her eyes closed, the brightness caused tears to stream down her cheeks. Allie felt herself swaying out of balance as the light danced across her eyes. She took a shallow breath and then pitched forward, planting her foot for balance, but then she fell back and crumbled to the ground, the flute still clutched tight in both hands.

Brady uncovered his eyes. The shadows and mist had fled. Sunlight shined through the evergreen canopy, casting golden rays onto the ground. A steady shaft of light illuminated Allie's slender body.

Brady dropped to his knees. "Allie! Wake up, Allie. Are you okay?"

Allie moaned and rolled over in the dirt, gripping the flute with one hand and covering her eyes with the other.

Brady nudged her and then pushed her harder. "Allie!" he said more forcefully. Standing, he kicked her gently as his eyes wandered around the scene.

Stirring, Allie's eyes opened a sliver and looked up at Brady, perturbed by the rudeness of the kick. As the spots of light faded from her eyes, she looked up but didn't speak. Brady paid her no attention. His eyes were fixed deep into the woods.

"Allie?" he whispered again and then kicked her harder.

"Knock that off," she said, pushing Brady's foot away.

Standing, she looked into Brady's face and then followed his gaze. As expected, the flute had caused the darkness to flee, casting out the mist of disembodied souls sent to frighten them. They seemed to be alone.

"You kick me again and I'll drop you," Allie said.

Brady grinned at the meaningless threat. "Shhh."

"And don't 'shhh' me."

"Okay then, shut up," he said, the grin absent from his face. "Is that better?" Allie prepared to respond, but Brady continued. "There's still something out there."

"I don't see anything," Allie said.

"I know. I can't explain it, but something's there. I can feel it."

Brady was right. A bizarre tension hovered in the air, a kind of palpable emotion radiating from some unknown source. It wasn't evil or menacing, but it wasn't friendly either. It felt like a lost child who had run away from home, longing to return but unsure how: uncertainty, loneliness, fear of rejection, rebellion—all wrapped into one pained emotion. "What an odd feeling," Allie said.

"Let's get out of here," Brady said. He offered his hand to help Allie up.

Allie looked at Brady's hand. *Right—you wish.*

She stood and brushed the dirt from her clothes. After a few cautious paces, her stride lengthened and her steps quickened. The path opened into a bright clearing.

Exiting the woods into the morning sun, Allie smiled with relief, happy to escape the gloomy forest.

In the clearing, the tall grass swayed, tickling her ankles. Allie gazed around the panorama. High on the upper rim of the crater, a valley notched into the side of the mountain, creating a steep pathway down to the islets leading to Wizard Island. Fallen pine trees littered the loose pathway like a precarious array of pick-up sticks.

"Oh, this is going to be fun," Brady said.

Walking farther away from the wooded border, Allie and Brady sat in the grass to rest before continuing their trek down to the shore.

* * *

From the border of the woods, two pairs of empty eyes spied, content to hide in the shadows and watch. They obeyed the command of their chief.

The souls of the prison slaves had failed in their mission to frighten the youth away. The hikers were approaching their final destination faster than expected. Wizard Island was close.

The two personages who had once been Nathaniel and Jenna lurked, careful not to interfere with the progress of the hiking kids. Hollow eyes sunk deep into their faces, punctuating their grayish, corpse-like skin. All youthful beauty and vigor had been sucked from them, leaving only a shriveled shell. They remained still and quiet within the wooded border, awaiting further instructions from the chief who pardoned them.

– 33 –

# Inner Visions

JORDAN MARCHED THROUGH THE PITCH-BLACK GULLET OF Crater Lake with the carefree safety of sleepwalking through a vast field. Nothing could hurt her or thwart her progress. Though her eyes had no vision, her mind was alive with images, guiding her along a true course. The necklace hanging at her chest knew the path.

Stars raced in circles, orbiting low in the night sky like distant rows of car headlights speeding along a midnight highway. On the ground, the bluegrass was illuminated as though the sun was shining. In the peripheral vision of Jordan's mind, an ancient scene unfolded to her left. A woman accepted a gift from a man as she held an infant child close to her body, but Jordan paid it no heed. To her right, a sheer mountain wall of rock exploded from the grassy field, but she cast the image aside and focused forward.

A white tree trunk rose from a rounded knoll, the top of the trunk splintered. The branches and leaves appeared to have been torn apart, pinched off like a dandelion head. Atop the trunk facing Jordan, a symbol was charred into the bark. She had seen a similar symbol before, yet it seemed foreign. As she drew nearer, she could see stones set in the hillside like steps leading up to the trunk.

Jordan was walking toward the trunk on the hill when the image faded. Then a new vision engulfed her mind.

* * *

On a throne set at the center of a rectangular slab of granite, balancing upon the peak of the highest mountain in North America, Chief Llao sat, gazing upon his territory. Forests and rolling hills extended to the blue ocean shore in the west, and to the east, a distant wall of mountain divided his domain from the rest of creation.

To the north, snowcapped mountains rose as watchtowers, stabbing at the horizon to protect his possessions from any enemy daring enough to enter his domain without permission. To the south, a mountain peak rivaled Mazama. Chief Llao rubbed the tips of his fingers together as the corners of his lips curled up. The southern peak, its lands and treasures, would soon be his.

Gathering at the base of Chief Llao's mountain fortress, every man and woman old enough to hold a weapon prepared for the long march to the southern peak. Mixed in with the strapping warriors were old men aided by walking sticks, while children, too young to be of any real use, clung to their mothers' sides, anticipating Chief Llao's order to attack. Chief Llao clenched his teeth as he assessed his forces and noted the absence of his most favored warriors.

Climbing onto his throne, Chief Llao placed a foot on each armrest. Stretching his arms from his side like wings, he closed his eyes, tilted his head, and arched his back. The mountain energy surged through him, causing every cell inside his body to accelerate. His chest heaved with angry breaths, and his body burned with the amplified energy and hatred that surged through him.

Rising above the throne, Chief Llao's feet lifted into the air as his eyes burst open. Clouds and sunlight collected above him in condensed radiance. Then Chief Llao inhaled, consuming the light. His mouth and eyes glowed with eerie brilliance.

The air grew stale and the sun shone deep purple. A peculiar green hue engulfed the sky and the mountain moaned beneath him. The tip of the mountain opened up and fell in upon itself, swallowing the granite slab and throne, as the chief hovered above. From deep inside the mountain, an orange burst of lava shot into the sky, enveloping Chief Llao. He soaked in the energy.

Moving his hands together in a slow clapping motion, Chief Llao unleashed his fury. He conducted destruction and mayhem like the instruments in a symphony.

Hurtling boulders the size of a house, Chief Llao assaulted the southern peak. Boulders crashed resulting in devastating damage. The barrage intensified as sprinkles of fire fell upon the forests, catching shrubs and trees ablaze and turning the mountainside into a hellish inferno.

Strangely, there was no retaliation. Chief Llao licked his lips and prepared to send in his troops.

At the base of Mazama, the earth swelled and then rippled outward. Chief Llao's warriors surfed hundreds of miles on a tidal wave of earth and rock. At the base of the southern peak, the warriors drew their blades and spears, searching for enemy combatants, but there was no one to fight. With a surge of confidence, Chief Llao's forces marched through the billowing smoke and blazing trees, up the mountain to victory.

Chief Llao gloried in the devastation he had caused and gloated in his superiority over Chief Skell. The balance of power had shifted. Dominance belonged to Chief Llao.

As his energy depleted and the barrage of lava and boulders ceased, Chief Llao lowered back onto Mazama. The green sky became blue again, and the purple sun shone brilliant white and yellow. Falling back into the hollowed mountain, the shooting lava abandoned the sky.

Weak from his exertions, Chief Llao rested while his minions prepared for his triumphant arrival onto the southern peak. Then, descending from the distant clouds, a pinpoint of white light shone. The light rested on the southern peak and brightened until the entire mountain was hidden by its brilliance. Screaming with frustration, Chief Llao grabbed a fistful of hair and gnashed his teeth with anger. Chief Skell had not been defeated at all. Llao braced for the retaliation.

With his feet planted on the southern peak, Chief Skell motioned with his hand, causing a ripple of energy to swell outward, increasing with speed and ferocity until it struck Chief Llao, causing Mazama to tremble. Then in a tsunami of earth and trees, Chief Skell evicted the intruding forces from the southern peak and sent them hurtling back toward Chief Llao.

Mazama crumbled. Through an opening large enough for the wave to enter, Chief Llao's warriors washed deep inside their hollowed mountain. With the warriors cast deep inside, the peak collapsed, swallowing Chief Llao.

Falling helplessly through the darkness, Chief Llao looked up in horror as the mountain collapsed around him. His outstretched fingers grasped for a handhold—or a stone, a tree, or, vine, or anything that would halt his free fall—but his hand caught only air. He plunged deep inside the bowels of the mountain.

With the last remaining power he could muster, Chief Llao softened his landing at the bottom of the inner mountain and shielded his body, pressing outward with an invisible force that protected him from the crushing rock. The mountain fell upon his protective shield, pressing him deeper into the ground.

As the rock stopped falling and the dust settled, Chief Llao shivered, lying on a black cavern floor. Grit and dust filled his nose and his pasty mouth was filled with dirt and just a touch of spit. His eyes blinked as he cleared his throat and then swallowed.

He groped along the walls, searching for a passageway, for some escape, but he found none. The moans and cries of his warriors surrounded him in the darkness. Chief Llao was entombed deep within his own mountain, but he was not alone.

* * *

Jordan continued along the blackened tunnel, images brightening her mind's view as she walked toward her predetermined end.

## - 34 -

# BATS

HITTING THE SIDE OF HIS FLASHLIGHT WITH THE PALM OF his hand, Jacob held his breath and then breathed again when the light flickered back to life.

Ethan listened intently. "Uncool," he said and then gulped.

With the beam once again lighting the cavern, Ethan and Jacob resumed their hike.

"You okay?" Ethan asked.

Jacob nodded, trying to convince himself. "Are we sure Jordan came in here? Shouldn't we have run into her by now? Maybe we should go back," Jacob said, his voice a little higher than usual.

Though Ethan understood the fear and uncertainty Jacob was feeling, now was the time for courage and determination, not weakness. Ethan looked at Jacob. "You can go back if you're scared, but I'm keeping the light."

"No, no. I'm fine. I'm just thinking out loud," Jacob said, his voice shaking. "I'm sure we'll find her."

Ethan nodded in agreement. The lava tube would either dead-end with a wall of rock or return to the fresh air above ground at some point. Ethan prayed for a safe return to the surface, but however it ended, Jordan was sure to be there.

The narrow cavern descended in a straight path with only subtle curves in either direction. From deeper inside the cavern, a pungent smell wafted toward the boys. Ethan became accustomed to the rank odor, but as they continued downward, the humid air thickened and the wall of the cavern glimmered against the light. Sidestepping to the edge of the stone corridor, Ethan placed his hand against the wall. It was wet. A drip of water hit him square between the eyes. He wiped the moisture from his face.

Jacob jerked as a drip hit him on the head and another on his arm. "Great." Shining his flashlight on the ceiling of the tunnel, Jacob groaned to see the drips increasing like a gentle rain. Then a mild flutter echoed from deeper inside the tunnel.

"Hey, Jacob, I meant to ask you," Ethan began, "what kind of animals live inside caves?"

Jacob thought for a moment and then answered, eager to distract himself from the spooky, inner-mountain hike. "Well, most animals will take shelter in a cave—bears, cougars, rodents. But we would have found most of those things near the opening of the cavern. I don't think they would wander this deep inside."

"Then what's that sound?" Ethan asked.

Jacob listened. He hadn't noticed anything, but then he heard a gentle flapping. "Oh, and bats," he said in a matter-of-fact tone.

"Bats?" Ethan groaned with displeasure.

"Yeah, of course. Did you know there are fifteen species of bats found near Crater Lake? Or maybe it's seventeen."

"Great. Thanks for the info."

Jacob smiled, recognizing Ethan's discomfort with the subject. "But don't worry, they usually leave people alone."

"Usually?"

Jacob's grin grew wider. "Yeah, usually." Jacob paused. "Wait, listen."

The fluttering sound grew stronger and more steady. Both boys stopped walking as they gazed deeper into the tunnel. The sound gathered, then like school students emptying into a hallway after class, the noise amplified into deafening chaos as the cavern filled with activity. Bats. Scores and scores of bats raced from deep inside the tunnel, filling it with flutters and flaps as they raced past the boys' faces and brushed against their bodies.

Ethan threw his hands and arms into a blocking position in front of his face, prepared to beat back the bats as they brushed by. Amazingly, the bats only grazed him with their wings and waves of beating air, never colliding even once. Ethan cringed with the creepy crawlies. From drips of water falling onto his skin to flying rodents brushing by, he almost panicked. Crouching in place, he covered his head as another wave of bats filled the tunnel.

"Ooohhh. Yuck!" Ethan shivered, but after another brief moment, the bats were gone. Ethan looked at Jacob, his lips pressed. "They won't bother us, huh?"

"What? I said 'usually.' Besides, they didn't *really* bother us," Jacob said.

"That didn't bother you?"

Jacob grinned. "Something must have disrupted them further down the tunnel."

The boys locked eyes.

"Jordan!"

- 35 -

# Descent to Wizard Island

In the tall grass overlooking Wizard Island, Brady sat, holding the ancient dagger. He wielded the short weapon like a knight inspecting his broadsword before battle. Brady turned the dagger in his hand, waving it slowly in front of his eyes. The black obsidian blade shone in the morning sun. Magnificent!

Looking at his hiking partner sprawled in the grass, Brady couldn't understand how she could sleep after all that had just happened. Eying Allie's comfort with jealousy, Brady stood, ready to go. He looked at the sleeping girl, wary of the consequences of waking her too soon, and decided it would be unwise to be the cause of her emotional collapse, especially while she possessed the magical flute that could turn him into an ice sculpture.

Brady looked at the intriguing instrument in Allie's hand. *Maybe we can wait another minute*, he thought as he bent down to pull the flute from Allie's fingers. After his experience with the blinding light in the forest, Brady believed everything Allie had told him about the flute, but he hadn't seen it in action. Not really.

Never had something so powerful been within his reach. He had to test the flute and unlock its full potential. Trying to convince himself of his own noble motives for taking the flute—and Allie's indifference at his borrowing the flute—Brady shook his head. Who was he kidding? She'd be livid. He grinned.

Brady appraised the ancient dagger sitting across his lap. Did the dagger hold special power like the flute? Holding the dagger up to his eyes, Brady looked at the black etching on the base of the hilt. What could the symbol mean? Was it some kind of clue, or maybe the artisan's signature? Answering those questions would have to wait.

Placing the dagger in the grass beside him, Brady lowered to his knees as he reached for the flute, his eyes wide with anticipation. He paused and then leaned closer, touching the flute with his fingertips. *Allie has no right to get mad. It's not like the flute belongs to her anyway,* he justified. Pinching the rounded shaft between his forefinger and thumb, Brady twisted the flute and pulled it toward him. The flute slid easily from Allie's hand. *Just a couple more inches. Easy—easy—almost got it.*

Brady glanced into Allie's face to confirm her continued sleep. Her eyes were still closed and her breathing heavy. Preparing to complete his delicate operation, Brady's eyes darted to the flute and then back at Allie. Her eyes were wide open, staring into his freckled face. Brady scampered back with surprise, falling on his rear with his hands propped behind him. *Caught.*

Stretching her muscles, Allie yawned as she sat up, never removing her eyes from Brady.

"Good, you're awake," he said, attempting to act cavalier. "We should probably get going."

Allie blinked and nodded in agreement, but she didn't say a word.

One red eyebrow rose on Brady's forehead. She didn't say anything about the attempted theft, so Brady figured he was in the clear. That was too close.

Rising to his feet, Brady extended his hand to help Allie up.

Ignoring the offered hand, Allie stood. Brady shrugged.

Tucking the dagger into his shorts, he turned and walked toward a black boulder at the side of the crater's cliff.

He assessed the narrow path through the ravine, the fallen trees, and the soft sediment. "This is going to be a blast," he said, shaking his head.

Joining Brady, Allie looked toward the brilliant blue water and the series of small islets stepping toward Wizard Island. Without saying a word, she took her first step downward, sliding as the loose sand beneath her feet gave way. On her backside, Allie continued to slide, scooting downward as her shoes filled with pumice and dirt. She looked up at Brady. "Well? What are you waiting for? Come on."

Hesitating for a moment, Brady stepped into the ravine, bracing himself with his hands as his feet slid. "This won't be so bad."

Looking down to the lake, Brady saw how far he still had to go. He moaned but pressed on, determined to keep up with Allie.

– 36 –

# The Second Eruption of Mt. Mazama

How old are the batteries in that thing?" Ethan asked as the flashlight flickered.

Jacob pounded the light with the side of his hand and the bulb came back to life. "Not that old, but we've been going a while down here. Don't worry, the batteries will last." As Jacob completed his sentence, the flashlight dimmed and then turned off, casting the boys into utter darkness. Jacob hit the light again, but it didn't revive, not even a flicker. He pounded it again as his heart raced.

"Really? They'll last?" Ethan yelled, each word swelling with greater volume.

"Shut up," Jacob replied in a high-pitched tone, his voice cracking. He pounded the light again. Nothing. Jacob felt around in the dark and found Ethan's shoulder. "Ethan, what are we going to do? Are we going to die in here?"

Ethan breathed shallow and fast. "We need to stay calm. Can you do that?"

"*Yeah—*" Jacob responded shakily. "Can you?"

Grabbing Jacob's hand from his shoulder, Ethan held it and pulled toward the side of the cavern. Standing side by side, arms outstretched between them, Ethan reached for the side of the tunnel. "Jacob, can you touch the wall?"

Jacob reached, his fingertips searching for stone. "No, I don't feel anything" he said. "You?"

"Yeah, I'm touching the wall right now. Pull me toward you and tell me as soon as you feel the wall."

Jacob followed the instructions, pulling Ethan sideways. After a few inches, Jacob's fingertips made contact with stone. "I can feel it."

"Good. We're only a few inches off the wall in either direction. If we hold hands and keep our arms out to the side, one of us should always be able to touch. We'll use the sides of the walls as our guide. We can do this," Ethan encouraged. "We'll just hope we don't hit our heads on a stalagmite or something."

"Stalactite."

"What?"

"Stalagmites are rock formations that rise up from the ground, whereas stalactites form as water and sediment drip from the ceiling. You meant stalactite," Jacob corrected, his voice sounding like he was reading from a science textbook.

"Whatever. Both would be bad," Ethan said, not bothering to roll his eyes.

Jacob nodded, but in the dark, Ethan was unable to see.

"We can do this," Ethan repeated before licking his lips and swallowing. He was happy Jacob couldn't see the fear on his face.

"Yeah, we *can* do it," Jacob said with a surge of confidence. "Hands out. Let's go." Jacob's high voice cracked again.

Ethan snickered, enjoying the inconsistency between Jacob's sudden courage and his feeble voice. Ethan covered his mouth, trying to silence his laugh, but he couldn't. Another brief chortle escaped from his lips.

"Shut up," Jacob muttered.

Ethan laughed harder. His laughing welled up inside and burst through the darkness, his amusement echoing down the black lava tunnel. "Sorry," Ethan said.

Ethan composed himself. "O-kay Jac-ob, let's mo-ve out,"

he said, forcing his voice to crack. Holding back his laugh, Ethan listened for a response and then smiled, as Jacob couldn't resist laughing himself. The tunnel boomed with laughter. It felt good—really good.

Holding hands with their arms extended, Ethan and Jacob walked down the tunnel using their fingertips pressed against the wall as their guide.

After a handful of successful steps, Ethan slowed his pace and then paused. "Listen," he whispered.

Jacob strained his ears to hear what Ethan heard. "What is it? Bats again? I don't hear anything."

Just then, Ethan's butt rumbled as a fart reverberated off the stone walls and encompassed the boys in an invisible cloud of noxious gas.

"Oh! Are you kidding me? That's terrible," Jacob accused, grimacing.

He attempted to pull Ethan further down the tunnel to escape the toxic odor, but Ethan held tight and wouldn't allow Jacob to move.

"So you heard it? The second eruption of Mount Mazama."

"I think Chief Llao heard it. Maybe we should make that part of our offensive strategy," Jacob suggested. Both boys chuckled.

Ethan knew he was acting childish, but it was fun, definitely better than cowering in fear or being overrun with sadness and worry. Still, the smell was rancid, and it followed the boys, choking them as they walked deeper through the darkness of the lava tunnel.

- 37 -

# WATA'M VILLAGE

BELOW CRATER LAKE, IN A CAVERN THE SIZE OF TWO PROfessional football stadiums, a small village exists. No one knows about it. How could they? Above ground, people visit the lake and gawk at the beauty of the crystalline water and mountainous cliffs, which create the cupping shape of the caldera. Hikers wander on scenic paths, oohing and aahing at the intensity of nature's beauty.

Visitors travel to nearby towns populated by remnants of the ancient natives. Some daring adventurers repel down the cliffs and some even scuba dive, swimming with the colorful Kokanee salmon and rainbow trout. Many are content to snap photos to show friends and family, proving the scenic superiority of the national park. Crater Lake is pristine. There is so much to see and experience, why would anyone suspect there was more below the surface?

Underneath the deepest lake in all the United States, a minisociety called Wata'm bustles with activity. Still dressed in simple leather garments, fathers and mothers toil to support their children, who will never grow up. Since Mazama erupted over seven thousand years ago, the Wata'mis have remained the same. No one grows old—no one matures—well, almost no one.

After the defeat of Chief Llao, most natives of Mazama were subjugated to the Below World. Life is as it always was, and the villagers have no idea there's anything better. Just like the tourists who gather to Crater Lake, the Wata`mis are content in their narrow view of reality. Why should they question or expect anything more?

There is no death, but there is no birth either. There is no sadness or pain, but there is neither joy nor fulfillment; there's only empty existence. Life under the lake is all the people have ever known, or at least, all they have ever remembered. In a way, it's merciful that Chief Llao's people are oblivious to the Above World. Everyone is content in his or her ignorance, except Chief Llao. He remembers.

Branching off from the main cavern, many smaller caverns connect via tunnels, like legs from a spider. Within these smaller caves and grottoes, workers gather to perform their assigned labors. Some fish in the cold freshwater ponds while others haul water back to the main cavern for drinking and cooking. The children play in the dirt and rocks. There is no vegetation, no grass—just bleak desert landscape.

At the top of the cavern, an expansive crystal window opens like a skylight into the bottom of Crater Lake. On a sunny day, when the water shimmers bright, a hazy blue sky is created for the people of the Below World. When fish swim by, it is as though the heavens are moving. But even at its brightest, the light that enters the cavern is never better than a summer evening before dusk. Life in the Below World is primitive and dreary.

Midway up the side of the main cavern, a two-sided throne is carved into the rock at the edge of a cliff. Chief Llao can either sit in his throne and gaze out over his busy subjects, working like drone bees, or he can sit on the opposite side of the throne and stare into the black tunnel that leads to the Above World. He longs for the Above World, and most days the high-backed throne hides him from the view of his people as he sits with his back to them, choosing instead to stare into the blackness of the tunnel.

Aside from cold staring or scheming for vengeance—should he ever escape the Below World—Chief Llao has another welcome distraction when he faces the tunnel. In the wide arm of his throne, an inlaid bowl is filled with water. On a clear day, when his powers do not fail him, the shallow bowl acts as an oculus, showing him the activities in the Above World. His roving eye wanders the lake above as he watches through his armrest. From the east shore to the Phantom Ship to Cleetwood Cove to Wizard Island, he watches and waits for the right moment to assert the limited power he has remaining.

Chief Llao waits patiently for his chance to escape into the Above World and challenge Chief Skell. But today, as interesting as the visions are, Chief Llao is focused on something different. Staring into the tunnel, Chief Llao drowns out the village noise and listens to the darkness. He can hear voices, and they're coming near.

# – 38 –

# Meeting the Spirit Chief

Jacob tripped and fell to the ground. Blood oozed down his shin, but he and Ethan advanced, searching the walls with their outstretched fingertips. They advanced slowly, but still, it was progress.

Along the path, Ethan and Jacob nearly separated as the tunnel connected with a second lava tube, which veered to the right. With Jacob touching the wall on the right, he attempted to follow the veering tunnel, but since Ethan was stronger, the boys remained on the original path. After a few steps of touching nothing but empty air, Jacob reconnected with the tunnel wall and the boys continued.

"I hope that wasn't our turn," Jacob said.

Ethan didn't respond, but he was hoping the same thing. With no light, no directions, and no clue, Ethan trusted his life to fate. If he was meant to find Jordan and return to the Earth's surface, it would happen. *Please let it happen.* But if he was destined to die a slow and grueling death, groping in darkness as he starved, well, it was a less attractive option, but fate would decide.

*Fate sucks*, Ethan decided. He preferred determining his own course. In his daydreams he was always the hero. Wits, strength, stamina, and physical prowess won the day as he worked, struggled, fought, and made difficult decisions. But now it seemed being a hero would only require dumb luck. He had no power to determine his own destiny. "What a rip."

"What was that?" Jacob asked.

"Oh, nothing." Lost in his thoughts, Ethan hardly noticed the dim light farther down the tunnel.

"Jordan!" Jacob yelled. "Is that you?"

Stunned by Jacob's yelling, Ethan returned his attention to the tunnel. His eyes widened with hope. Far in the distance, the total blackness brightened to a dark, charcoal gray. It wasn't a light so much as a slight absence of darkness.

"Jordan!" Ethan echoed. There was no reply.

Releasing Jacob's hand, Ethan kept his palm pressed against the wall and began jogging. Sacrificing safety for speed, Ethan raced forward as Jacob's disgruntled cries fell further behind. Ethan couldn't risk losing Jordan again.

"Hey you, little brat! Stop!" Ethan yelled. His words raced ahead of him, but still no response came. His jog quickened to a steady run as his palm scraped against the wall. The charcoal gray brightened with each passing moment, turning to a faint granite color and then light heather gray. Instead of a mere absence of darkness, Ethan could now discern actual light up ahead. His feet sped into a full sprint, and Jacob fell further behind.

Slowing, Ethan neared the light source. "Jordan," he whispered as he approached another intersection of tunnels. To his surprise, the original tunnel curved to the left as the new tunnel peeled off to the right with a sharp turn. The light came from the new tunnel, so Ethan followed it.

With each snaking turn Ethan navigated, the light grew brighter. His eyes adjusted easily from the complete darkness to the softness of the new glow. "I love light," Ethan mumbled. A faint smile covered his face.

Rounding one last curve, Ethan stopped. His eyebrows scrunched together, and he stood like a statue. What he saw couldn't be real.

Hunched over in a high-backed chair made of stone, the silhouette of a frail old man motioned for Ethan to come closer. Ethan didn't budge. His back leaned toward the bend in the tunnel as he prepared for a quick getaway. But although he wanted to, Ethan couldn't turn away from the man. His eyes fixated on the peculiar figure in front of him.

With the light illuminating him from behind, the man motioned again with his bony finger, urging Ethan to step closer, but Ethan kept his distance. Shadow hid most of the man's face, and Ethan was grateful. The man looked like an absolute lunatic—the creepy kind. Wiry white hair poked out horizontally from the man's head with kinky curls, except down the middle where a thick black streak smoothed against his scalp. It looked like a reverse Mohawk, but not as cool.

The man set his hand on the arm of the chair. From behind, the light illuminated the chair's stone arm and the man's thick yellow fingernails as he tapped. His mouth moved, but no audible sound came out.

Ethan stepped closer, curious to hear the man's silent ramblings. He took another step closer, still unable to hear, but he could see through the shadow and into the man's face. Ethan's lips curled down with disgust as he noticed the man's teeth. Some were corn yellow, while the others were dead gray. The gray teeth matched the man's pallid complexion. His thin, colorless lips were pasted between hollow cheeks. In the corner of the old man's mouth, white foam gathered and drops of spittle crusted on his chin. His eyes were black; the complete absence of white was odd—disgusting.

"Nish . . . imawi . . . wata`m," the man muttered.

"What?" Ethan didn't understand.

The raspy voice seemed to be in another language. Maybe it was just nonsense, the incomprehensible expression of a crazy old man. The phrase repeated, "Nish . . . imawi . . . wata`m." Ethan couldn't understand.

Transferring his gaze from the crusty oldster, Ethan crept

along the side of the tunnel wall near the cliff's edge, looking with wonder at the scene below. Stick huts, white smoke rising from cooking fires, children running? "What is this place?"

Stepping closer to the old man, Ethan leaned over, placing his hands on his knees as he looked into the vacant black eyes. "Who are you? Where are we?"

The man's head tilted with confusion. "Nish . . . imawi . . . wata`m."

Ethan was getting nowhere, but he was getting nauseated. The man's breath was a wave of gaseous bile. The foul odor almost knocked Ethan to the ground. Standing upright, Ethan stepped backward to escape the stench. He backed right into Jacob. Ethan jumped and let out a high-pitched squeal but then recovered his cool. "You made it," he said, his breathing heavy.

"Yeah," Jacob said, smirking. Then his mouth fell open as he acknowledged the old man and the village scene below. "I made it . . ." he said, his voice trailing off.

"Let me introduce you to the crazy old man I can't understand," Ethan said, motioning to the figure on the throne.

"I am not crazy," the man said in perfect English.

Ethan's face flushed, embarrassed the man understood his insult. "Oh, you do speak English. I'm sorry, I didn't mean to . . ."

"What is English?" the man asked in a whisper.

Jacob looked confused. "It's the language we're speaking right now."

"No—no English. I speak my native tongue," the man insisted.

"But how?" Jacob asked as he set his canvas bag on the ground with a thud. He moved closer. "How can we understand each other?"

The black eyes moved to the canvas bag. "What is that?"

"It's a bag," Ethan said. "This guy isn't too bright," he whispered, leaning close to Jacob with a hand covering his mouth.

The man gave a perturbed sigh. "No, I mean, what is in the bag?"

"Oh, of course," Ethan said sheepishly. Bending over he picked up the bag and reached inside. "It's just some personal stuff." Ethan first pulled out the flashlight, held it up, and placed it back in the bag. Next he pulled out a package of dried fruit, and then put it back. He then pulled out the glassy stone rectangle with a hole in the center.

The man's black eyes widened, and his lips quivered as if beholding a long lost child. "My translator! You found my translator. Hee hee!" he said with giddy excitement.

"Um, I think it's just a stand to hold a stone bowl," Jacob corrected.

The man shot Jacob a scathing glare. His voice lowered as his long yellow fingernails reached forward. "You have my bowl? May I see it?"

The two boys looked at each other, unsure whether or not they should answer. "No. We don't have the bowl," Ethan said, but his lie was unconvincing, even to him.

"That translator is what allows us to communicate. I speak in my language—you speak in yours. We all understand," he said, smiling. His thin lips rose into what was supposed to be a smile, flashing the gray and yellow teeth at Jacob. "You, with the translator, walk around that corner. I will keep talking."

Although he didn't understand why, Ethan walked around the tunnel corner with the stone translator in his hand. He listened as the man continued to speak, and his words instantly became unrecognizable. Stepping back around the corner toward the man, Ethan was again able to understand. "Whoa."

"Please, let me touch the translator," the old man requested.

Holding the stone, Ethan leaned toward the man and extended the translator. The man's feeble hand shook as he reached, but he wasn't quite able to touch, so Ethan moved closer. Jumping from his seat, the old man grabbed Ethan by the wrist. Ethan struggled to pull away, but the old man's grip tightened.

Holding Ethan, the man straightened his posture. Standing tall, he reached for the translator with his other hand. He stared into Ethan's frightened eyes while Jacob watched.

"Welcome to my island under the lake. I am Llao."

## - 39 -

# THE CONJURER'S EYE

ETHAN WRENCHED HIS ARM, ATTEMPTING TO ESCAPE from Chief Llao's grasp, but the bony fingers locked in place. With each motion of his arm, Ethan felt the yellow fingernails dig deeper into his skin. Attempting to stun Chief Llao into letting go, Ethan kicked frantically, but Chief Llao blocked the kicks. The bone on bone contact sent painful shivers down Ethan's leg. With fear filling his eyes, Ethan turned to Jacob.

"Jacob! Help!" he screamed, his eyes pleading. Glancing back to Chief Llao, Ethan's blood ran cold as he looked into the face of death. The old man seemed to be enjoying the fear he was inflicting, like it was the best show he'd seen in a thousand years.

Still gripping the translator, Ethan was heartened by the emerging look of determination on his friend's face. Jacob pushed his glasses higher on his nose, tightened his fists, and clenched his jaw. Jacob's eyes were sharp and his mouth angry, but even at his fiercest, Jacob looked like a Chihuahua preparing to attack a Doberman pinscher, albeit a super old Doberman pinscher.

Setting his back foot, Jacob pushed off and ran at Chief Llao, his fists flailing as he screamed an intimidating war cry. The chief shrieked with laughter. Jacob pounded away at the chief's midsection, punching, clawing, and kicking. Ethan also fought, but nothing he did could loosen the chief's grip on his wrist.

A putrid stench expelled from behind Chief Llao's gray, smiling teeth. Then without warning, he released Ethan and grabbed hold of Jacob's neck. Chief Llao tightened his grip, lifted Jacob into the air, and stared at the thrashing boy.

Jacob wheezed for breath as his body convulsed.

Ethan beat on Chief Llao with every ounce of energy and strength he possessed, but the chief ignored him. Walking to the edge of the cliff, Chief Llao dangled Jacob over the bustling village. Jacob's eyes fluttered, and then he went limp.

Still aided by the translator, Chief Llao spoke. "Your friend will die unless you give me what I want." Llao squeezed Jacob's neck, and his fingernails dug in. Ethan thought he heard a mild crack.

Ethan backed away. "Fine, what do you want from us?"

"Not much. Show me the stone bowl." Chief Llao waited. "Unfortunately, you do not possess the bowl. Most unfortunate." Chief Llao grinned menacingly. "Your friend will die." He squeezed again, causing Jacob's legs to twitch.

Racing to the canvas bag, Ethan bent over and pulled the bowl from inside, leaving it on the ground in plain view. "There. There it is. Now let him go," Ethan demanded. "Now!"

"I am disappointed with your deceitfulness. You had the bowl and you lied to me? Very unfortunate."

"I showed you what you want, now let him go. Take the bowl!" Ethan screamed, looking at the limp boy dangling over the cliff. "Take it!"

Chief Llao responded with a whisper. "No. I cannot take it. Give it to me."

Picking up the stone bowl, Ethan walked to Chief Llao and set the bowl in his outstretched hand. The chief closed his eyes, feeling the power of the bowl tickle his bony fingers. Facing the cliff and the village below, Chief Llao flung his upraised arm backward and released his grip, sending Jacob crashing to the floor near Ethan. Jacob's head slammed on the ground with a crack and blood started to flow from it.

Kneeling at Jacob's side, Ethan listened for breath. There was none. He felt for a pulse, but Jacob's body was still. There was no life left within him. The small boy lay crumpled on the ground, dead.

Tears streamed from Ethan's red eyes and his chest heaved with raw anger. Although he had known Jacob for less than a day, it felt like he had lost a brother. Ethan's eyes narrowed with defiance as he scowled at Chief Llao. "I *will* kill you," Ethan said as he stood.

"No. You won't."

Ethan growled. With his arms outstretched, he raced toward Chief Llao, prepared to push him over the cliff.

Turning toward Ethan, Chief Llao raised one hand. An invisible force sent Ethan flying backward through the air, slamming him against the corner of the tunnel.

Sitting up, Ethan rotated his sore neck and stretched his limbs. He prepared for a second attack. With his hands clenched, Ethan took a heavy step toward Chief Llao, but then he stopped, his head tilting with confusion. Instead of standing tall with power, Chief Llao once again shriveled over, holding the bowl in one hand. With his other hand, he reached while shuffling his feet toward the stone throne. He eased himself onto the throne.

Chief Llao crumpled over in the chair, his chest touching his knees. The old man coughed and wheezed. Ethan approached the throne with confidence. He cocked his clenched fist backward, ready to pound the feeble killer.

"You will not destroy me," Chief Llao whispered.

Ethan noticed the old man trembling—his bony fingers, his body, and even his crazy hair shook softly but uncontrollably.

"I can help you," Chief Llao said. "We need each other. I will prove it to you." Chief Llao motioned to the inlaid bowl in his armrest. "Look."

* * *

Brady's long legs stepped over two downed trees. The white hemlock trunks were separated from their roots, and with just a few dead branches remaining at the top, it seemed the trees would roll down the ravine if jarred loose. Straddling another trunk, Brady flung his leg over and stood on an intersecting tree trunk. He walked along the tree like a tightwire acrobat until he was once again on the soft dirt.

"Do what I did," he yelled back to Allie.

Without hesitation, Allie scrambled up the fallen tree, mounted the other trunk, and then began descending. She walked gracefully along the trunk, but as she neared the end, she felt it wobble beneath her feet. She jumped off the tree and onto the loose ground. "Piece of cake."

"We're almost there," Brady said as he rested. "You keep up pretty good for a girl. How are you doing?" he asked.

Allied frowned but kept moving, speeding her descent. *Let's see if you can keep up with me.* With Wizard Island straight ahead, Allie felt renewed energy. They were close; their mission would soon be accomplished, and her parents would be freed from the Prison of the Lost. She would have her normal life back, and she wouldn't have to listen to Brady's male chauvinism—bonus!

"Hey, Allie, hold on a minute," Brady said, falling behind as he struggled to keep her pace. Sitting on his behind, Brady allowed gravity to pull him downward on the sandy surface.

Allie looked back at him, her face stern.

With each passing minute, Wizard Island grew larger and greener. From the plateau high above, the pine trees that stuck up like crew cut hair had seemed small, and the island had appeared to be a hill that would be easy to hike. Now Allie could see the trees were tall and dense in most areas, and the hill was a small mountain. Allie's hope deflated as she gazed upon Wizard Island.

"Finding the conjurer's home may not be as easy as we thought," Allie said with a sigh. Hearing a screeching sound above her, Allie raised her eyes into the sky. Three sets of four large hawks circled. "Brady, check this out," she said, pointing to the sky. "It looks like our friend has come back to join us. COWARD!" she yelled.

"Yeah . . . great . . ." Brady said.

Allie grinned and continued trudging along.

* * *

Ethan raised his eyes from the inlaid bowl. The magic that permitted Chief Llao to watch the Above World also allowed Ethan to search out and view his friends. In the water, Ethan watched Allie and Brady descending the ravine toward Wizard Island.

"I want to see my sister," Ethan demanded. "Show me."

Chief Llao smirked. "No."

Ethan's eyes bulged and his jaw locked.

"I cannot. My eye sees only the Above World. Your sister is below."

"Your eye?" Ethan asked. The riddle from the bowl artifact pounded inside Ethan's head. *Stab the conjurer through the eye . . .*

As if sensing the angry thoughts inside Ethan, Chief Llao wagged his bony finger. "I see here," he said, motioning to the armrest, "but the eye is above. As long as Chief Skell protects the eye, my imprisonment continues."

Glancing again at the image of Allie and Brady inlaid in the armrest, Ethan wiped his eyes as he felt a surge of boldness. "You say we need each other, but my friends are doing fine without you," Ethan said, glaring at Chief Llao. "You can't even stand for more than five minutes. You killed my friend. Why do I need you?"

Waving one hand over the water, Chief Llao licked his dry lips with a pasty tongue. He watched Ethan. The image in the oculus changed. "Behold."

The scene changed. Ethan no longer viewed his friends approaching Wizard Island. He now watched a scene *on*

Wizard Island. His lower lip dropped. An army of massive, pale-skinned zombie warriors waited with bizarre weapons held in a ready position.

Brady and Allie were walking into a trap.

# - 40 -

# ALLIES

ETHAN TUGGED AT HIS THICK, CURLY HAIR, HIS EYEBROWS scrunching.

"I was not always this weak," Chief Llao said. "Soon, my power will return. I am a better ally than an enemy."

"What did you say?" Ethan asked with disbelief. "You think I would ever trust you? Crazy coot."

Chief Llao stared at Ethan through his cold, black eyes.

"You are the problem," Ethan growled as his face reddened with anger. "You sucked my parents into the Prison of the Lost. I watched you kill Jacob. You squeezed his neck with your bare hands and threw him to the ground like a piece of garbage."

Ethan approached the frail man and pulled him to his feet, walking him to the edge of the cliff. "You see, I think that if I throw you off this cliff, you'll die. If you die, your hold on my parents will end, and they'll be freed."

"Or be lost forever," Chief Llao whispered. "You cannot know for sure. But your friend Jacob, he will certainly be lost."

"Jacob's dead. He's gone. Nothing I do can help him now."

Chief Llao cackled as he managed a thin smile. "Really?"

Ethan turned away with repulsion.

"You do not know as much as you think you do." Chief Llao paused. "If I save your friend, will you listen to what I have to say?"

Ethan considered the offer. What could it hurt to listen? "If you save him, I will listen. I make no other promises. If I don't like what I hear, I'll throw you off the cliff," Ethan threatened. As he heard the words come out of his mouth, his own lack of conviction struck him as pathetic.

"Good. The bowl," Chief Llao said, pointing at the stone container. "Bring it to me."

Ethan obeyed.

"I need water. You will get me water. Then I can continue."

Pulling a bottle of purified lake water from the canvas bag, Ethan handed it to Chief Llao. "You think I'm stupid, don't you?" Ethan accused. "He's dead. He can't drink the water. It can't heal him."

Wagging his forefinger at Ethan, Chief Llao continued. Pouring the clear liquid into the bowl, Chief Llao raised the bowl to his forehead, closed his eyes, and then lowered it, placing his lips on the rim. He gulped the water and began to transform.

Ethan groaned. "What have I done?"

The wiry white hair turned black and fell smoothly down the side of Chief Llao's face, stopping at his shoulders. His gaunt cheeks filled, and the deep creases smoothed as his skin changed from deathly gray to a deep, healthy brown. Color returned to his lips, and his teeth became perfect and white. Even the stench of his breath turned sweet. Ethan watched in horrified amazement. Chief Llao's eyes became beautiful, like chocolate. His feeble frame broadened with muscle, his bony fingers became thick and strong, and the crusty yellow fingernails remained long but became flesh colored and white, strong and sharp. Chief Llao stood in front of Ethan, a youthful man—a powerful man.

"I give up," Ethan said, placing his hands in front of him like a prisoner about to be handcuffed. "Just kill me. Quickly. Please."

Chief Llao smiled at his young captive. His smile was captivating and warm. After casting off his ghoulish form,

Chief Llao was handsome and strapping. Reaching toward Ethan, Chief Llao grabbed his hand and held it. "I thank you."

"For what? Being an idiot?" Ethan asked. He shook his head, irritated with his own foolishness.

"For giving me strength to help you," he said, watching for Ethan's response.

Ethan lowered his head in shame.

"You see me, and I am strong."

Ethan nodded.

"I could do with you whatever I desire. Yes? Think about that." Chief Llao waited, giving Ethan time to consider his words. "I told you I would save your friend. I am a man of my word. I will save him."

Kneeling next to Jacob, Chief Llao dipped his fingertips into the stone bowl, where a small amount of water remained. Placing his middle finger on the bridge of Jacob's nose, the two closest fingers on Jacob's cheekbones, and the pinky and thumb on Jacob's jaw, Chief Llao pressed down and squeezed his powerful fingers into the flesh of Jacob's face. Removing his hand from Jacob's face, Chief Llao then held Jacob's head and tipped it back, allowing the mouth to hang open. Raising the bowl above Jacob's mouth, he tilted the vessel and dripped the remaining water from the bowl into the boy's mouth. He waited.

Ethan's eyes filled with hope as he watched. A slender streak of Chief Llao's hair turned white, and then Jacob's eyes shot wide open. Jacob looked at Ethan, then at Chief Llao. Sitting up, he hugged Chief Llao.

A look of surprise covered Ethan's face. *Do you know that's the same guy that just killed you? Probably not.*

"Thank you, Chief Llao," Jacob said.

Jacob *did* recognize the man who killed him. Weird. Sitting next to Jacob, Ethan embraced his friend, the sides of their faces touching. Embarrassed by the realization that the hug wasn't very manly, Ethan pulled away, but Jacob clung to him as a tear ran down his face.

"Thank you, Ethan," Jacob said.

Chief Llao watched with satisfaction. "Ethan, will you now listen to what I have to say?"

Ethan hesitated, but Jacob didn't. "We'll listen."

Smiling at the young men, Chief Llao began, "You think I am your enemy, but I am not. For centuries, I have been too weak to cause much mischief in the Above World. I am imprisoned with my people," he said, motioning to the cliff and the small village beyond.

"Then why did you take our parents?"

"The ground ate them," Chief Llao responded.

"Why?" Ethan yelled, his voice breaking.

Placing one hand on Ethan's shoulder and his other hand on Jacob, Chief Llao lowered his head. "I killed Jacob, because I needed to gain your trust. Likewise, your parents were consumed into the Prison of the Lost, because I need your help."

"Strange way to ask for help."

Chief Llao nodded in recognition. "If I had asked for assistance, you would have denied my request."

Ethan lowered his eyes. Of course he was right.

"But I knew I could save Jacob, just like I can help you save your parents. Now, our desires are aligned. Together we are strong."

Ethan considered the Chief's offer of alliance. "Those . . . those . . . things on Wizard Island waiting to ambush my friends . . . whatever you call them . . ."

"They are Grankars."

"Yeah—I don't care. Just call them off. Tell them not to hurt Allie and Brady," Ethan demanded.

Chief Llao shook his head with disappointment. "I do not control those creatures."

"What do you mean? If you don't control them, then who does?" Ethan asked.

"It must be Chief Skell. Those creatures were once part of my army, but like me, they were imprisoned long ago. Chief Skell imprisoned them, so only Chief Skell could release them."

"Why would he release part of your army?" Jacob asked.

"Simple. So he can use them. They will be loyal to the one who released them. Chief Skell's army was caught unawares for the challenge I wage. He is not prepared, so he uses my warriors against me. Chief Skell is devious. Dangerous."

"Kind of like you, huh?" Ethan said with a glare.

The muscles in Chief Llao's jaw bulged. "It is ironic."

"What do you mean?"

"Your friends will soon battle against ghastly fiends in an effort to defeat me."

"Yeah?"

"In actuality they will be fighting against the forces controlled by Chief Skell. The irony is this: your friends are trying to defeat me, though I am trying to help you," Chief Llao explained and then laughed. "Even better, the army of Guardians will unwittingly fight for me against their master, Chief Skell." Chief Llao continued to laugh. "It is a beautiful thing."

"But why?" Jacob asked. "Why is Chief Skell trying to stop us from freeing our parents?"

"Simple. When you unlock the Prison of the Lost, you will also free my people and me. Skell does not care about your parents. He only wants to defeat me and keep me in prison. You see we are now allies, fighting for the same cause."

"Look, I don't care who wins your little power struggle with Chief Skell. All I care about is freeing our parents," Ethan blurted. "Our friends on Wizard Island need our help. If you want to help, then help."

"I cannot. My power is limited. I am still a prisoner of the Below World. My treaty with Chief Skell binds me here. As long as he upholds his end of the treaty, I must remain."

Jacob's face brightened. "There's a tunnel. Follow us, and we will get you out. We'll lead you to the Above World."

"That is a kind offer; however, I must remain. If I attempt to leave, I will return to the shadow of myself you saw earlier," Chief Llao explained.

Ethan and Jacob looked at him skeptically. "You just brought Jacob back to life, and you're telling me you can't walk down a tunnel?"

Standing, Chief Llao walked to the corner where the tunnel led away from the small throne cavern. He held his hand out for the boys to view. It was muscular and thick. Holding up one finger, Chief Llao reached around the corner into the tunnel and then pulled his finger back. He held it up for the boys to see. All muscle seemed to have dissolved, leaving a long, bony finger. The fingernail was coarse, yellow, and brittle.

"I cannot leave. But I can help you in other ways," Chief Llao said. "I will be a powerful ally. Together we will defeat Chief Skell and release your parents from prison."

"I don't give a rip about you or Chief Skell. I'm in this for my parents," Ethan blurted.

Chief Llao smiled. "Of course you are."

"What do we do? How do I rescue my dad?" Jacob asked.

"Continue to Wizard Island, stab the conjurer through the eye, and watch him perish. His inheritance will become yours," he said, quoting the inscription from the stone bowl. "You will need the artifacts you have gathered from my Phantom Ship—all of them. Find the old man and stab him in the eye. When you do this, I will have greater power to help you."

"But I thought *you* were the conjurer. I thought it was your eye we needed to stab. Are we to claim your inheritance?" Ethan asked.

Chief Llao smiled. "Yes, I am the conjurer. But though I may be blinded from viewing the Above World after you stab me in the eye, I will be free again. Everything I have will become yours. When you free your parents from the prison, you will also free me and my people."

"And our parents? Will the artifacts really unlock the prison?

Can you guarantee that we will get our parents back?" Ethan questioned.

Opening his mouth to speak, Chief Llao halted and raised the bony finger. Walking to his throne, he looked into the watery oculus in the armrest. "Look!"

Scurrying to the armrest, Ethan and Jacob gazed into the water. They watched as Allie and Brady waded from the shore into the lake. Waist deep in the water, the pair made their way toward the first small islet on the way to Wizard Island.

"They made it to the shore," Jacob exclaimed. "They'll be to Wizard Island soon."

Ethan's eyes locked on to Chief Llao's. "Not good."

"You must hurry. Follow the tunnel to Wizard Island. Save your friends. Find the old man. Follow the signs. Stab his eye. You must go—now!" Chief Llao said.

Gathering the stone bowl, the translator, and the empty water bottle, Ethan threw them into the canvas bag. Inside the bag, the flashlight came to life, shining bright. Removing the light, Ethan glanced back at Chief Llao. The chief nodded, urging him on.

Racing around the corner with Jacob close behind him, Ethan navigated the tight turns, his flashlight illuminating the way. The boys exited into the main tunnel and sprinted through it toward Wizard Island.

- 41 -

# The Guardian Warriors

Che-tan squawked as he hovered above Wizard Island. Two other flocks of birds understood and dove toward the island, skimming just above the tree line, scouting for possible danger.

One hundred yards from the shoreline tongue of Wizard Island, a band of ghoulish warriors hid behind large boulders and in thick groves of trees. The birds lowered into the forest for a closer look and then lofted upward, squawking, eager to tell Che-tan what they had found.

On the upper ridge of the crater, near the ravine where Brady and Allie had begun their descent to the lake, a line of animals assembled. Three dozen oversized cougars and a score of large black bears lined the ridge, awaiting orders from Che-tan.

Circling the kids, Che-tan swept down close. The scowl of disgust and betrayal on Allie's face was unmistakable.

Rising into the sky, Che-tan joined the flight of the other hawks. Communicating in brief bird tones, he then flew to the crater's rim, uniting with the army of animal Guardians. Che-tan dove to the ground, each bird crashing into the other as they fused into human form.

Standing at the front of his Guardians, Che-tan spoke, "Chief Llao underestimates us. He thinks we are weak. He thinks we are no threat to him. Let us show him what we are capable of. Brothers, sisters, on to Wizard Island!" Che-tan yelled as he waved his arm forward.

One by one, the cougars and the black bears leapt into the ravine and raced to the shore below.

A mixture of sadness, apprehension, and fear swelled within Che-tan as he considered the opponents his army would soon face. Once again, Che-tan burst into a flock and lofted upward, overseeing the movement of his army. The Guardians were strong. They would find a path to victory. Che-tan's fear gave way to pride and hope for his soldiers.

* * *

Trudging over the first islet, Brady and Allie reentered the water on their way to the second. With the exception of Che-tan buzzing overhead, Allie felt they were alone, unaware of the armies assembling on each side.

– 42 –

# ARRIVAL

WITH HER EYES SHUT TIGHT, JORDAN FOUND A HANDGRIP and then a foothold. She pulled herself up and then repeated the process, over and over. The lava tunnel had been easier to navigate; in fact, she didn't recall the journey at all. Sleepwalking to her final destination, Jordan only remembered her visions: a large field of bluegrass bathed in light, the base of a hill, and the trunk of a solitary white pine with a symbol burned into the bark. Jordan knew it meant something important, but what? She remembered fire, lava, and boulders spitting from the majestic mountain. She focused on the images like trying to remember her favorite dream, but with each passing moment of consciousness, they faded from her mind.

Unlike her swift sleepwalking through the lava tunnel, Jordan's climb was slow and arduous. She used muscles she didn't even know she had; her fingertips and legs, her arms and torso all quivered as she reached for her next handgrip. The sun beat down upon her, filling her closed eyelids with orange, flesh-colored light. Reaching again, she found a handhold and pulled herself up. With each movement upward, the light became broader and brighter.

Clinging to the wall, Jordan's eyes pressed together, releasing welled up tears of frustration, exhaustion, and pain. She considered giving up or at least resting for a moment. But how?

She could keep climbing, dangle from the wall, or fall to her death. Climbing was her best option.

Jordan had been immersed in darkness for so long, her eyes adjusted slowly to the brightness of daylight. She forced her eyes open to see where she was, but the sunlight burned and her eyes watered, so she closed them again. It couldn't be much farther. Jordan climbed, ignoring her burning muscles and watering eyes. After another moment, the wall angled outward, making her climb easier. Her arm reached for the next handhold but found only a fistful of air. Jordan whimpered with happiness. Crawling out of the crevasse, Jordan lay on her stomach and shielded her eyes with both hands. She rested for a brief moment but then propped herself up on her elbows as she took in the panoramic view.

Sitting atop the cinder cone that is Wizard Island, Jordan looked out to the calm blue lake and the crater cliffs rising from the water. She glanced back to the hole from which she had just emerged. How odd. Jordan didn't know whether she should laugh or cry. Wizard Island is a volcano inside the crater of a collapsed volcano. Uncle Bart hadn't mentioned that.

"How did I get here?" she wondered aloud.

Sitting at the mouth of the dormant volcano, she looked deep into the blackness of the volcano's mouth, and then her gaze moved across the water to the Phantom Ship in the distance. The last thing she remembered was being on the shore near the Phantom Ship. *How did I get here?* She didn't want to think about it, and she didn't want to think about sitting at the mouth of a volcano.

Jordan gasped as she looked around, realizing she was alone.

– 43 –

# Battle Lines

With laces tied together, Allie's shoes hung around her neck as she emerged from the water onto the last islet before reaching Wizard Island. Between the islets, the water was shallow. Only once did the frigid water reach to her chest. Her wet clothes clung to her, chilling her in the breeze, but after a few minutes drying in the sunshine, she began to warm.

Even though Allie's clothes were wet, her shoes remained dry. "You're going to be sorry you didn't listen to me," Allie teased. "You're going to want dry shoes and socks."

Brady took a heavy step, the water sloshing from his saturated shoes. "Yeah, well, at least I have a dry, warm shirt," Brady said. "Besides, I hate the gooey mud between my toes. It's . . . icky."

Allie laughed. "Icky, huh? That's kind of my favorite part."

Brady pulled the shirt hanging over his shoulder and pretended to snap it like it was a wet towel. He moved in slow motion, flexing with each movement, but Allie refused to show even a hint of admiration. Brady was definitely showing off, but his shoulders and chest were already burned dark pink. Allie grinned. He deserved it.

Every few minutes Che-tan flew low and circled the hikers. Allie thought Che-tan was taunting them, and Brady even took a swing, trying to hit the birds as they flew close, but he missed.

"Why doesn't he just leave us alone?" Allie asked. "We made it this far without him. Can't he see we don't need him?"

"Maybe he misses you," Brady offered.

Allie smiled and then walked the ten yards through the shallow water, anxious to step foot on Wizard Island. "So, Brady, do you have any good ideas?"

"I always have good ideas," he said with playful arrogance. He waited a moment. "About what?"

"About how we'll find the conjurer's home. This looks tougher than I thought," she admitted, noting the vast size of the island with its dense forest vegetation.

"Oh, yeah, sure. Well, let me ask you this . . . if you had an island like this and could build a house anywhere you wanted, where would you build it?"

Allie considered the question for a moment. "Near the water. You always need water, right?"

Water. That's a good point, but not what Brady was looking for. Allie's answer sounded smarter than his. "I suppose that could be true, but if I were to put my house somewhere, I'd put it as high as I could."

"On top of the mountain?" Allie asked.

"Well, yeah. What's wrong with that? Rich people always build high. They want a good view," Brady suggested.

Allie tucked her blonde hair behind her ear and raised one eyebrow. "Your entire strategy for finding the conjurer's home is based on where the best view would be?"

It did sound a little silly when she said it like that, but what's wrong with a view? Brady's mind scrambled for a smart response. Shielding the sun from his eyes, he scanned the mountain and then gazed at Che-tan hovering above. Then it came to him. "Well, of course you want a view—for security. If you were in a battle, would you rather have the high ground where you could see an enemy approach, or would you want to be low, where others could gain a better position on you? I bet the conjurer has all kinds of enemies he has to watch out for." Brady nodded his head, pleased with his response. Allie even seemed impressed by his intellectual recovery.

*Rich people also build on the water—oceans, lakes, rivers*, Allie thought, but she was too tired to argue. "Okay then, lead the way," she said as they stepped onto the main island.

Finding a downed tree, Allie sat and put on her shoes while Brady covered his chest with the warm, dry shirt. Like everywhere else they'd been at Crater Lake, Wizard Island looked deserted.

Near the string of islets, a long tongue of land extended to the rounded, volcanic mountain. It looked like at one time, the tongue and the islets had connected Wizard Island to the shore. *That would have been easier*, Allie thought. She finished lacing her shoes and caught up with Brady.

Leaving the island tongue, Brady approached the base of the mountain but stayed near the shore, just in case Allie had been right about the prime location of a home being near the water. Allie strolled next to him but wandered away when she noticed a small dock with a rowboat and a couple of canoes. The boats bobbed as the lake water splashed against the dock. Allie got excited as a small building came in to view, but she soon realized it was only a double outhouse.

"So much for building around water," Brady mumbled.

"At least right here," she retorted. "Hey, Brady, check this out," Allie hollered. "It's a path."

Walking toward Allie, Brady eyed the worn trail past the outhouses. "Looks like it winds around a bit, but it should take us up the mountain. Well done, Allie," he said and then patted her on the back, like a teacher complimenting his student.

Allie nodded, but when Brady turned away, she pretended to gag. "Let's do it."

As they started for the path, Che-tan swooped low, dive-bombing the trailhead. Instead of flying single file as the flock usually did, the birds lined up horizontally, clearing a wide swath. Allie covered her head and ducked, but Brady dove to the ground as the birds approached collision at full speed.

"I'm going to kill that . . . that . . . birdman!" Brady yelled as he got up and brushed the dirt from his clothes.

"Good one," Allie mocked. "Birdman? Ooh, you're so mean," she chuckled, but Brady didn't smile.

Determined to climb the trail, Brady ran up the path when he noticed two more flocks flying toward him in a similar wide path. Brady stepped off the trail, and the birds passed.

"What's going on here?" Brady huffed.

"If I didn't know better, I'd say Che-tan is sending us a message. He doesn't want us going up that path," Allie suggested. "But why?"

"CHE-TAN! COME HERE!" Brady screamed into the breeze, with his eyes squeezed shut and his head cocked backward. "Let's ask him."

Within moments, three lines of birds assembled above the trees and flew toward the kids. Brady's eyes widened, unsure if he could evade so many at one time. But as they approached, all three flocks slowed into their own single files and then plowed into themselves at ground level, assembling into human forms.

Three figures stood in tight formation, cloaked in dark brown robes. Removing the coarse fabric from his head, Che-tan approached Allie and Brady while his companions remained behind him, their faces obscured by the dark hoods. Standing face-to-face, Allie, Brady, and Che-tan watched each other but didn't speak. Allie's lips puckered, but she couldn't remain silent.

"Are you insane? What are you doing, attacking us like that? You are the biggest creep I've ever met. Leaving us in the forest! Attacking us! Lying to us!" Allie yelled into his face.

She was just getting started when Che-tan raised one hand to silence her. "I apologize for my methods," he said. "Please understand that everything I have done is to help you free your parents and friends."

"But you left us. We needed you," Allie said, her voice faltering. Though still loud, her tone was wounded, desperate, but not angry. "We're all alone, and when we needed you most, in the forest, you left us. You abandoned us," she said as a tear rolled down her cheek. Crying in front of people usually embarrassed Allie, but not now. She didn't care. Che-tan stepped closer and held out his arms. Allie leaned in and hugged Che-tan.

"What the heck?" Brady wondered aloud.

"Truly, I am sorry, Allie. But you are mistaken. The forest was not the time you needed me most. You need me now," Che-tan said. Turning back to his friends, he motioned for them to come closer. "These are my fellow Guardians," he said with a grin. "We are all here to help you."

Standing beside Che-tan, the robed figures removed their hoods, exposing their faces. The girl looked young, but the boy appeared to be even younger, maybe twelve years old. Like Che-tan, they had striking Native American features with long black hair. Each had a ponytail tied in back.

"Warriors?" Allie asked.

"More like middle school students," Brady said as he coughed.

"What do we need warriors for?" Allie asked.

Che-tan raised one finger. Then, bursting into pieces, he took flight, rising straight into the sky like a rocket. He then dove toward a large boulder along the path. The sounds of growling and hissing grew louder as Che-tan flushed out the enemies from behind rocks and the nearby groves.

One ghastly personage emerged from behind the boulder, and then another, and another, and another, forming a battle line. Allie watched with horror as the line of enemies continued to lengthen. Ghoulish creatures emerged, adding to the line, and then more formed a second battle line behind the first. Allie thought the creatures appeared somewhat comical at first—their heads were much too small for their powerful bodies—but her amusement quickly faded. Their mouths were sealed, smoothed over by scarred flesh, and their ears turned in on themselves, allowing little sound to enter. Their faces were gaunt, their clumpy hair was bluish gray, and they all wore clothing that seemed to be peeling away from their bodies like rotting flesh.

Most held nothing in their hands, but others gripped long poles with unusual instruments on top. One instrument looked like a giant butterfly net, and another was a huge metallic hook. Allie couldn't imagine what the instruments could be used for, and she didn't want to find out.

Reassembling at Allie's side, Che-tan motioned toward the horde of creatures assembled across the mountain path. They pounded their chests, screaming and hissing, ready for battle.

"Oh," Allie said, her mouth gaping open.

"And you brought two warriors as reinforcements?" Brady asked, the pitch of his voice raising an octave. "Good thinking."

Che-tan ignored Brady but grinned at Allie as he turned toward the crater's shore. Black bears and cougars lined the waterfront. Flocks of birds perched on evergreen boughs. Allie even thought she saw bats hanging upside down in a pine tree. She took a closer look. The dead tree looked full and healthy, but only because it was filled with so many bats.

"Bats in the middle of the day?" Allie asked.

Brady nodded with approval. "Sweet!"

Raising one arm high over his head, Che-tan waved to his waiting warriors. In a sea of motion, birds and bats took flight, darkening the sky. Some of the cougars and bears waded into the water, while others leapt from islet to islet, quickly reaching the long tongue of Wizard Island. Che-tan screeched and then watched as many of the birds flew overhead and alighted in the branches of pines behind enemy lines.

"We have them surrounded," Che-tan said, with an approving nod.

Pulling the dagger from his belt and unsheathing it, Brady gripped it tight as the thrill of impending battle overtook him. "Let's do this."

"No. We wait."

"What? Why? Che-tan, we have them outnumbered. Let's attack," Brady urged.

Looking around at the Guardian warriors gathered on the island tongue and in the tree branches, Che-tan's face grew long and solemn. "Friend, do not be eager for battle. We must not be the aggressor," Che-tan said, his eyes squinting as he caught the gaze of the enemy leader. "We have greater power as we defend what we love. If the enemy is bold enough to challenge us, we will take the battle to them with all of our might. Until then, we wait."

Bloodcurdling screams and inhuman growls, hissing taunts and the rattling of weapons echoed in Allie's ears. For the first time she considered the possibility of her own death. There was nothing to look forward to in battle. "Brady, I think Che-tan is right."

The enemy cries of hatred and evil escalated toward bloodshed. Brady resheathed the dagger. He swallowed and then inhaled. "We'll wait."

- 44 -

# Reunion

Groaning with relief as his hand reached the top of the rock wall, Ethan climbed the rest of the way out of the volcano's mouth and rolled onto his back. Moments later, Jacob joined him.

"Where are we?" Jacob asked.

Ethan smiled. "We're here. We entered the bowels of death and emerge at the top of the world. Wizard Island! Victory!" Ethan yelled, throwing his arms into the air and kicking his legs. He had never been so thrilled to be lying in the dirt with the sun beating down on him.

"A little over the top, don't you think?" Jordan asked, her thick curly hair sticking from her head like the mane of a lion. Rising from the flat rock where she had been sitting, she walked over and stood above Ethan. She bent over him, blocking the sun.

"Over the top? Maybe. But it feels gooood," Ethan said, rising to his feet. He embraced his sister and then held her by the shoulders at arm's length as he stared into her eyes. Then his tone changed. "What's wrong with you?"

The question took Jordan aback.

"We've been chasing you since the shoreline near the Phantom Ship. We followed you into the mouth of the earth and walked through complete darkness to find you. Jacob even died," Ethan said.

"It's true. I died. How do I look?" Jacob quipped.

Jordan's lower lip quivered. She looked at Jacob and then her brother. When her eyes met Ethan's, she burst into tears. "I'm sorry. I don't know what happened. I don't remember anything." Throwing herself into Ethan's chest, Jordan wrapped her arms around him. "I'm sorry, Ethan. I didn't mean it. I'm sorry."

Recognizing his greeting wasn't as kind as it could have been, Ethan reached out and held his younger sister's hand. He hunched to look her in the eye. "Hey. It's all right. We found you. That's all that matters. And we're on Wizard Island. Somehow you led us right where we needed to go." Ethan patted his sister's head and then awkwardly kissed her forehead as he whispered. "I'm glad you're safe, Jordan."

Snuggling into her brother's embrace, Jordan startled as four hawks squawked overhead. The lead bird's wing tilted downward and then up.

"Is it waving?" Jacob asked. The flock disappeared, skimming along the treetops down the west side of Wizard Island.

"It's Che-tan," Jordan said. "He's here. Do you think Allie and Brady made it too?"

Jacob and Ethan looked at each other and smiled, then bumped fists in victory. "We all made it?" Jacob stated in a way that sounded more like a question.

"We need to find them—fast. We still have work to do," Ethan said, looking up at the sun. "Our families don't have much time. We need to find the conjurer's home and stab him through the eye to unlock the prison gate before noon."

Wiping the dirt from his legs, Jacob stood and took a step toward the mouth of the volcano. He peered into the complete darkness of the Below World. "After what we've been through already, we can do anything. We are destined to succeed."

Ethan smiled at his friend's surge of confidence and wished he felt the same way. "If Chief Llao was honest, and right, the last twenty-four hours may have been the easy part. Gathering the artifacts from the Phantom Ship, hiking through the Below World . . ."

Jacob nodded. "Unlocking the prison gate will require everything we've got. Courage, strength, smarts."

"That's right. We're going to be tested . . . big time." Ethan stretched his limbs and cracked his knuckles as he looked over Wizard Island. His nose scrunched and his lips sagged into a worried scowl. "Chief Skell will be difficult to defeat," he said. "He has everything to lose."

## – 45 –

# The Approaching Storm

With her flute in hand, Allie watched as dark clouds blew toward Wizard Island from the east plains above Crater Lake. The warm sun beat down on her, but distant bolts of lightning webbed through the sky as a veil of shadow lowered to the ground. The pulse of rain beat upon the crater's rim but seemed to pause before invading further into the lake. Then after a brief reprieve, tall clouds and a heavy line of rainfall marched into the crater toward Wizard Island.

Watching as ghoulish adversaries positioned in battle lines upon the hill, Allie's heart sank. The creatures became more hostile with each passing moment, roaring through their flesh-covered mouths with a fury that eclipsed the thunder of the approaching storm.

Allie found Brady's hand and squeezed.

# - 46 -

# MUDSLIDE

AS THE STORM ADVANCED TOWARD WIZARD ISLAND, ETHAN questioned the wisdom of standing atop a mountain during heavy lightning. He considered his options, but unless they all climbed back into the mouth of the volcano, there was no place to take cover.

Down the east side of the mountain island, heavy forests of pine could provide some shelter from the storm. Down the west side, much of the mountain was barren, the forest appearing to have been washed away by previous torrents. A landscape of loose sand led most of the way down to the island's tongue, which extended in the direction of the crater's shore.

"If Brady and Allie are on the island, that's where they'll be," Ethan said, pointing in the direction of the island tongue.

"Not much cover over there," Jacob said, yelling over the sound of the approaching storm.

"What should we do?" Ethan yelled back.

In an instant, the veil of driving rain and wind descended upon the top of the mountain, drenching the three kids at once, as though a fire hose had been unleashed upon them. The unnatural storm marched to encompass all of Wizard Island. Lightning sizzled in the sky, and then a flash struck the ground near the volcanic vent.

"We have to get out of this," Jacob hollered back. "We need cover."

Ethan nodded. Grabbing Jordan's hand, Ethan descended the east side of the mountain, away from the island tongue. Jacob followed close behind. The dense pine forest offered some protection, but as the ground became saturated with rainwater, the steep slope turned into volcanic mud, causing Jacob's feet to slide out from under him. Unable to reach Ethan's outstretched hand, Jacob fell to the ground and slid through the mud, coming to an abrupt stop when his back crashed sideways into the thick trunk of a tree. He lay motionless as a steady stream of water and mud flowed past him.

"Jacob!" Jordan yelled.

The water loosened Jacob's position against the tree and dragged him farther down the mountain. He slid until his head crashed against a large, black rock. His body rotated and then came to rest against a tree. Ethan scurried toward his friend, but with each unsure step he risked falling victim to Jacob's same bad fortune.

"Jordan, follow me," Ethan yelled. He slid down the mountain on his backside until he reached his injured friend.

Jacob stared up at Ethan, his eyes frantic and his mouth clenched tight in agony. His face lay against the ground with water and mud rushing around.

"I've got you, Jacob. You'll be all right," Ethan hollered.

"Bowl . . . water . . ." Jacob gasped, his lips dripping with mud.

Lifting Jacob's head, Ethan positioned himself behind his friend. Jordan then straddled Ethan, forming a short train. Holding Jacob under the arms, Ethan slid down the mountain, steering with his heels like the rudder on a boat. Gaining speed and momentum, they headed toward the shoreline that came into view at the bottom of the mountain. Digging his heels in deep, Ethan attempted to put on the brakes and slow the trio to a manageable speed, but to no avail. Sliding over a small bump of ground, the three friends went airborne before crashing in a pile and sliding past the shoreline and into the water.

The water wasn't as frigid as Ethan remembered it being the night before, but it was still cold. Looking back to make sure Jordan had survived the slide, Ethan saw her scampering back up to the shore. Holding Jacob's head above the surface, Ethan cupped a handful of water and washed it across Jacob's face, removing some of the mud and grime. Then, pulling the canvas bag from Jacob's shoulder, Ethan reached inside and removed the healing bowl. Dipping the stone artifact into the lake, Ethan placed it next to Jacob's lips and tried to coax him into sipping.

The water entered Jacob's mouth, but it dribbled out the sides.

"Come on, Jacob! You have to drink," Ethan screamed over the pounding rain.

Tipping his head back, Ethan poured a small amount of water into Jacob's mouth and then pushed up on his chin, closing the mouth. Pinching Jacob's nose shut, Ethan waited, hoping Jacob would instinctively gulp the water down.

Ethan held his breath, waiting, and then Jacob swallowed.

The pained look removed from his face in an instant. "More water," he whispered.

Accepting another mouthful, Jacob swallowed with ease. His eyes brightened as he looked through the stinging rain into Ethan's worried face. "Thank you . . . again."

Ethan nodded. "Here, hold on to this," Ethan said, handing Jacob the healing bowl. "You seem to need it the most."

Jacob accepted the bowl gladly. "I hope the others are doing better than we are."

"Yeah, me too."

## – 47 –

# Battle on Wizard Island

The veil of rain encompassed Wizard Island like the steel bars of a jail cell. Just beyond the island, Allie could see blue sky, but it felt distant, unreachable. Rivers of muddy water rushed from the mountain over the shoes she had tried so hard to keep dry. She frowned.

The devilish creatures waiting high on the path were no longer content to bellow and scream in fits of intimidation. Their growls were now hungry. The beasts were on the move; the torrents were their signal to attack.

"Those guys are ug-ly," Brady murmured to himself, cringing at the site of the ghoulish creatures. "Chief Llao must be very proud," he said for his own amusement.

Che-tan gave Allie the sign. Raising the flute to her mouth, she placed her finger over the proper hole and blew all the breath from her lungs. Shooting from the flute, thick sheets of ice covered the ground just below the approaching enemies. Allie breathed deep and blew again, broadening the covering of ice.

With his dagger unsheathed, Brady joined the cougars and black bears. He listened to the enemy growls and chuckled nervously, and then growled himself, mocking the monsters. He awaited Che-tan's order.

Holding his hand high above his head, Che-tan waited for the perfect moment. The hordes descended upon the ice, crashing and sliding on their backs over the icy ground. Chetan's hand lowered. The Guardians pressed forward, descending upon the fallen creatures, digging their claws and teeth into the foul flesh. Slower than the rest, Brady raced toward the enemy, eager to aid his fellow warriors.

Drawing closer, Brady scowled with disgust, surprised to see the hordes of enemies rise to their feet and continue to fight, despite gaping wounds and missing chunks of tissue. Watching as a bear reached its jowls around a small enemy head, Brady flinched when the head disappeared and then the bear spewed it out onto the ground. Headless, the creature continued fighting. Sneaking beside the headless enemy, Brady plunged the dagger into its back, slicing the flesh easily. The creature slumped into a gray puddle on the ground before being swallowed by the saturated earth.

All around Brady, muscular, corpse-like creatures fought with devastating strength. The bears and cougars were valiant, but they were no match. The field winnowed as beautiful animals collapsed into bloody pools. Hawks and bats smothered their opponents, scratching at their faces and plucking their eyes. The enemy swatted at them like flies, occasionally knocking one from the sky.

Brady watched as a powerful predator hawk fell, sputtering on the ground after being sliced across the breast with a metallic hook. The remaining birds in the flock were unable to continue without the one. Falling together, the hawks reassembled into a young teenage girl with a mortal wound in her torso. Brady recognized her. She was beautiful but pathetic, lying dead in the mud.

Anger boiled inside, and a nauseous bile rose in the pit of Brady's stomach. Tightening his grip on the dagger, his muscles bulged. Brady screamed as he surged into the battle, slicing at every ghoulish creature within his reach. Each creature he sliced with the ancient dagger fell into a heap on the ground before disappearing into a whirlpool of mud and water. After the ground consumed the enemy, only a dimple in the earth remained.

Between slashing ghouls, Brady searched the field of battle and found Allie. With her flute in hand, Allie fought to give the Guardians an advantage. She blinded the enemy with an explosion of light while the bears mauled on their putrid flesh. She lit the enemy ablaze in a ball of scorching flame. She froze them in place, stopping them in their tracks.

Brady cheered from a distance and then rubbed his nose, hoping to rid it of the smell of burning zombie flesh.

After a few swift encounters, Allie realized the ice worked best. Blinding them served no lasting purpose, and the torched creatures seemed only fiercer and smelled horrible. But the ice halted their progress well enough, even though the enemy's destruction wasn't permanent.

With many of Che-tan's animal warriors bleeding on the ground, Brady assessed the battlefield. The enemy continued to press forward, but what were they trying to accomplish? Most of Che-tan's wounded forces were still alive, at least for now. Once in a while a bird or a cougar or a bear transformed back into human form, and Brady knew they were dead, but the enemy didn't seem concerned with killing. They were after something else.

The attacking forces encircled Allie and her flute. Fending off the enemy by turning them into freakish ice sculptures was working for now, but Brady wondered how long she could keep it up.

Brady fought alongside the battling animals, slashing the fiendish creatures. Each slash collapsed another enemy into the mud. Brady raised the dagger high into the air and cheered on the Guardians. A gnarly smile covered his face, and then he saw it.

Across the battlefield, away from the fighting, a few of the enemies roamed in search of divots where their ghoulish colleagues had fallen. Piercing a long metal hook into the ground, one of the creatures yanked upward shooting the fallen creature into the air on a fountain of mud and grime before returning to the earth in a ghastly heap of tissue and bone. With the large butterfly net instrument, a companion covered the heap, leaving it to rest for a few moments. Then, removing the net, a resurrected fiend emerged, again ready for battle.

Brady shook his head and blinked in disbelief, but then he witnessed the same process again. His shoulders slumped, and his face drooped in discouragement, realizing his efforts were in vain. He hadn't accomplished a thing—nothing. Che-tan's forces were losing. The battle felt hopeless.

# - 48 -

# Search for the Old Man

AFTER TAKING TURNS SIPPING LAKE WATER FROM THE BOWL, Ethan, Jordan, and Jacob were refreshed and energized, but the rain was relentless, beating across their faces. Taking cover beneath a pine tree a few feet from the shoreline, the three kids huddled together.

"What now?" Jordan asked. "Where do we go? What do we do?"

Jacob and Ethan stared at each other. Ethan shrugged. After a long moment of silence, Ethan spoke up. "Our goal hasn't changed. We have to find the conjurer's home and stab him through the eye—whatever that means. Somehow, that will unlock the prison and our parents will be freed."

"But we don't even have the dagger. I'm pretty sure we'll need the dagger," Jordan said.

"True, but the dagger's useless until we find where to use it. We have to find the old man first," Jacob said.

"What did you just say?" Jordan whispered, but Jacob didn't respond. He was already on to his next thought.

"I've been thinking . . . I don't think the eye is really an eye at all. The eye must be some kind of a locking mechanism. How else would stabbing it release our parents from the prison? Maybe we should be looking for an actual gate or door that has some kind of a lock."

Ethan nodded his head in agreement and started to speak, but Jordan cut him off. "What did you just say?" she repeated, louder.

Jacob thought for a moment and then explained again about how the eye of the conjurer was a lock, not a physical eye.

Shaking her head, Jordan placed a hand on Jacob's shoulder and stared into his eyes. "No. You said we have to find the 'old man.' Why did you say that?"

It's the kind of question a teacher asks in class that is so simple no one wants to answer, but Jordan was willing to wait for a response.

"Old man—conjurer—wizard. It's all the same, isn't it?" Jacob said, looking at Jordan, but she didn't seem satisfied with the reply. "Look, we're supposed to find the conjurer's home and stab him in the eye. When I think of a conjurer, I think of a wizard. When I think of a wizard, I think of a long white beard. Who wears long white beards? Old men. That's it. That's all I meant. No big deal," he said defensively.

Jordan watched him for another moment, and then a large smile enveloped her face. "You're right. All this time we should have been looking for the 'old man,'" Jordan said.

"All-righty then," Ethan said. "Why don't we—"

Before he could finish, Jordan stood and spoke up. "Ethan, don't you remember what Uncle Bart told us about the 'old man'?" Ethan stared. If Uncle Bart had mentioned it, Ethan sure hadn't paid attention. Jordan laughed as she considered the simplicity of the riddle. "The 'old man' is a log that floats in Crater Lake."

"A log? We're looking for a log?" Jacob asked. "Jordan, no offense, but that may be the dumbest thing I've ever heard. Seriously."

"Yeah, a log that bobs up and down in the water. Listen, people started noticing this huge white tree trunk bobbing in the water all over the lake. One day it was in one area of the lake and the next day it was somewhere else. Uncle Bart said the wind blew the 'old man' from place to place. If you saw the 'old man,' it was considered good luck." Ethan's bewildered expression gave him away. Jordan shook her head. "You don't pay attention very well, do you?"

"Guys, we don't have a lot of time," Jacob said, yelling against the rain. "Somehow we ended up here on Wizard Island. I think we are meant to find the 'old man' here on the island. When we do, we can unlock the prison. Even if we wanted to, we don't have time to search the entire lake for a bobbing tree trunk." Looking at Ethan, Jacob muttered, "It's ridiculous."

Jordan bristled at the dismissal of her idea. "Guys, listen to me, please. I'm not talking crazy. This makes sense. The 'old man'—it's the answer to the riddle. You need to listen to me."

"Look, Jordan, Jacob's right. We don't have time to search the lake. We don't even have a boat. That's just not a real option for us. Let's search Wizard Island. If we can't find anything, then we'll figure out a way to search the lake. Okay?"

Folding her arms tight across her chest, Jordan sat on the other side of Ethan and stared out into the vast lake. Past the wall of rain, the lake brightened with sunshine. "No one ever takes me seriously," she grumbled.

Turning toward Jacob, Ethan motioned with jittery hands as he thought about how little time they had. "Chief Llao said we have until midday to free our parents. My watch is busted. I don't know what time it is now, but we've got to be getting close," Ethan said. "We're out of time."

"It's 11:40," Jacob said, looking at his watch. "When did Chief Llao tell you midday?"

"Maybe when you were dead," Ethan answered.

Jacob scowled. "Then we better get moving." His eyes gazed heavenward, trying to match the location of the sun with his wristwatch, but the blackened clouds and heavy rain made it impossible to determine what time it was by looking at the sun.

"So we need to search for the conjurer and find his eye. Jordan and I will go to the left. Jacob, you search to the right.

Stay along the shoreline so you don't get lost in the rain," Ethan suggested.

"I can't see twenty feet in front of me," Jacob said.

"I know. Be careful. We'll meet back here in about fifteen minutes," Ethan said. "Let's go."

Turning away from Jacob, Ethan twisted back to the place where Jordan had been sitting. "Um, Jacob, where'd Jordan go?"

"She got up a minute ago. I thought you noticed. She went down to the water to splash her face," Jacob said.

Ethan looked around but couldn't spot Jordan. "Not again. JORDAN!" Ethan screamed. "Are you kidding me? Jordan! You little brat. JORDAN!"

Jacob looked at Ethan.

"Okay, new plan. Jacob, follow me."

– 49 –

# Teamwork

Slashing his way through the hordes, Brady assumed a defensive position next to Allie. While Allie iced her opponents, Brady dodged and ducked the slow but powerful blows of the craven beasts. Slicing and stabbing at any fleshy target he could reach, Brady wielded the dagger masterfully, sending the grotesque enemies to a temporary grave.

"This isn't working," Brady hollered over the pouring rain. "We have to stop the resurrectors."

"The what?"

"The bad guys with the hooks and nets. We have to kill them and get rid of their instruments. If they keep bringing the enemies we kill back to life, we don't stand a chance," Brady yelled.

Spotting the silver hook and net held by a pair of resurrectors twenty yards away, Brady raced ahead. Using two large black bears as moving shields, he sliced through the muscular ghouls in his path. "Allie, follow me."

With her hands positioned through the large grips on the side of the flute and her finger placed over the proper hole, Allie kept the flute ready in her mouth, zapping fiends with ice. She followed as Brady cleared the path to the nearest team of resurrectors.

Brady lunged at the resurrectors with his dagger but was knocked to the ground by the large hook. He rolled into a deep puddle of mud as the resurrector attempted to slash him with the hook. Brady tried to stand but instead collapsed face-first into the puddle as the second resurrector moved toward him. Lifting the net over its head, the resurrector hammered down but stopped before hitting Brady. The fiend's torso, arms, head, and weapon froze instantly. Looking up from the mud, Brady lifted his blade and slashed the beast's foot, collapsing him into a pile of fleshy rubble. Then it was gone. Only the net remained.

Taking courage, and learning from his mistake, Brady pushed toward the resurrector's companion and motioned for Allie to freeze him. In an instant, the creature's upper body was frozen and Brady moved in for the easy kill, stabbing at the flesh.

"Che-tan!" Brady screamed.

Hearing Brady's call, a flock of four birds dove toward the ground and picked up the unusual weapons. Gripping the staffs in their talons, the birds flew out toward the center of the lake and dropped the instruments, burying them in the watery depths.

Waving to the birds as a sign of gratitude, Allie and Brady advanced with their animal bodyguards to the next set of resurrectors, eager to finalize the deaths of their enemies.

# – 50 –

# The Fog

Sliding across the mucky ground, Ethan raced along the shoreline in the only direction Jordan could have gone. Even with the gloominess of the pounding rain, Ethan was sure he would have noticed if she had stepped into his line of sight.

Sloshing behind Ethan, Jacob squinted as he lowered his hat to keep the stinging rain from hitting his face. There wasn't an inch of his body that wasn't waterlogged. His fingertips were shriveled prunes and his toes sloshed inside his socks with each step. "She couldn't have made it far," Jacob screamed. "She has to be close."

Jordan was gifted at getting lost. *Very annoying.* Although Ethan knew they had to find Jordan, he hoped it wasn't at the expense of rescuing his parents, Jacob's father, and the other Scouts. Jacob hadn't said anything, but Ethan figured he was thinking the same thing.

Stopping, Ethan wiped the water from his face and turned to Jacob. Then, as though the fire hose had been shut off at the hydrant valve, the rain stopped and the clouds dispersed, showering the two boys with sunshine instead of rain. Ethan closed his eyes as he basked in the warmth of the sun. He reopened them in time to see Jordan step into the lake, holding the necklace around her neck.

Ethan raced to the spot where she jumped into the water.

His arms swung back as he prepared to dive, but Jacob grabbed him.

Ethan turned in anger but noticed the look of caution on Jacob's face. Looking back at the lake, Ethan saw what Jacob was seeing. Fog—thick, pea soup, blinding fog. Jordan was swimming into its eerie heart.

"Wait here," Ethan said as his eyes focused on Jordan's feeble stroke.

Without further warning, Ethan kicked off his shoes and dove into the water, swimming to catch up with his sister before she disappeared from sight.

After a few frantic moments, kicking and pulling his arms through the water, Ethan looked up to judge the distance between him and Jordan. She was pulling farther away. *Impossible.* The dense fog settled over the water like a shroud over a corpse, but a thin line of clarity hovered between the water and the fog.

Lowering his face into the water up to his eyes, Ethan could see beneath the pall of murkiness. Rotating toward the island, Ethan thought he could still see Jacob's feet standing at the shore. The rest of his body was hidden behind the foggy shroud. Realigning his body in a straight path with Jordan, Ethan swam with the intensity of an Olympic swimmer. *No way is Jordan faster.*

Ethan was determined to catch Jordan. Hopefully soon.

– 51 –

# CASUALTIES

Salty water ran across Brady's lips. Though the rain had stopped a few moments before, the rainwater drizzled down his face, mixing with his sweat. Licking his lips and then spitting into a puddle, Brady stared at the ancient dagger, still clenched in his hand. Knowing how lethal the weapon was, Brady admired it even more. As a warrior in the throes of battle, he couldn't ask for anything more than a solid weapon, except maybe even odds.

As a team, Brady and Allie had killed dozens of fiendish enemies, maybe hundreds, but it was impossible to tell since the enemies were sucked into the earth after death. In a way, it was nice not having to look at the dead creatures heaped upon the ground, but it was tough on morale. Instead of seeing his success, the only thing Brady could see was the destruction of his warrior friends. They were beautiful animals, lying crippled on the ground, or worse, young teens lying motionless in the mud.

Brady wiped a mixture of sweat, rainwater, and tears from his cheeks as he beheld the carnage of his suffering friends. Each animal was also a teenager, like him. But despite their courage in battle, the strapping bears and cougars lay in pools of blood, their lungs sputtering for air. Among the animals, a few had returned to human form, signifying their ultimate sacrifice. Some of the teens looked like kids from school. The sight of death was absolutely final. Brady's chest heaved. There were no do-overs.

Even Che-tan had taken a beating. Hovering above the carnage, part of Che-tan's flock drifted behind the others, a bad wing . . . or something worse? It was impossible to tell. Like the rest of his army, Che-tan was unable to issue a single deathblow to the enemy. He was merely an irritant to the ghouls while they advanced toward Allie and Brady. Even now, birds and bats filled the trees, resting. The heavy rain had beaten them down; every minute flying in the storm was like a punch to the gut or face.

Despite the lack of body count, the system of attack Brady and Allie devised worked well: Allie froze the fiends with the flute and Brady finished them off with a dagger slice. It worked beautifully—gruesome, yet beautiful. But despite Brady and Allie's success, the remaining ghouls continued to advance.

Allie's long hair matted to her head like the soggy clothes on her body. Her breathing was heavy and her arms rested at her side. She held the flute loose in one hand. Her lungs were exhausted, and her chest was sore. Even her arms ached from lifting the flute for so long. She watched as a broad line of enemies encircled her and Brady.

Allie rotated, keeping her back against Brady's and her vision focused on the encroaching force. Weary and sore, Allie raised the flute to her mouth. "Any bright ideas?" she asked as her feet shuffled.

"No."

She didn't know why, but Brady's answer made her laugh. It was so . . . short. "Seriously? 'No' is the best you can do?" Allie teased. "Would you care to elaborate a little bit?"

Brady grinned. "What can I say? I have no idea how to beat these guys."

Allie pursed her lips. "Can I ask a stupid question?"

"I doubt I could stop you. Haven't been able to yet," Brady responded.

With a quick jab of her elbow into Brady's back, she turned her head toward his ear. "Do we really have to beat them?"

Intrigued by the question, Brady's eyebrow rose. "Well, it's better than losing. What do you mean?"

"We never intended to be in a fight with . . . with . . . these monsters. We came to Wizard Island to release my parents and your friends from prison. We have to find the conjurer's home and stab him through the eye, right?" she asked, still rotating.

"Yeah."

"Well, maybe we've lost sight of what we're trying to do." Pausing from her thought, Allie blew through the flute in three quick bursts, turning four approaching fiends into ice. Two were standing so close to each other that Allie had frozen them together with one blast. "I mean, we're spending our time and energy trying to defeat these guys, when we should be trying to find the conjurer," Allie said, not missing a beat.

"You think this whole battle is a distraction?" Brady asked. His voice sounded harsher than he intended. "Sorry. I didn't, uh, mean . . ."

"I said it was a stupid question. I'm just wondering," Allie said.

"So if we're not trying to defeat them, what should we do?" Brady asked.

"Escape."

## – 52 –

# DISTRACTED

With the nearest ghouls turned to ice, Brady stepped into their midst, thrashing and swinging his dagger, his blows connecting with tissue and bone. With each cut the fiends collapsed to the earth and then disappeared.

"Che-tan!" Allie yelled.

She continued firing short bursts of ice, keeping her perimeter secure while waiting for Che-tan to lower to the ground and form into a man.

"Che-tan! Hurry," she yelled, but although Che-tan flew as quickly as he could, it wasn't very fast.

Keeping one eye on Brady as he slashed through the ghoulish enemies, she turned away in disgust as his dagger sliced clean through a muscular arm, dropping it to the ground. For the first time, Allie realized there was no blood or pus, only flesh and bone. That was gross enough.

Finally, the first three hawks crashed into each other on the ground, assembling into Che-tan, but he was incomplete. Allie's eyes widened as she watched Che-tan hobble on one leg. With his body hidden beneath a brown cloak, Allie couldn't tell if the missing leg was traumatized and gory or a smooth stub. The final hawk floated downward. Instead of crashing into Che-tan with the force needed to reassemble and make him whole, the bird bumped into his chest and fell, flapping on the ground.

Allie gasped as she saw the human leg lying next to Che-tan.

With his eyes closed, Che-tan breathed to control his pain, willing himself not to be sick. "What can I do for you, Allie?" he asked.

Lowering her eyes, Allie wondered whether she should even ask.

"Allie, what is it?" he asked again.

"Che-tan, I'm so sorry about your army, and your . . ." She couldn't say it, but she pointed to Che-tan's leg lying beside him. "I hope you'll be okay. We kind of need your help."

"Of course. What can I do?"

"We can't beat these things. We've tried, but we can't," she said, her voice choking on the words. "We need to find the conjurer. This whole battle has distracted us from what we're really trying to do." Allie raised the flute to her mouth and exhaled two deep breaths. Again, approaching enemies were stopped in their tracks.

Che-tan took in the devastation of his young army. "These warriors did not die as a distraction," he said, motioning toward two young teens piled on the ground. "These warriors lie in their own blood. They have given all they can. You say their sacrifice was meaningless?"

Allie's head lowered as she spoke reverently. "No. Not meaningless. Just misguided." She looked at Che-tan with assurance. "But it's not their fault. It's yours—and mine." She paused to give Che-tan time to digest her words.

Che-tan's lips tightened and his eyes narrowed. Allie couldn't tell if he was in pain or angry. "Che-tan, we must rescue our loved ones from the prison. That is everything. Winning a battle will be meaningless if we lose our families," she said.

Che-tan thought about her words. His lips loosened and his expression softened. "We have lost many, but our losses in this battle will be vindicated with our success at the prison gates."

"Yes," Allie said, barely audible.

"What would you have me do?"

– 53 –

# The Old . . . Stump?

Wrapping her arms around the vertical white stump, tears cascaded down Jordan's cheeks. "How did I get here?" she screamed into the fog. She listened, but the fog didn't answer. Unable to reach all the way around the stump, Jordan held tight as it bobbed in the cool water like a buoy. She pressed her face against the damp wood and closed her eyes. Surrounded by thick white fog, she couldn't see anyway. Trying to remember the vision that had brought her here, Jordan calmed her breathing as she spoke to herself in peaceful, gentle tones. Her crying stopped as she reentered her vision.

* * *

Stepping from the sandy beach, Jordan splashed into the warm tropical surf and stood waist deep. Small waves crashed against her. As one large wave drew near, she turned her back and jumped, allowing the wave to lift and push her back to the shore. She felt weightless. There were no worries, only sand and surf, and a warm sun overhead.

After a few playful moments, Jordan heard a terrifying scream. Squinting in the sunlight, Jordan stared in the direction of the screaming. Far out, beyond the breaking ocean waves, a man reached his arms high, flailing them in the air to get attention. His head dipped below the surface, and then he rose again.

After a moment of screaming and splashing, the man lowered into the water and disappeared from sight. Glancing around the beach, Jordan searched for a lifeguard or any adult who could help the man, but the beach was deserted. No one could help. It was up to her. Diving into an approaching wave, Jordan emerged on the other side of it and began paddling toward the man. He rose from the water, screaming and waving, but then he disappeared again as he submerged below the waves.

"I'm coming," Jordan hollered between strokes. "Hang on." She looked for the man, and once again his head was above water, gasping for air.

Approaching the man, Jordan considered grabbing onto him but paused, keeping her distance from his flailing arms. Diving deep under the water, Jordan kicked and pulled with all her strength, pushing herself beneath the man before emerging behind him. She grabbed him from behind where his panicked arms couldn't reach to pull her underneath the water. Holding his head from behind, Jordan attempted to tow him back to shore, but she couldn't move. Maybe he was too big, or she was too small, but she could tell she wasn't moving. She tried harder but still could not move the old man. No longer flailing and panicking, the man remained still as Jordan wrapped her arms around his broad chest and pressed her face into his back.

* * *

"Jordan!" Ethan screamed as he reached for her, but speaking and swimming really don't mix. Ethan swallowed a mouthful of water, causing him to cough. "Jordan, are you okay?" he asked, placing one hand on her back.

Opening her eyes, Jordan once again saw she was clinging to the white tree trunk in the water, not wrapped around a man's chest. "Ethan? What happened? How did we get here?"

"I know how I got here. I followed you," he said, wrapping his other arm around the trunk. "What were you doing? I have no idea."

Jordan wiped tears from her cheeks.

"We're together now. We're going to be fine," Ethan said in his most reassuring voice.

Pushing herself back from the trunk, Jordan looked at the top of the white pole. Burned into the white flesh of the wood, Jordan saw the same symbol she had seen in vision earlier, while sleepwalking through the Below World. "Ethan, I've seen this before."

"What do you mean? Where?"

"In my vision. I saw a tall trunk on a grassy hill. And I've seen this symbol before. I think we found the 'old man.' I think this is the conjurer. "

Rotating around the trunk to face the symbol, Ethan's eyes brightened as he looked up. Near the top of the trunk was an image of a chubby salamander lying on its belly, encircled by its tail with an arrow at the end. Inside the circle created by the tail, three thick dots created a triangle, the top point poking the salamander in the belly. Above the salamander, four icons that looked like the artifacts from the Phantom Ship lay side by side.

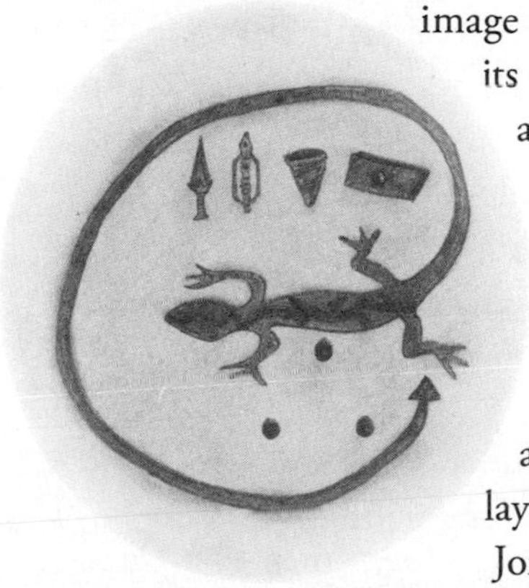

Jordan studied the pictogram. She had seen it in vision, but she had also seen something similar. She closed her eyes and searched her memory. It was close, but just out of reach. Then her eyes widened with excitement as she remembered. "The dagger!"

"What about the dagger?" Ethan asked.

"On the base of the dagger's hilt, there's a picture—a symbol."

"The same symbol is on the dagger?" Ethan asked.

"No. It's better." Jordan thought for a moment. "Together, I think they tell us how to unlock the Prison of the Lost." She stared at her brother. "We need that dagger."

## - 54 -

# RETREAT

"GO! NOW!" BRADY YELLED TO ALLIE AND CHE-TAN AS HE slashed another fiend across the back, turning it into a puddle of gray goop.

Taking his cue, three hawks burst from the ground, flying high within seconds, while the fourth struggled for movement. After a moment convulsing on the ground, the dismembered leg also transformed and took flight, straggling behind the other members of Che-tan's flock.

Entering the trees, Che-tan squawked, sending the bats and various flocks of birds into the sky. After lofting high as a cohesive body and casting Wizard Island in shadow, the flocks separated. Some flew into the pine forest, weaving and ducking through branches. Some stayed near the battlefront, and others flew over the fog that was just beginning to blanket the island. Bats flew over the lake, rising and falling through the fog with ease. In a grid pattern, the bats began hunting for the mysterious conjurer and his prison gate.

In one fluid motion, Allie raised her flute and blew, spreading thick sheets of ice across the ground in a semicircle around her, creating a slippery obstacle for any fiend who dared to approach. She continued to spew frozen water vapor, creating steady lines of ice on either side of her. She walked along the only pathway cleared of ice.

Looking to her left, Allie saw Brady sprinting toward her, swiping at the fiends' outstretched hands, occasionally catching one and causing it to collapse to the ground. Between her and Brady, three large beasts stood shoulder to shoulder as if daring Brady to a game of Red Rover. To Allie's astonishment, Brady accepted their challenge. Cringing as she watched Brady run toward the beefy ghouls, Allie covered her eyes, unwilling to watch Brady's certain demise. But peeking through her fingers, she saw Brady slide beneath one of the enemy's legs like a baseball player stealing second base. He swiped his knife. Allie couldn't keep from smiling at Brady's gumption, while simultaneously shrinking away and averting her eyes as the beast plopped into a mess of carnage the instant Brady was through its legs. Allie breathed a deep sigh of relief and then grinned again as she saw a giant smile cover Brady's face. He looked just as impressed as she was.

Hopping up as his feet slid off the ice and onto firm ground, Brady grabbed Allie's hand in one smooth motion, never breaking stride. Together they raced along the path Allie had cleared, while hundreds of birds and bats continued to swarm the faces of the fiends as a diversion. Glancing backward, Allie was pleased to see the oafish beasts sliding and falling on her icy obstacles. Mission accomplished . . . almost.

With the flute gripped at her side, Allie ran as fast as her weary legs would allow. Splashing through puddles and weaving through a grove of white aspens, Allie followed Brady's lead. Returning to the small dock with the double outhouse nearby, Brady untied a wooden canoe and stepped inside. Sliding to the back, he stabilized the shaky canoe, propping one ore against his lap as he held the sides of the canoe for balance. Allie climbed in carefully—slowly.

"Hurry up, Allie!" Brady hollered. Over Allie's shoulder, he could see two fiends racing toward them. Bats hovered around their eyes, blocking their view, but it didn't seem to slow them. Looking at Allie, Brady could see her hesitance. "Now, Allie! Sit!"

Allie plopped onto a mesh seat, rocking the canoe as it threatened to capsize. Brady remained still as he willed the canoe to become calm. Then, removing the paddle from his lap, Brady pushed off from the dock, sending the canoe floating away from the ghouls' outstretched hands.

Sitting, Allie faced the center of the canoe, looking into Brady's face. She didn't know much about canoeing, but this position had to be wrong. Brady was bound to make a smart remark, but for now, he was focused on stroking his oar through the water. At the dock, the fiends climbed into a rowboat that had been moored next to the canoe.

"Allie, can you take care of that?" Brady hollered.

Twisting in her seat, Allie leaned back toward the dock and raised her flute. "This ought to be good," she muttered under her breath. Placing her finger over the hole, Allie blew. Fire burst from the flute like a flamethrower, connecting with the wooden dock and the rowboat that was still connected. Along with the boat and the dock, the fiends caught fire. Allie immediately wished she hadn't used fire. Flames rose from the burning fiends, but they didn't stop. Climbing into the rowboat inferno, the flaming creatures began rowing after the canoe. Panic nearly stopped Allie's heart.

Turning in his seat, Brady faced what was now the front of the canoe. Looking over his shoulder, he could tell the fiends were already gaining. "Allie, row! Right side."

Digging the oars deep into the water and pulling backward with all their strength, Allie and Brady lurched forward. "Row. Row. Row," Brady said in cadence.

As their strokes became rhythmical, the canoe glided through the water, but looking to the rear, they saw that the flaming rowboat had narrowed the gap. One of the fiends sat in the center of the boat, rowing both oars with unmatched power while the other hovered near the front of the boat, ready to pounce as soon as they were close enough. Flames rose from his head like a torch, but even through the fire, Allie could see the hate-filled eyes beaming at her.

"Brady—faster!" Allie screamed.

The rowboat was close enough that Allie could smell the burning enemies. She was so hungry, the burning flesh smelled like steaks grilling on the barbecue. The aroma made her mouth water, but the thought made her nauseated. She looked back again.

"This isn't working!" she screamed.

Brady was breathing too hard to respond. His shoulders and arms burned as he continued to row. Although Allie rowed with her full strength, Brady was much stronger. With each stroke the canoe turned a little in Brady's direction so he began rotating strokes on either side of the canoe to straighten their path.

"Keep rowing," Allie said as she placed her oar back in the canoe. Brady didn't have to be told; he kept rowing. Turning in her seat, Allie fumbled for the flute, which slid across the canoe floor. She leaned and reached, but each time she did, the canoe threatened to capsize. Holding as still as she could, moving only in slow, smooth motions, Allie reached behind her and grasped the flute with her fingertips. Pulling it closer, she picked up the flute as she saw the fiendish torch upon her. Lifting the flute to her mouth, Allie positioned her fingers and blew. Frozen water vapor shot from the flute and hit the front of the rowboat. An instant iceberg formed in the water, causing the boat to crash to a halt. The fiend standing at the front of the boat flew over board and sunk into the water as it reached for her. Allie waited to see if it would emerge and swim after her, but it didn't.

"Maybe drowning is another way to kill them," Allie said, but she didn't know for certain if it had died. Maybe the fiend was walking along the bottom of the lake. No matter.

"Nice one," Brady complimented.

Even though the rowboat had disappeared from view, Brady continued to row. The soupy fog made it impossible to know where he was on the lake. For all he knew, they could be thirty yards off the shoreline of Wizard Island, or maybe the Phantom Ship.

"Is there anything you can do with that thing to help us see?" Brady asked.

Allie looked at her flute and the four holes. She knew about the ice and fire features of the flute, and also the blinding light. What did the final hole do? She had been too nervous to test it, but in the middle of the lake, with nothing around, what could she possibly hurt? Placing her finger over the last, untried hole, Allie turned sideways in the canoe and blew into the fog.

Gusts of wind began swirling around the canoe, so much that a small whirlpool formed in the water, spinning the canoe in place.

Pulling in his oar, Brady held on to the side of the canoe as it began spinning faster. "What are you doing?" he yelled.

"I don't know."

"Well, stop it," Brady pleaded. The canoe spun so fast that his cheeks pulled tight and flapped against his face.

"Too late. Hold on."

Allie enjoyed the dizzying motion. It reminded her of a ride at the state fair. Brady closed his eyes and held his breath as the canoe spun out of control. It was a good thing there was nothing in his stomach, because the vomit would have sprayed everywhere. After another minute of ferocious spinning, the canoe slowed and the whirlpool subsided.

Opening his eyes, Brady marveled at the clarity of his vision. The sun shone high, the fog was gone, and a warm breeze blew across the lake. It could have been like any other day on the boat with his dad, except for the reminders of the Phantom Ship looming a short distance away to his right, and Wizard Island behind him. Looking around, it appeared the canoe was dead center in the watery crater.

"Whatever you did, worked," Brady said as he held his queasy stomach.

"Brady."

Still consumed by the unsettled feeling in his stomach, Brady didn't answer.

"Brady," Allie said more forcefully, jabbing him with her oar.

"What?"

"Look over there!" Allie said, pointing and smiling.

Squinting against the sunlit blue water, Brady searched the watery horizon in the direction of Allie's pointed finger.

Allie laughed. "There they are."

Ethan and Jordan were wrapped around a log sticking out of the water.

"Jordan! Ethan!" Brady yelled. "I can't believe it."

Jordan shrieked with delight at the sight of her friends.

"Hold on. We're coming!"

# – 55 –

# ASSASSINATION

STANDING WITH THE TOES OF HIS SHOES IN THE WATER, Jacob gazed across the blue lake in hopes of spotting Ethan and Jordan. Time was running out, but alone on the island, he felt helpless to do anything. With the fog cleared by the sudden gusts of wind, Jacob once again saw wispy clouds brushed across the sky, and he noticed the multitudes of bats and birds passing overhead. Heavy shade floated above as swarms of the animals gathered into one giant flock and then flew over Wizard Island back toward the rim of the crater.

"This place is so odd," Jacob said to himself. He had been so excited when his troop arrived at Crater Lake for their overnight camp, but now, all Jacob could think about was rescuing his father and leaving Crater Lake forever. He never wanted to see this place again.

At the center of the lake, amid the calm water, Jacob could see movement. Straining his eyes and ears, he even thought he heard the muffled sounds of distant yelling, though he couldn't make out the words. Was it Ethan and Jordan? It was too far to see any detail. Jacob considered diving in to swim toward his friends, but his healthy fear of water wouldn't allow it.

Jacob had already died once today, almost twice. His stroke was a weak doggy paddle, and he didn't dare tempt death again by trying to swim. It was time to get back to work.

"Might as well be useful," he muttered, turning from the water. Starting along the shoreline to resume his search for the conjurer and the prison gate, Jacob stopped in midstep.

Standing in front of him was a tall, freakish figure. Jacob gulped with shock as he stared into hollow eyes. The creature's gray skin sagged on the muscular physique. Its lips were narrow and the cheeks thin, and dark, corpse-like hair dangled from the scalp over a blue bandana. The creature didn't utter a sound or even approach, but Jacob felt threatened all the same. Turning in place, Jacob attempted to retreat but was blocked by a second creature. A ponytail slapped against the side of its neck as its head turned. This creature had once been a woman, and though she looked like she had been dead and buried for at least a year, Jacob could tell by her high cheekbones and delicate features that she had once been beautiful.

A wave of fear washed over him. He considered the thought for the first time that maybe this is what happened to all the adults at Crater Lake. Was it possible his own father was wandering the woods as some kind of half-dead zombie? Jacob's breathing raced as he pushed the hideous thought from his mind.

With zombies in front of and behind him, the steep mountain on his left, and the vast lake on the right, Jacob considered his options. Easy choice. Attempting to scurry up the steep hill, Jacob made it only a few feet before slipping downward in a mass of loose lava rock pebbles and mud. Looking back at the creatures, Jacob turned to the water. What other option did he have? What were the odds that a zombie could swim and give chase? Not good, he decided.

Jumping into the water with his canvas bag still wrapped around his shoulder, Jacob reached his arms forward in an awkward paddling motion, but he was too slow. Glancing back up to the shore, Jacob gasped as he saw a large gray hand reach over his face, shoving him beneath the water.

Grabbing and scratching frantically for the surface, Jacob's panicked eyes looked into the hand of the creature holding him down. After only seconds, his breath was depleted. Looking helplessly into the eyes of his murderer, Jacob's arms flailed and scratched at the large hand pressing him beneath the water. The water was so clear, it seemed as though he was peering through a pane of glass, except for the ripples caused by his hysterical movements. Holding his breath the best he could, Jacob knew he couldn't hold out much longer—fifteen or twenty seconds, maybe less. Then his breathing reflex kicked in. Even though he knew he couldn't breath in the water and survive, he couldn't help it. Jacob's mouth opened wide and gulped the water into his lungs as though it were air. His body convulsed violently as he inhaled. Jacob's second death took him quickly.

Removing his hand from the boy, Nathaniel stared with indifference at the lifeless face floating just below the surface. Jenna stepped alongside her companion and gazed into the water. Satisfied with the assassination, they both turned to leave. Chief Llao had not told them why he wanted Jacob dead, but it wasn't their place to question. The job was finished.

- 56 -

# Power Struggle

Pulling the canoe next to the "old man," Brady reached for Jordan and Ethan, but the siblings clung to the white stump, ignoring his offer.

"Give me your hand," Brady called, reaching for Jordan. "I'll pull you up."

"Come on, Ethan. Grab hold," Allie urged, but neither budged.

"It's good to see you guys," Ethan said, his eyes narrowing into thin slits of accusation.

"Hey, sorry we ditched you guys last night, but it was for your own good," Brady offered.

Ethan grunted, and Jordan scowled.

"We had to leave you," Allie continued. "Che-tan said . . ."

As if hearing his name, Che-tan squawked high above, drawing the attention of all four kids. He swooped low and then flew off to Wizard Island behind the rest of the flocks.

Raising one hand, Ethan waved off Brady and Allie's explanations. "There's no time for excuses," he said. "Do you still have the dagger?"

Pulling the dagger from his shorts and unsheathing it, Brady showed the weapon. "Yeah, I got it. This little baby is AWESOME!" he said.

"Great. I'm glad you like it. Can I see it?" Ethan asked with his hand outstretched.

Brady eyed him as he considered the request. "Why?"

Looking at Jordan, Ethan gave a subtle nod. Jordan's eyes brightened as she started to explain. "We found the conjurer. It's time to unlock the gate," she said and then let out a happy yelp.

"That's great!" Allie said, laughing with excitement. "Where is it?"

"You're looking at it," Ethan said, motioning to the white stump with his head. Jabbing his hand forward, Ethan again requested the dagger. "The dagger, please. I'm going to stab the conjurer through the eye. It's time."

"What? This stump is the conjurer? That doesn't make any sense," Allie said. "How could stabbing a stump possibly be the same as stabbing the conjurer through the eye? And more importantly, how will stabbing the stump unlock the prison gate? You can't be serious."

"Yes, I am. Trust me, the stump is the conjurer's eye, but there's no time to explain. We can exchange stories later. Guys, this is it. Give me the dagger," Ethan urged. "We're running out of time."

"Just like that?" Brady asked, dubious of both Ethan's motives and the reality that the stump bobbing in the water was the conjurer. "You're going to have to do better than that if you expect me to give this baby up. This thing has saved my life a thousand times. I'm not letting it go because you said so, just to have you accidentally drop it in the water while trying to stab a stump," Brady said with a smirk.

"Brady, give me the dagger," Ethan demanded again. "I need it now. There's no time to waste," he said, looking at the sun overhead.

"If we don't hurry, we won't be able to unlock the prison gate and free our family," Jordan said.

"No. You can't make me," Brady said, sounding like a

kindergartner throwing a tantrum. Allie raised an eyebrow to confirm the childishness of his comment. "What I mean is, there's time. Explain what's going on. I need to know."

Ethan thought for a moment. "Fine. I'll tell you what I know. Listen close because I'm not going to repeat myself."

– 57 –

# A Proper Burial

Approaching Wizard Island, Che-tan saw a zombie crouching near the water, his arm dripping. The creatures looked different than the fiends he had just battled, but still, they were grotesque and unwelcome. Che-tan swooped low, extended his talons, and ripped across the male creature's back, removing a hunk of flesh just below the shoulder. The assassins strode into the forest, disappearing into the trees, never fighting back or even acknowledging the presence of the hawks.

Slamming into each other at ground level, the three strong hawks reassembled into Che-tan, who fell to his knee near the water. Seeing Jacob's dead eyes staring back at him below the surface, Che-tan reached into the water and grabbed Jacob under the arms. Lifting the boy part way out of the water, Che-tan pulled him by the hands the rest of the way onto shore.

Jacob's lifeless body lay in the mud. The canvas bag hung from his shoulder, and his hat dangled around his neck. Removing the canvas bag, Che-tan examined the contents, finding the bowl artifact inside. Lowering his ear to Jacob's mouth, it was clear the boy wasn't breathing. Che-tan prepared to fly away but paused, looking down at Jacob. Lowering on his one leg, Che-tan replaced the canvas bag over Jacob's shoulder and then clenched his fingers around the boy's belt. He couldn't leave him. With the boy grasped tight, Che-tan separated into his small flock and lifted off—or at least attempted to.

Three large hawks flew close in formation, each holding a piece of Jacob's clothing in their talons, but despite their size and strength, the boy was a heavy burden to manage. Che-tan attempted to fly higher but was unable to get the lift he needed. As his flapping wings dipped uncontrollably, Jacob's feet dragged across the clear lake water, creating a small wake.

Che-tan flew toward the "old man" with no one—and nothing—around that could help.

## – 58 –

# STAB THE CONJURER

BRADY SHOOK HIS HEAD. "WAIT A MINUTE. I THOUGHT WE were fighting against Chief Llao, but now you say Chief Llao wants us to succeed in stabbing him through the eye? So who were we fighting on Wizard Island?"

"Chief Skell marshaled the forces on Wizard Island to stop us from helping Chief Llao." Ethan thought about it for a moment. "By helping us to stab the eye, the treaty that binds Chief Llao inside the mountain will be broken and Chief Llao will be freed."

Allie grimaced as she scratched her head. "This is insane. I don't know who to trust."

"All I care about is stabbing the stupid conjurer in the eye and freeing our parents. That's it. Llao, Skell, and everyone else can do their own thing. I'm done with them," Ethan said.

Brady nodded in acceptance of Ethan's explanation, though he didn't fully understand.

"Brady, the dagger please," Ethan requested once again. Brady was still hesitant. "We're out of time, Brady."

"What's wrong with you?" Allie screamed. "Give it to him, Brady. Now!"

Looking at the symbol on the bottom of the dagger's hilt, Brady then examined the pictogram on the "old man."

"Brady, what are you doing? Give Ethan the dagger. Please," Allie said.

"Guys, I want to stab the conjurer. Please, let me do it," Brady requested.

"Fine. Whatever, just do it already," Ethan said.

Moving to the back of the stump, Jordan got out of the way as Brady maneuvered the canoe, butting it sideways against the "old man." Swimming out behind the canoe, Ethan got into position so he could watch the deed.

With the pictogram at eye level for Brady, he raised his dagger and slammed it against the center of the symbol with a harsh stabbing motion, but it glanced off as though he were stabbing solid steel. Embarrassed, Brady's freckled face turned red as the others looked at him impatiently. Gripping the dagger even tighter, Brady cocked his hand back and stabbed again. The blade stabbed straight into the center of the pictogram, but again, it could not penetrate the wood. Instead, the impact sent rattling shivers through Brady's arm. He looked at the blade, wondering if it had been damaged, but the tip was still needle sharp.

"Stop messing around," Ethan blurted. "Hurry!"

Brady swiveled around to meet Ethan's gaze with a cold stare of his own. Cocking the dagger again, Brady attempted shorter, swifter stabs, but none penetrated the white wood. "There's something wrong with it. This dagger's not working. I think it's broken."

Ethan looked up into the sky, noting the position of the sun. "Maybe we already missed our chance. Maybe we're too late," he said with defeated resignation.

"No. It will work. We're just doing something wrong," Jordan said.

"I agree," Allie said. "There must be more to it. Ethan, you said the symbols were instructions for stabbing the conjurer. Are we following the instructions exactly?"

"Of course," he huffed. He thought for a moment. "Well, the instructions don't actually start until after the dagger's in the wood. Once it's in, we'll twist it counterclockwise, and that should do it."

"How do you know?" Brady asked, still rubbing his arm.

"Look, the salamander sits at the top, and its tail wraps around until it ends with an arrow pointing counterclockwise," Ethan said.

"Okay, fine. But what do these three dots mean? It looks like they form a triangle. And what are these?" Allie asked, pointing to the icons above the salamander.

"We think it's the artifacts," Ethan said.

"Think?"

"Yeah. 'Think.' I'm sorry, but I don't speak pictures, or hieroglyphics, or anything else," Ethan said with frustration. Looking at the bottom of the dagger, he noted the rough symbol etched into the hilt. It looked like a pine tree sitting on a hill. "I don't speak the language," he muttered again, his voice choking on the words.

"We heard you the first time," Brady snapped.

"Wait," Ethan said, a smile forming on his lips. He chuckled as he stared upward with thought and concentration. "Of course! Chief Llao said we would need *all* the artifacts." Digging into his pocket, Ethan pulled out the flat stone translator that had helped him read the bowl and also understand Chief Llao. "I don't speak the language, but maybe the translator does." He looked at the smooth black stone in his hand. "It's worth a shot."

Swimming around the canoe, Ethan squeezed between the canoe and the log. Raising the translator from the water, he reached as high as he could and held it next to the symbol. "Allie, can you see anything?"

Allie shook her head, indicating she couldn't.

"Try this," Ethan said. Removing the translator from its place against the wood, he handed it to Allie. "Look through the hole in the center. Hold it up to your eye," he instructed.

Placing the hole against her eye, Allie peered at the pictogram and smiled. "Got it. It's so easy," Allie said, and then continued admiring the pictogram through the translator.

"Great!" Ethan said, prodding Allie to continue, but she didn't take the hint. "Come on, Allie. What's it say?"

"Oh, the artifacts are all pieces to the same key. Stabbing the conjurer requires all artifacts working together."

"I just said that," Ethan huffed.

"I have the flute," she said, picking the instrument off the floor of the canoe and holding it up for all to see. "What else do we have?"

"We have the translator," Ethan said.

"And I've got the dagger," Brady said. They each looked at each other, waiting for someone to claim possession of the stone bowl. "Well, who's got the bowl? Jordan?" he asked, peering around the white stump where she was still clinging.

"I only have this necklace," she said, propping the necklace out of the water. But we didn't get this from the Phantom Ship."

"Hey, where *did* you get that? That's mine," Brady said, reaching out his hand.

"I don't think so," Ethan said with a glare. "We'll deal with the necklace later. Where's the bowl? I just had it." Placing his wet hand against his forehead, Ethan moaned. "Oh no, Jacob has it. He kept getting hurt, so I thought he should hang onto it."

"It's a healing bowl, you know," Jordan said from around the stump.

"There's so much to tell you guys," Ethan said. "But not right now. We have all the pieces except for the bowl. Allie, do we really need it? I can't imagine what a bowl would have to do with stabbing the conjurer's eye."

Allie didn't answer.

"Allie, do we need the bowl?" Ethan repeated. Again she didn't answer. Her eyes were fixed on the water near Wizard Island. Following the direction of her gaze, Ethan saw what she was looking at.

"Oh. That doesn't look good."

## – 59 –

# The Ice Runway

JUST ABOVE THE WATERLINE, A SMALL FLOCK OF BIRDS FLEW toward the group, dragging a body across the water and gripped the boy near the center of his waist. The floppy body was bent nearly in half. The hands and feet dragged across the water and a hat dangled from the neck. At moments even his head seemed to skim the surface.

"It's Jacob!" Jordan yelled in dismay, tears welling in her eyes.

Brady's head shook. "I don't think they're going to make it."

Ethan's eyes squinted, and his face tensed. He watched the approaching birds. "The bag. I see the bag. Jacob had the bowl inside. Guys, we need the bag."

"If they don't make it to us, that bag's going to sink straight to the bottom of the lake. We'll be totally hosed," Brady said.

"He's right," Allie said.

"What do we do?" Jordan asked.

"I know what to do," Allie said. Pushing away from the "old man," Allie looked at Brady. "I need you to row in line with the birds. Can you do that?"

"Of course I can do that," Brady said as he picked up his oar and placed it in the water.

"Jordan, Ethan, I need you to get away from the 'old man.' Just for a minute," Allie said.

Not questioning, Jordan and Ethan swam away from the

log and treaded water. They watched as Allie raised the flute to her mouth and blew, sending frozen water vapor into the lake near the white stump. Thick ice formed, encircling the trunk.

Brady rowed toward the dipping birds as Allie blew short bursts of ice into the water, creating a smooth but narrow runway to the "old man."

"Faster, Brady! We need to intercept Jacob."

Shaking his head, sweat flew from Brady's brow. The runway grew longer as they raced toward the struggling flock.

Although Che-tan carried his burden the best he could, it wasn't good enough. He squawked, and as one, the hawks increased their flapping, lifting Jacob just above the water, but then dipped again, dragging him even deeper. Fast approaching the start of the icy runway, Che-tan squawked again. This time, the flock was unable to raise the boy from the water. They had to raise him higher, or Jacob's crash into the ice would be like hitting a concrete highway divider. The runway loomed, just seconds away.

Che-tan squawked again, and the birds lifted, raising Jacob so only his fingers and toes dragged in the water, but they began to dip again when the fourth hawk rejoined the flock. Struggling just to stay aloft, the fourth hawk dug his claws into Jacob's back, just below the neck, and lifted, raising the front of Jacob's body fully from the water, just as they reached the icy runway. Collapsing, the fourth hawk lay across Jacob's back as the other three lowered Jacob onto the ice and released their grip, allowing him to slide across the runway until he came to a stop just yards away from the log. Jacob lay motionless, his bag still wrapped around his shoulder.

Climbing out of the water, Ethan then pulled Jordan onto the icy platform. Racing the short distance across the ice, Ethan slid on his knees and plowed into Jacob, almost pushing him over the edge. Grabbing tight to Jacob's shoulders, Ethan held him, searching frantically for any sign of life. He felt for pulse and breath, but there were no positive signs. Holding Jacob's arm, Ethan looked at the wristwatch on his dead friend's wrist. 11:55 a.m. There was still time!

Forming back into a man, Che-tan landed on the ice near the two boys as Brady and Allie turned their canoe and began rowing back to join the group. Standing, Ethan cupped his hands to his mouth and yelled, "FIVE MINUTES!"

Looking at Che-tan's sweaty face, Ethan dropped to his knees and dug into the canvas bag, pulling out the stone bowl artifact. Leaning over the edge of the ice, Ethan dipped it into the lake, filling it with water. Scooting toward Che-tan, Ethan extended the bowl. "Drink."

Che-tan looked at the bowl and then accepted it. Ethan nodded. Raising the bowl to his lips, Che-tan drank. His droopy eyes widened with life, and he stood taller on his one leg. Guzzling the water, Che-tan smiled with amazement. Within moments, the fourth hawk took flight and then crashed into him, making him whole again.

Satisfied with Che-tan's renewal, Ethan looked to the fast-approaching canoe. "Hurry up, guys."

Waiting for the reunion of all essential artifacts, Ethan grabbed the bowl from Che-tan and dipped it again in the water. He poured a small amount into Jacob's mouth, but the water ran out the sides of Jacob's lips. Ethan tried again, but it was no use. Jacob was even deader than when Chief Llao had brought him back to life. Ethan's head dropped in defeat. Then, loosening Jacob's wristwatch, Ethan strapped it on and checked his pocket to confirm the translator was still there. And with the bowl in his hands, he turned away from Jacob and walked to the white log poking from the water.

Standing on the ice that surrounded the "old man," Ethan grabbed Jordan's hand and squeezed as Brady and Allie wafted sideways into the ice. After Brady and Allie climbed out of the canoe, Che-tan and Ethan held it still. Then the five teens crowded around the conjurer's pictographic eye.

"We have to do it now," Ethan commanded as he glanced at

the watch. "Two minutes until noon."

Following Allie's instructions, Brady stepped to the front of the group and placed the tip of the dagger in the center of the pictogram, between the three dots that formed the triangle. Moving beside Brady, Ethan raised the bowl in his hand and tapped the hilt of the dagger three times with the bottom of the bowl. Looking at the emblem on the dagger's hilt, Ethan realized it wasn't a picture of a tree on a hill; it was an image of the bowl striking the dagger. On the third tap, the dagger sunk deep into the wood. Ethan tested it, attempting to wiggle the dagger, but it wouldn't dislodge. Stepping aside, Ethan made room for Allie.

Placing the tubular handle of her flute over the dagger's hilt, Allie held on to the end of the flute and turned. Whether it was the added torque gained from using the flute as a lever or maybe some mystical power within the flute that was meant to twist the dagger, Allie didn't know, but the dagger turned smoothly. Like removing a lug nut from the wheel of a car, the more she turned, the easier the dagger spun until it spun out of control. Unable to keep up with the rotation, she removed her hands from the flute and watched as the dagger and flute continued to turn. Then it stopped abruptly.

Brady stepped up to the dagger and tried to remove it. "Is it supposed to do something?" he asked. "How do we know if it worked?"

Ethan shrugged his shoulders.

"If the prison gate has been unlocked, we will surely know," Che-tan said.

"But how?"

"Be patient," Che-tan instructed.

Glancing at Jacob's watch, Ethan's head shook. Noon. His eyes narrowed with worry and his lips quivered. "We failed."

"Keep watching," Che-tan urged.

Allie, Jordan, Brady, Ethan, and Che-tan all stared at the embedded dagger and stationary flute. Then, the handle on the flute broke off and the flute fell to the icy ground. Inside the circle of the salamander's tail, the white trunk began to glow like a hot ember, and the black etching paled as the dagger brightened into a blue flame. The hilt sucked into the trunk as a loud hissing cry echoed from inside. It almost sounded like laughter. Jordan grabbed Ethan's arm and held tight.

A white-blue flame engulfed the entire trunk, but although the heat from the trunk didn't scorch the kids, the ice that surrounded the "old man" melted. The trunk slipped through the ice, sinking into a watery grave.

The kids encircled the round opening in the ice where the white trunk had just been and stared into the crystal clear water, watching as the "old man" fell deeper and then disappeared from view.

"Is that it?" Che-tan asked.

As if sharing a brain, Brady, Allie, Ethan, and Jordan all swiveled their heads and looked at Che-tan. He was the one with answers. "What do you mean?" Ethan asked.

"You're the one who said 'we shall surely know,' " Brady said in a mocking tone. "Don't *you* know?"

Che-tan looked at his inquisitors, made a face, and shrugged. "Friends, I am sorry. I thought there would be more. Something spectacular. I thought . . ."

Before Che-tan could finish his thought, the volcanic cinder cone that *is* Wizard Island began to moan. Ash, dirt, and rock belched high into the air. Wizard Island erupted with fury.

- 60 -

# Prison Break

Deep within the bowels of Crater Lake, Chief Llao sat on his stone-carved throne. With the cliff behind him and the inhabitants of Wata`m Village scurrying below, Chief Llao faced the blackness of the lava tunnel and stared at the oculus on his armrest. He could see Ethan tapping the dagger straight into his eye and then the oculus became a muddy pond.

Above ground, the eye of the wandering "old man" provided Chief Llao his only vision of the Above World. For seven thousand years, he had been trapped beneath the earth's surface, his powers subdued by tons of imprisoning rock. Chief Llao rubbed the tips of his fingers together with gleeful anticipation.

Staring into the murky pool as it turned blood red, Chief Llao felt all the latent power he possessed surge through him, raising him from off his throne. Hovering in the air, Chief Llao floated over the edge of the cliff and descended gradually. His subjects gathered to greet him as he lowered into their midst. Little did the villagers know their lives were about to change forever.

The eye had served its purpose, keeping Chief Llao apprised of the events atop Crater Lake, but now, with the dagger blinding the eye permanently, Chief Llao could no longer view Crater Lake from the Below World. Chief Skell had broken his treaty, and the prison gate opened.

With a hearty laugh, Chief Llao tilted his head backward, stretched his arms at his side, and arched his back as he lowered onto the ground amid the villagers. The people surrounded their chief. Then without warning, the entire village lofted into the air and shot through the tunnels like lava escaping the inner pressure of the earth. The energy could not be contained.

The prison bonds were broken. Chief Llao and his people were free.

- 61 -

# Death of the Conjurer

STANDING ON THE ICY PLATFORM, ETHAN, BRADY, ALLIE, and Che-tan gazed at Wizard Island. After the preliminary burp of rock and ash, the eruption seemed to fizzle. The eruption was a dud. Though relieved, Ethan couldn't help being a little disappointed.

Kneeling on the ice, Jordan removed Jacob's glasses and held his head in her lap as she stroked his wet hair. His skin was cold and pale, but she remembered his warmth and enthusiasm, his skill and knowledge. His quick thinking saved the lives of Ethan and Brady after their swim to the Phantom Ship, but now he was dead. Jordan's lips tightened, and she clung to Jacob as she felt the ice beneath her rock.

The water around the platform rippled and gentle waves lapped against the ice as the entire lake trembled. The sun shone deep purple, and the sky became green. Unlike the gentle moan emitted from Wizard Island just before spewing the rock and ash, the sound of screeching nails on a chalkboard became deafening. Covering their ears, Allie and Ethan dropped to their knees while Che-tan and Brady stood on the rocking ice platform, balancing like surfers.

The percussion of the volcanic explosion knocked Brady and Che-tan from their feet, and it even toppled Allie and Ethan from their knees onto their stomachs. Wizard Island bulged with pent-up gas and lava. Then, like releasing the nozzle on a hose, molten magma and rock burst through the vent opening at the top. Red and orange flames blew into the sky in a molten stream of lava. The fountain burned through the clouds, and large boulders of volcanic rock shot in every direction like a Roman candle. Some rock landed with great impact atop the crater's ridge or in the pine forests, while other boulders splashed harmlessly into Crater Lake.

Scooting close to Jordan, Ethan grabbed her hand and tried pulling her toward the rest of the group, but she wouldn't leave Jacob. With his eyes still fixed on the eruption of Wizard Island, Ethan's eyes widened with fear as the cascade of fire intensified. It was as though they were at the center of a meteor shower with no place to hide. Small burning rock crashed into the water all around them.

Rising through the stream of molten lava, Chief Llao and his people emerged from their underground prison, shooting high into the air. Larger than life, Chief Llao gloried in his escape, stretching his arms at his side, soaking in the energy and heat of the molten rock and ore. At the top of the fountain, Chief Llao looked upon Crater Lake and its surrounding forests and cliffs. Then, shooting from the lava stream to a secluded place along a grassy plateau, Chief Llao led the villagers to their new home.

Ethan watched with wonder as a flurry of glowing rock burst from the lava, shooting numerous bolts into one small area overlooking the lake. Ethan's sense of wonder and awe was short-lived when he refocused his eyes upward. Two large boulders rained upon the ice platform and his group of friends.

"Jump!" Ethan screamed to the group, and he yanked Jordan toward him. Holding his sister by the waist, Ethan leapt into the water as a ball of fire crashed upon the icy runway. The impact of the boulder's splash created a wave that caught him and Jordan, sweeping them further away from the platform. Trying to look back to see if the others had made it off the ice platform in time, Ethan swallowed water as a second waved engulfed him, pushing him beneath the surface. Ethan's hand gripped Jordan's, but he couldn't hold on. The churning water and crushing waves pulled Jordan away.

Rising to the surface, Ethan gasped for air and immediately searched for Jordan. She was close. Swimming to her, Ethan grabbed his sister by the shoulders and held on as another wave crashed upon them, pushing them further away from the platform. Glancing back at the runway, all that remained were random pieces of ice floating in the water. The icy runway had been pulverized. There was no sign of Jacob or the others, but Ethan didn't have time to worry about them.

Preparing for the crash of another wave, Ethan took a deep breath. Wrapping both arms and legs around Jordan, he held his breath as the wave churned him underneath the water. He tried to remain aware, but after the repeated underwater somersaults, he had no sense of direction. He didn't even know which way was up. His eyes bolted open, the cold water stinging them as he searched for air. Panicking, he struggled not to inhale.

For a moment, everything went black and quiet. Then, like a boat pulling onto a sandy beach, Ethan floated onto dry ground, still wrapped around Jordan.

Fifty yards away, the Phantom Ship loomed ominously in the bright sunlight. Ethan knew exactly where he was. Just up the trail his parents had been devoured, sucked into the ground by a consuming mouth. He had returned to the origin of his nightmare.

Ethan gasped for air. Looking into Jordan's face, he smiled as she opened her eyes. He squeezed her tight, thankful she was alive.

Jordan hugged back at first but then scolded him. "Get off of me. Geez."

Ethan didn't mind his annoying little sister. He was just happy she survived. But what about the others? And Mom and Dad?

Ethan glared at the Phantom Ship. He wanted to forget this place, but he knew he never would.

- 62 -

# CONDOLENCES

BRADY OPENED HIS EYES AND LOOKED INTO THE WOODS with bewilderment. The last thing he remembered was Ethan yelling, "Jump!" as a flaming ball of lava rock crashed onto the ice platform. He had seen Allie dive into the water, and Che-tan explode into a flock of birds, but for some reason, he hadn't moved. *Why?* He couldn't. His fear wouldn't allow him to jump as the fireball crashed onto him. Brady thought about that, disappointed by his lack of courage. He shook his head again as he sat up. His clothes and hair were dry.

"Am I dead?" he wondered aloud, but quickly realized this was far from heaven.

Rising to his feet, Brady heard the squawk of birds flying above, but he couldn't see them through the thick forest canopy. Maybe it was Che-tan, but it could have been any one of the other teenage warriors, or even a real flock of birds. It didn't matter. Looking around the forest, Brady saw a familiar rock outcropping. He had been here before. In fact, he had dug his latrine here before. Jacob had sat against a tree while waiting for him to finish his bathroom business. Brady laughed as he thought about the obnoxious little know-it-all. He remembered Jacob's frustration at his slow bathroom break and even slower walk back to the path. His eyes turned red and puffy at the thought. Jacob wasn't so bad.

Snapping out of his memory trip, Brady realized he was close to the path. Though he didn't know how he ended up in the woods near Mt. Scott, Brady knew how to get back to the ranger station. At least that was something. Hiking through the trees, Brady passed another rock formation with a large flat stone balanced at the top. He pressed forward, but his pace slowed as he listened to what sounded like voices ascending from the trail. Stopping, he concentrated on the sounds. *Yeah, definitely voices.* Jumping over a downed log, Brady raced toward the voices. He emerged from a small grove at the place where his troop had been waiting for him.

The Scoutmaster looked up as Brady approached, but the other boys continued hefting the black lava rock, chatting and laughing as though nothing had happened. It was as though they had never been sucked into the Below World as prisoners of a demented Spirit Chief. Brady shook his head in disbelief. They were all here: Jacob's dad, the assistant Scout leader, and the older boys. The fog of the last day felt like a dream. Everyone was present, except Jacob. Brady knew it was real. Descending to the trail, Brady was dumbfounded as his eyes met the Scoutmaster's gaze.

"Where's Jacob?" the Scoutmaster asked.

Brady's mouth hung open as he stared at Jacob's dad.

"Brady, Jacob is your buddy. Where is he?" he asked again.

Unable to answer, tears ran down Brady's face as he raced into the arms of Jacob's dad, hugging him tight. Jacob's dad was oblivious to his son's death, so the comfort was completely for Brady's benefit. Brady looked into the father's eyes, but he didn't know what to say, so he simply held tight and cried.

– 63 –

# VICTORY!

BRUSHING THE SAND FROM THEIR CLOTHES, ETHAN AND Jordan zigzagged up the hill toward the Sun Notch Viewpoint. Turning back to the ship, Ethan paused. It had all started right here: the earthly consumption, the fear, the magic, the quest. Ethan's head hung low as he held Jordan's hand. He studied each deliberate footstep.

"Come on, kids! We've got to be getting back."

"Let's go! Get the lead out."

"Huh?" Gazing up at the overlook, Ethan saw his parents looking down upon them, waiting impatiently for the kids to return.

"It worked?" Ethan said, turning to Jordan. "Seriously? It worked!"

Jordan jumped up and down, screaming with joy. Ethan couldn't help himself, so he joined in. He knew he was acting like a little girl, but he didn't care. His parents were alive! Alive and well!

Sprinting up the hill, Ethan and Jordan didn't slow down as they zigged and zagged. Maybe the water from the artifact was still giving them supernatural energy or maybe it was the excitement of seeing their mom and dad. Probably both.

Rising onto the cement pad at the outlook, Ethan and Jordan surprised their parents with a tight embrace. Mom and

Dad looked at each other with confusion but hugged their children anyway.

"Are you *my* son?" his dad quipped as he tried to pry loose of Ethan's grip. There was no way Ethan was letting go.

Huddling together in one big family hug, Ethan's mom smiled. "Could today be any better?" she wondered aloud. Ethan didn't respond. He just kept hugging.

Stepping from the corner of the outlook, Allie's parents peered over the stone wall, looking for their daughter.

"Allie!" her father hollered down to the trail, but there was no response. "Enough messing around. Come on. It's time to go." He continued looking downward, expecting Allie to emerge from behind a boulder or a clump of trees, but she was nowhere to be seen.

"Allie?" Ethan muttered, locking eyes with Jordan. "Where's Allie?"

Pushing away from their parents, Jordan and Ethan looked over the wall, hoping to find their friend. They had been lucky to end up at the Phantom Ship overlook, but maybe Allie ended up on the opposite side of Crater Lake. *Maybe she's dead*, Ethan thought. Between the raining lava rocks and crushing waves, surviving the past hour was not a sure thing.

"Kids, where's our daughter?" Allie's mom asked with a touch of concern.

Ethan's father put his hand on his son's shoulder. "Ethan, do you know where Allie is? She was just with you."

Ethan shook his head. What the adults believed to be only a few minutes, Ethan knew was an entire day. Thoughts and memories of their adventures flooded Ethan's brain. He thought of all the explanations and stories he could tell to help explain the various possibilities of where Allie could be, but nothing seemed adequate. How could he tell Allie's parents that she might be dead?

"I don't know," was all Ethan could say.

"I'm right here," Allie said as she appeared from far off the trail. Allie flashed Ethan a knowing smile, and Ethan shared one of his own. She wrapped her arms around her parents.

Jordan ran up and hugged Allie's back, joining in Allie's family embrace. Quietly, Jordan said, "I'm glad you're not dead."

Allie bent down and gave Jordan a tight squeeze and a pat on the back. "Me too. I'm glad you're okay." Allie's smile broadened as she looked up at Ethan. "We did it!" Allie exclaimed, and she jumped into Ethan's arms.

Ethan's dad looked on with pride. His eyebrows rose. "Way to go, son!" he said, nudging Ethan with an elbow. "Uh, what did you do, exactly?"

Ethan tried to answer, but he couldn't stop smiling long enough.

"Mom, can we go now?" Jordan asked.

"Well, I suppose. But don't you want to see Wizard Island?" she asked.

"NO!" all three kids blurted in unison.

"Okay. Then let's go."

Jordan leaned in close to her mom and tugged at the bottom of her shirt. "Mom, can we take Ethan with us?" she whispered. "Please don't make him stay here all week."

Her mom looked at her with a perplexed expression. "But just this morning you said . . ."

"Please. I'll never ask for anything again."

Jordan's mom placed the back of her hand against Jordan's forehead. "Hmm. Are you feeling okay?"

Jordan nodded.

"I think Uncle Bart would be disappointed, but let me talk to Dad."

Jordan smiled at her mom.

Placing his arm around his little sister, Ethan looked down at her as they walked. "I can't wait to tell Uncle Bart everything."

# - 64 -

# Rebuilding

IN A GRASSY MEADOW AT THE CENTER OF THE LIVING FOREST, high on the northwestern plateau of Crater Lake, Wata`m Village reassembled. Within minutes of landing in their new home, Chief Llao's people began rebuilding the village. Some tilled the ground for planting, while some gathered water and others hunted for game in the woods. Even the children were involved, foraging for berries and edible plants. But most villagers were already laboring to build Chief Llao a new fortress at the center of the village. Their huts surrounded a pergola, topped with evergreen boughs for shade. Beneath it, Chief Llao sat on a simple wooden throne, directing the preparations and construction of his new fortress. Most of his people worked hard, but there were a few who sometimes needed to be motivated. Chief Llao provided excellent motivation.

Chief Llao enjoyed his newfound freedom in the Above World, but his people would never be free. They belonged to him.

Chief Llao sighed. Even though the loss of his powers was temporary, he missed the energy surging through him. He thought of his young allies and laughed. The promised inheritance would be more than they bargained for. Their inherited powers would make them potent allies and ensure victory in the dethroning of Chief Skell.

Chief Llao looked heavenward as four hawks wafted downward in a spiraling motion. Sneering with satisfaction as the hawks approached, he extended his right arm in front of him and waited. One hawk landed on the outstretched arm while the other three alighted on the back of the wooden throne. Chief Llao smiled at the bird and stroked its head.

"Che-tan, welcome back," the chief said as distant workers bustled with activity. Che-tan squawked in response, but the chief understood. "You have succeeded beyond my greatest expectations. Well done." The bird lowered its head with a reverent bow. Chief Llao admired the beautiful hawk.

Squawking, Che-tan responded, "Thank you, Chief."

"We have one year to prepare. Chief Skell will wish to renegotiate our treaty, but I refuse to be imprisoned again. Will your people be a problem?" Chief Llao asked.

Che-tan squawked. "Very few Guardians remember you personally. Those who do remember will be rewarded for their loyalty. The others do as I command because they trust me."

"And your mother? Will she stand in your way?"

"No, Father, she will not."

Chief Llao laughed. "Well done, my son. Well done." He gazed into the bird's eyes. "And the dead boy? You confirmed he is still dead?"

The bird's head lowered with shame. "No, Father. His body was lost in the depths of the lake. He is dead, but I cannot confirm."

"What?" Chief Llao screamed. "You lost him?"

"Father, I held his body. He is truly dead. There is no threat to you."

"We shall see," Chief Llao said, his head shaking with disappointment. He huffed as he considered Che-tan's failure. Then, in an attempt to calm his growing rage, Chief Llao changed the subject. "We caught Chief Skell unaware. We will not have the benefit of surprise the next time we go to battle. Now go. Prepare your armies," Chief Llao commanded.

Raising his arm, Chief Llao bid farewell as Che-tan flapped his powerful wings and lifted off. The three hawks from the throne joined him, circling Chief Llao.

Rising into the sky, Che-tan hovered above Crater Lake. Over Wizard Island, Che-tan confirmed the absence of ghoulish warriors. They had been sucked back into prison by Chief Skell to await their next battle. Wizard Island was cleansed. Ghouls and animal warriors alike were removed from their deathly heaps. Those who perished fighting with Che-tan were buried in the depths of Crater Lake, while the injured returned home to recover from their wounds.

Flying above the ranger station, Che-tan watched as a line of cars exited the park. One abandoned vehicle remained, but the college sweethearts were unlikely to ever reclaim it. They were now as much a part of Crater Lake as the trees and rocks, and just as incapable of acting or thinking for themselves.

Though the four young teens were leaving Crater Lake for a season, they would be back, whether they liked it or not. There would be no use fighting against their collective destiny. They would forever be tied to the mystical powers of Crater Lake and the evil forces of Chief Llao.

Catching a wind current with his powerful wings, Che-tan turned and glided away.

# ACKNOWLEDGMENTS

MANY PEOPLE PLAY A SIGNIFICANT ROLE IN THE PUBLICATION of a book, and I am grateful for the contributions that brought *Crater Lake: Battle for Wizard Island* to life.

Stephen King talks about writing with our "ideal reader" in mind. The ideal reader is the person we think about as we're writing. We wonder, "Will they laugh about the second eruption of Mount Mazama?" or "Will they cringe when I describe the slaying of the ghastly fiends into piles of fleshy rubble on Wizard Island?" I am grateful for the support and feedback of my ideal readers, Mica and Lindsay. They have lived the creation of this book with me every step of the way and even provided the illustrations found inside.

I would also like to acknowledge those fellow writers and friends who helped to critique the story as I was editing and putting on the final touches. Their expertise and creative ideas were a great help. Also, many thanks to the LDStorymakers who provided insight and wisdom on a myriad of subjects and topics pertaining to the writing craft, editing, critiquing, and everything in between.

Finally I would like to thank the great team at Cedar Fort for their professionalism and vision in publishing *Crater Lake*. Every step of the way, from acquisitions and editing, to cover design and marketing, Cedar Fort has been a class act.

Crater Lake is a beautiful location and one of God's most stunning geographic creations. I am thankful for the beauty of this world and the opportunities we all have to enjoy them. I am also grateful for the Native American tribes local to Crater Lake for the intriguing legends that add mystery and wonder to the natural beauties God has provided.

# ABOUT THE AUTHOR

STEVE GREW UP AND GRADUATED FROM HIGH SCHOOL IN Salem, Oregon. He enjoyed hiking and camping with the scouts in the Oregon mountains, but his least favorite campout was a snow camp on Mt. Hood that is now referred to as "Camp Hypothermia." Instead of building a snow cave like he was taught, Steve and his friends dug a wide ditch and placed their sleeping bags inside, figuring the ditch would protect them from the wind. It did. But it didn't protect him from the rain. His down sleeping bag became a freezing pile of mush, and by 9:00 p.m., he was warming his freezing body next to a small camp stove.

"That camp was the longest night of my life," Steve remembers. When exhaustion set in, Steve gave up the heat of the stove and found a small corner in his Scoutmaster's snow cave where he huddled on the ice in a puddle of water with no blankets or sleeping bag. The Scoutmaster treated Steve for hypothermia, and the entire camp ended early the next morning when the Scouts cross-country skied out of camp and back to warmth.

Steve now lives on a small farm with his wife and four children, chickens, dog, cats and a duck. Steve has officially retired from snow camping.

0 26575 59605 2